Problems

RUTHLESS DADDIES 2

BREA ALEPOÚ
SKYLER SNOW

Cover Artist: Charli Childs

Editor: Breathless Lit

Proofreader:

Formatter: Brea Alepoú

Sit down, get comfortable, and be a good slut for daddy. 🖤

WARNING AND TRIGGERS

Warning: This book contains daddy kink with mild age play(middle), mafia themed violence, and torture.

Tropes: Age gap, forced proximity, a lot of fucking kink bitch idk

Please note, *we are not experts on the mafia lifestyle. The purpose of this book is for romance entertainment* ***only****. This is a work of fiction. Enjoy your time out of reality.*

PROLOGUE
RONAN

"WHAT DO YOU DO FOR A LIVING?" The man that sat across from me wasn't who I was constantly thinking about, but he was going to be my replacement for the night. I was at my wits end with Jack O'Brien. I was hired to protect him, and everything had been going great until he grew up and started flirting with me. Not to mention he pulled at parts of me that needed to stay far away from him. His dad was my boss, the head of the Irish mob in New York. There wasn't a more off-limits man than Jack.

"Is it a secret or something?" His eyes widened as he looked me up and down. "Do you work for a celebrity?"

"No."

His teeth sank into his pouty bottom lip and I couldn't help but picture Jack instead. His pout was cuter. His nose always wrinkled up and the freckles on his face made him look younger. *No, no, don't start thinking about him.*

I sat up in the chair forcing myself to move on and forget. Impossible. Fuck, who was I kidding? I'd been trying to forget my desire for Jack for well over a year. I was no closer than I'd been back then.

"Are you not into this? I can go," the guy said.

1

I hadn't even bothered to learn his name. I knew why; it wasn't Jack, and no matter how often he told me his name I was more than likely to forget it. When did this even happen to me? When did the wayward teen I was tasked with watching turn into a bratty man that lit a flame of desire in me?

"No stay. I'm sorry. I'm not normally like this." I wasn't. If my dear mam saw me she'd slap me in the back of the head. I didn't treat people like this regardless of my troubles.

"Are you sure? If you're not into this…"

I wasn't but I needed to try something. "I work in security."

The man stared at me for a long while before smiling. "Okay, I'm guessing it's a secret or else you'd boast about what company or celebrity you work for." His head tilted to the side and his light brown curls fell over his forehead. "Want to just get out of here?"

I was taken aback by his forwardness. Then again, he was younger than me. Maybe the wine and dine era was over. I knew I was old fashioned. I wanted to get to know a person and understand their likes and dislikes before sleeping with them.

"Are you finished with your drink?"

He glanced down at his watered-down amaretto sour and shrugged. "Are you wanting to sit here any longer? We don't have to kid ourselves. You're hot and this is a one-night stand, right?"

I barely held back the flinch at the mention of a one-night stand. "You deserve—"

The man shook his head. "What is up with you? You're giving total daddy vibes, and that's great, but you're not available for that, right?" His head tilted to the side as he studied me. It was as if he was trying to see who I was.

Right, it wasn't supposed to be more than getting Jack out of my system. I'd chosen a man who looked similar enough that I'd be able to squint and pretend it was Jack. It would be one and done. Simple, and yet I hadn't made a single move to get up from the table.

"Never mind, you're too hard to read." He huffed in annoyance when I kept my face impassive and my body relaxed. "We don't even know each other's names, you don't have to think this hard about it."

The man reached over the table and wrapped his small hand around mine. They were too soft. Jack had calluses on his fingers from holding pencils for long hours. I stared at our joined hands as my stomach rolled in unease. I had to stop this. Nothing would ever happen between us. I could never let it happen.

"Okay."

The man smiled brightly up at me and flagged down the waiter. He reached into his pocket, but I already had the cash out and laid it on the table.

"My drink wasn't that much."

I glanced down at the two-hundred-dollar bills. It wasn't a lot, but it was more than enough to cover the two drinks the man had. I felt bad for wasting everyone's time. We didn't even get to try the food at the restaurant.

"I'm starting to regret not knowing your name."

The guy winked at me as he stood up. I was nearly a foot taller than him, another thing that was different than the boy I shouldn't want. Jack was tall and lean. He was only a few inches shorter than me.

I'm messing this all up.

"Did you drive?" the man asked. He wove his arm through mine and pressed against my side.

Ants instantly crawled up my side and the need to pull

away ate at me. I forced the repulsion down. *Maybe this won't work if his touch feels wrong.*

"Yes."

"Good, I took a taxi." Maybe he was one of those people who needed to fill the silence with talking because his lips kept moving. I was normally a good listener, but it was taking everything in me not to think about Jack.

I sped up, leading him to the car as fast as possible. The moment we reached my black BMW I unlocked it and unwove my arm from his. I held the door open for him.

"Thank you." He blushed, and I instantly felt bad.

All I'd been thinking about was getting off of him, because he didn't feel like Jack. I plastered a smile on my face and nodded, not sure what else to say to him. Once I shut the door I rounded the car mentally coaching myself. *I can do this.* It was for a cause, so I didn't fall prey to Jack's flirting. I sank into the seat behind the wheel. My fingers tightened around the wheel, and once again I reminded myself I could do it. That I'd feel better once I got Jack out of my system. I glanced at the other man and guilt twisted my insides. It felt wrong to use him to get over someone else, especially someone as amazing as Jack O'Brien.

The man buckled up filling my car with his scent. It was sweeter than Jack's. I ground my molars. Why couldn't I stop comparing every man I met lately to him? It was a problem and I had no idea how to solve it.

He rattled off his address and I swallowed back my guilt and uncertainty. I wouldn't know until I tried. Who was to say after sleeping with him I'd be able to face Jack's advances with ease? I wanted to laugh at myself. I knew without trying it wasn't going to work, and the closer we got to his place the more I felt it deep in my soul. Everything moved at breakneck speed. One second we were stuck in traffic and the next I was parked in a garage.

My fingers tightened around the wheel as I glanced over at the man I was going to take to bed. The one I was going to use to forget the boy of my dreams.

The man unbuckled, hesitating as he reached for the handle. He glanced over his shoulder at me. "You coming up?"

My mouth opened, no and yes battling it out, making it impossible for me to say anything. I'd never been so indecisive in my life. It felt *wrong*. Ringing penetrated the air, bypassing the soft music playing in the background. I took my phone out of my pocket knowing only a few people had this number. The main person who I knew would call was Jack.

Instantly my heart started to race. I wanted to peel out of there and go to him to make sure everything was okay. Hold him and comfort him. Ever since he'd come home from college, he'd been trying to show Declan he was more than a pampered prince. It had led to a few arguments that left Jack hurt and floundering about. I could only be the support he ran to. I had no way of changing Declan's mind, not that I wanted to. I agreed with the boss, Jack wasn't meant for this life. He was gentle, caring, and delicate: all things that the underworld would chew up and spit out.

The phone buzzed in my hand and I hesitated. If I ran back, I'd be at square one. I'd be wrapped back in the web of desire Jack spun. It was my night off. I clicked off the screen and checked the tracker app. Jack was at home and Declan had his men surrounding the place. He was safe, there was no need to panic and run back to his side.

"Do you need to get that?"

I hesitated. I knew the moment I heard Jack's voice there was no way I'd be okay going home with a knockoff. He wouldn't feel right, wouldn't smile as brightly or let out soft moans that made the base of my spine tingle.

I answered and brought the phone up to my ear.

"How long are you going to be gone?" Jack asked.

The question didn't concern me as much as the sound of his voice. The audible strain as if he was holding back tears.

"Did something happen?"

"I need you, Ronan."

Everything else immediately fell away. Jack needed me. I nodded and put the car in reverse. It wasn't until I was out of the garage and about to merge into traffic that I remembered the man next to me. He stared at me with a perplexed look on his face.

"I'm on my way. Go sit down and grab your sketchbook."

A frustrated groan came over the line and I knew instantly Jack was having issues with drawing. I mentally went over the projects he'd been working on.

"Ronan—"

"You don't have to say what's wrong right now. I'll be there soon. Wait for me and be good."

Jack let out a heavy sigh. "Okay."

I was reluctant but I ended the call. The more I heard, the more I wanted to get back to him.

"You don't have to say anything. That guy is lucky to have someone like you," my date said.

"It's not like that." Or at least it couldn't be, no matter how my heart said otherwise.

The man opened his door and slipped out. He leaned down and gave me a sad smile. "If it doesn't work out, call me."

I wouldn't, I knew that without thinking about it. The moment the door closed I drove off and headed toward Jack. It didn't matter what he needed. Until the day I was no longer his bodyguard, I'd stand at his side. Even if every day I couldn't have him as mine was torture.

CHAPTER ONE
FINNIAN

I STARED at my boss as he rounded the desk and sat down. The air felt heavy, tension thick between us as he stared at his computer screen. Somehow, I had become this man's second, the one closest to him in our organization. He always said he saw something in me. I wasn't so young that I was bold and stupid, but I wasn't so old that I only dwelled on the old ways. At thirty-five, I was significantly younger than him, but he never faulted me for it. Declan saw things in people, the good and the bad. Whatever he saw in me had me right by his side making sure things ran as smoothly as possible.

"What are we waiting on?" I asked as I made my way to his desk. He'd stuck a cigarette in his mouth. I took out the gold, square lighter I kept in my pocket and flicked it open before lighting his smoke. "You were vague in your message."

Declan glanced at me. The weary look in his gaze made my stomach tie into knots. *What was that expression? Whatever is going on, it can't be good.* Declan rarely looked worried. To the world he was a man without a care, but I knew that look entirely too well. Something was going on, something big. Shit was about to change.

"You needed me, Dad?" Jack burst into the door, swaggering in as it slammed behind him. He nodded briefly at me before I was quickly forgotten. "What's going on? I'm supposed to be working."

"That can wait for now." He looked at his son carefully before his eyes fell on me. "Where are Ronan and Cian?"

"I'm right here, sir," Ronan called as he walked through the door. "Sorry, Jack gave me the slip downstairs."

"You shouldn't be so slow, old man."

"That's not the point," Ronan said evenly. "You know you're supposed to stay beside me. How many times do I have to tell you that?"

"A hell of a lot more," Jack said as he twisted in his chair and grinned at Ronan.

Ronan and I exchanged a look. Jack was a handful on a good day. No one knew how to tame him to tell the truth. Ronan seemed to run after him more than anything. Personally I stayed out of his way. Jack was a smart ass with a sharp tongue and a rich upbringing that included an unlimited black card. He was the type of young man I'd like to drag over my knee and punish. Not the kind of man that I wanted to hang around or have a conversation with.

Cian breezed through the door. He turned the lock as soon as he was inside and ignored both me and Ronan as he walked over to Declan's desk. He moved to a chair and sat down, not a concern in the world.

"You wanted to see me?" he asked, his deep voice filling the room.

That one is just as arrogant as Jack. Maybe more so.

Cian irritated me. He was what we called a reaper, an assassin who could take out damn near anyone if he had the right financial motivation. Otherwise he was stuck up, arrogant, lazy, and a pain in the ass to work with. It was rare we had to work together, but when we did, I made it quick so I could get away from him as fast as possible.

"Now that you're all here I can tell you." Declan stood up as he looked at each of us. "We're in the midst of a war."

"What?" I asked.

"The Vitale's and The Triads are at each other's throats. I've been called upon to basically pick a side. We have dealings with both parties. Right now, I cannot justify choosing one over the other."

I frowned. "If you don't pick though—."

"We become a target." Declan nodded before he tapped the long trail of ash from his cigarette. "And if we're a target," he nodded toward his son, "Jack will be too."

"So let me fight," Jack said as he sat up a little straighter. "I know how to handle a gun. And I want to be part of the business."

"No," Declan said at the same time Ronan did. They glanced at each other before Declan continued. "This is not the time or place to prove that you've got a set of bollox. You know I want better for you."

"I've never asked for that!" Jack snapped as he jumped up from his chair. "Let me fight!"

I clenched my jaw. Pain radiated up the side of my face as I stared at the spoiled little brat. The way he talked to his father with no respect made me want to sit him down and tell him to shut the fuck up. Declan's word was law. The last person who needed a say in that was Jack. He wasn't built for our world when half the time his head was stuck in the clouds and he was in la-la land.

"That's enough," Declan said gently. "Sit down."

"No," Jack growled defiantly. "I'm not going to get shoved out this time. This is my family. My business. Why won't you let me in?"

"This is not a life you want," Declan said evenly before he glanced at me. "Finnian."

I moved forward. He reached into his desk, dug around, and pulled out a sheet of paper. I read over the itinerary, a frown on my lips as I realized he'd booked four tickets.

"Where are we going?" I asked.

"Not me, you. I want you to take Jack out to the property in Arizona. It's far enough away from here that no one should come looking for him."

"I'm not going!" Jack shouted.

"Stop," Ronan whispered.

I ignored the two of them. "What do you want me to do?"

"Not just you. Ronan and Cian will go along. The three of you are the most trustworthy men I have. I don't want my son in the hands of just anyone." Declan passed over a bag. "Cash. By the time you arrive I'll have TSA agents who only work for me. You'll get through without question. I want you all to pack a single bag and go. Now. The plane takes off in three hours."

"What?" Jack whispered. "You're sending me away? I'm not a child!"

"Then do not act like one!" Declan snapped. "This is for your own good. For your safety. Besides with you here and my worry for you, I can't concentrate. That's what I need right now. You're going. And that applies to everyone. Do I make myself clear?" He asked as he glared at us.

"Yes," Cian said. "Anything you need."

"I go anywhere Jack goes," Ronan said.

I frowned. "What about you? Who's going to make sure you're safe?"

Declan grabbed my shoulder and squeezed it hard. "I have people to watch my back. Thank you for giving a shite about me."

I laughed. "When have I not?"

Declan and I weren't close in age, but we were close nonetheless. I'd grown up under him, studied everything he did, learned from him and grew. My job was to look after him as much as it was to look after the organization. Being separated from it, and him, wasn't something I looked forward to.

I took the itinerary. "You heard him. Let's get going."

"Who the fuck said you're in charge?" Cian asked. He grinned. "I know more about this shit than you do. Why don't you—."

"Finnian is in charge," Declan said. "He'll make sure everything is in order like he always does. Listen to him. All of you."

I stuck my chest out a bit. *Yeah, shut the fuck up you twat.* Cian looked at me as if he'd somehow read my expression and knew exactly what I said, but I didn't give a damn. No one liked to challenge Cian, and I kept my cards close to my chest, but if there was one person I wanted to knock down a few pegs, it was him.

"Like I said, let's get going." I tucked the itinerary into my pocket. "One bag. Everyone lives fairly close, so forty minutes and then we're racing to the airport."

Cian's eyes narrowed. "Asshole," he muttered under his breath.

"What was that?"

Cian grinned at me even harder. I lived for the day when I wiped that look off his face and put him in his place. Someone needed to do it.

"Come on, Jack," Ronan said as he stood and smoothed his suit. "We should pack."

Jack however wasn't looking at Ronan or any of us. He glared at his father. The two of them hadn't taken their eyes off of each other. A storm brewed between them threatening to break at any moment. I stepped in.

"Enough," I said carefully. "Jack, we have to go."

"I'm not going anywhere," he said through gritted teeth. "I've been saying for years that I can take care of myself."

"You're young," I cut in. "Barely a man. At twenty-two I didn't know my arse from a hole in the ground. Neither do you. Your father wants what's best for you. Why don't you respect his worry and go quickly and quietly?"

His dark gaze cut to me. "I'm not going to go."

I groaned internally. Leave it to Jack to be a pain in the ass. I could already see Declan was struggling and that he didn't really want to send Jack away. The more he stood there, the more I could see the worry, fear, and hurt. However, he was right. We were caught in the middle between dangerous factions that would have no problem destroying us from both sides. Even if he chose, things would still be dangerous. No, we needed to get Jack out of here.

"Come with me or be carried," I warned Jack.

"You're not going to lay a hand on me," he growled. "Do it and I'll end you."

My gaze flickered to Declan. The look on his face said "do it". That was all the permission I needed. I dropped down, shoved Jack's thighs over my shoulder and hauled myself to my feet.

"Let go of me! Ronan, make this motherfucker put me down!"

"Is that really necessary?" Ronan muttered. "He can walk."

"Sure, look I'm just gonna go ahead and carry him. We'll get out of here faster."

Jack's fists hammered against my back as I marched toward the door. I wasn't interested in seeing what the hell anyone else thought. We were given orders and I would follow them.

"Put me down, you fucker!"

"Calm down," I grunted. I took one last glance at Declan. "You sure?"

Declan nodded. "Sure as anything."

I nodded. "We'll be in touch."

"No," Declan said sternly. "No phones for any of you. Pick up burners when you get to Phoenix. We'll keep in contact only when we have to. Someone will bring more money and my burner number when I'm sure it's safe. Otherwise, just watch over my son. And Finnian?"

"Yes?"

"Don't let anything happen to him. Any of you." He looked at us. "I'd hate to have to kill you all."

CHAPTER TWO

JACK

PHOENIX, Arizona was hell. I felt like I was standing on the surface of the sun. My face hurt from it, my arms burned, and I was ready to punch someone in the face. Ronan loaded the bags into the rental that had been arranged for us. I stared at it. A janky little car that barely had enough room for all of us. It looked like it had last been used ten years ago. However, Finnian insisted it was perfect. Just what we needed to blend in and stay below the radar.

"Fuck, it's hot!" I groaned as I climbed inside. "Turn up the AC!"

"What do you think I'm doing?" Finnian asked.

"Don't be an asshole."

Finnian glared at me in the rearview mirror, but he didn't say anything. I knew he wouldn't. He turned up the AC. A blast of cool air went right to the backseat where I'd opted to sit since it was next to the only empty space waiting for my bodyguard. Ronan. He climbed into the car and froze when he saw I'd moved into the middle seat.

"Go back to your side," he said gruffly.

I frowned at him. "What? You don't want me close to you?"

"That's not what I said," Ronan muttered. "Go back to your side and put your seatbelt on. Please."

Boring. Ronan loved to pretend he wasn't interested in me, he always had. I'd been after the man since I was seventeen years old. Back then I understood when he didn't make a move, I was underaged and all. Now? Well, there was no reason to keep distance between us when I was a legal adult.

I laid a hand on his thigh. "I don't know how to work my seatbelt. Will you fix it for me?"

Ronan quickly removed my hand. "You are old enough to buckle yourself in. How many times do I have to say that?"

"At least a few more," I said as I grinned. "I forget things quickly."

Ronan stared straight ahead, his lips pressed together in a thin line. Sighing, I shoved myself back into my seat. *Of course he's the same as always. All business, no fun.* I crossed my arms over my chest as I stared out the window.

"Are we going?" Cian asked.

"Of course we are," Finnian snapped back.

I stared up at the two of them. I never saw Finnian lose his temper as much as he did around Cian. Normally he was upright, controlled, boring. Once he was around Cian though? It was an entirely different story. Finnian adjusted the glasses that sat on the bridge of his freckled nose. He had red hair, a red beard, and deep green eyes that were honestly kind of sexy. Too bad he was an uptight asshole or I'd want to ride his dick as badly as I wanted Ronan's.

Finnian's eyes met mine in the rearview mirror. I grinned when he looked away first. Both he and Ronan acted like they were scared of me lately, I wondered why? My gaze turned to Cian. He stared straight ahead, his face impassive as the radio played. His darkish-brown hair was short on the sides and longer on top where it was pushed back. He had a beard and mustache too, but it was short compared to Finnian's. Tattoos covered his skin, snaking underneath the short sleeves of his shirt as they wrapped around his buff arms.

I wouldn't mind him bending me over either.

I fidgeted in my seat. I didn't mean to be a horny night-mare, but it was hard when I was surrounded by three hot as fuck men. Did they all annoy me? Hell yeah. Were they all sexy daddy material? Also, yeah. Finnian was a pain in the ass, but Cian was hot and Ronan wanted me. I knew he did, even if he denied it every single day.

"Where are we going?" I asked.

"To a house," Finnian answered.

"Where is it?"

He glanced in the rearview. "Have you been here before?"

I shrugged. "Not since I was a kid."

"Then what does it matter? We'll be there soon enough."

I glared at him. "Do you always have to be such a jerk?"

Finnian ignored me. Instead he turned up the radio. With no phone, I was left on my own. I slammed my back against the seat again feeling like a teenager. When was the last time I'd existed with no phone, no computer, nothing? It made me want to claw my own eyes out. How was I going to stay sane with no technology?

Ronan handed me a crossword puzzle. Reaching into his jacket, he pulled out a pen and passed that over too. I stared at him as I clutched the items. *How the hell did he know I was bored?*

"Are you hungry?" Ronan asked.

I nodded. "Fucking starving."

"You don't have to swear," he said as he winced. "Finnian, can we stop for food or will there already be something at the house?"

"Declan said there would be food already stocked, but we should get more shortly. Or I can run back and grab food. Jack doesn't need to be seen."

I gestured to the hoodie I wore. "Hello?" I asked as I pulled the hood over my head. "No one can see me. Come on, man. I want a burger."

"Come on, man," Cian mimicked me as he grinned at Finnian. "He wants a burger."

"Keep it up and I'll put you on the side of the road," Finnian said evenly. "I'm sure I can come up with a story for why your body was found in a ditch."

"Stop bickering like an old married couple and stop for something to eat. I want a shake too," I added.

"You're not getting anything until we have you somewhere safe. Do you think this is a vacation?" Finnian snapped. "Right now is all about making sure you're out of harm's way. That's what your father wanted."

"Fuck him," I muttered. "He didn't want my help? I don't give a shit if he gets fucked up."

The car jerked to the right. We drove over bumps that rattled the car before it careened to a stop. Finnian's door opened before he reappeared by me, yanking open my door as I shoved myself away from him. Finnian's face hadn't changed, but as he grabbed my shirt and yanked me toward him, I froze.

"What did you say?"

I swallowed thickly. "Let me go."

Finnian yanked me forward. "Repeat your words," he growled. "Go on. Act like you have an ounce of balls and repeat what you said. I want you to."

Even though his face was calm, a fire burned in his eyes. I instinctively shrank away, trying to put distance between us even as rage filled my chest and threatened to spill over. All of them underestimated me. My father brought fear to people in less than a second, but I was just his weak, punk ass son. No one cared about me. No one feared me. I might as well be invisible.

"Get off!" I yelled at Finnian. "Fuck off already."

"Enough." Ronan removed Finnian's hand from my shirt. "He's hot, tired, overwhelmed, and hungry. Besides, we don't have time for this shit. Drive."

Finnian stared at him. "I'll decide when we drive and when we wait," he said calmly. "If you have a problem with that, let me know." When Ronan stayed quiet he turned his attention to me again. "I suggest you keep your mouth shut. Your disrespect won't be tolerated by me. Ever. Do I make myself clear?"

"Whatever."

Finnian dragged me close, his face inches from mine. "Do I make myself clear?"

"Fine," I spat. "Clear!"

Finnian released me. I fell back against the seat as he adjusted his glasses and slammed the door. If I was angry before, I was pissed now. My fists tightened as I stared ahead. Finnian took his seat, glanced back at me, and I returned his gaze.

"You can glare all you want. My job is to take care of you and make sure you're safe. I'm going to do that no matter how you feel about me. I suggest you let it go before you do something stupid. Like try to fight me."

I released my fists and decided to glare instead. Like I'd told my father, I was good with a gun. Fighting? Not so much. I spent my time at boarding schools getting my ass kicked when I wasn't at home. In college I didn't have bullies, but I didn't learn how to fight either. Whenever I tried, Dad lost his shit. He didn't want me to have anything to do with his life. Instead, he chose to shut me out; to make me an outsider. Not even his men respected me.

I was a joke.

An arm wrapped around my shoulders and tugged. I resisted Ronan's tug for a moment before I gave up. He pulled me to his side. I laid my head on his arm, staring out the windshield as the sun blasted landscape whipped by. All of my irritation drained away as Ronan's fingers pushed into my hair, scraping across my scalp. It always calmed me when he did that. It also made me insanely horny. I moved my head to lie on his lap.

"Jack," he growled.

I rubbed my face against his crotch. "Yeah?"

Ronan pulled me up and pushed me away. "Enough."

I frowned at him. "I was relaxing."

"Yes, well you lost the privilege didn't you?"

"Fuck, everything sucks," I groaned.

"Watch your language," Ronan snapped.

Oh fuck off.

I STEPPED out of the car and glanced at the house that we would be staying in. On the outside it was just like any other place, a nondescript place in some boring suburb with an HOA, rules, and annoying neighbors. I stared at it, hating every bit of its muted beige colors and perfect manicured rock lawn. A lizard skittered over the sidewalk and disappeared as quickly as it had arrived. A shudder ran up my spine.

I hate this.

"Get inside, Jack," Finnian said as he nodded toward the house. "Your room is in the middle."

"Am I supposed to know what the fuck that means?"

"Jack," Ronan called.

"Fine, fine."

I stepped into the house and wandered around. The house had a pretty simple lay out. A long hallway led to a kitchen and then dining room. I took a right. There were three bedrooms in a row. Between the center two there was a long bathroom connected by two doors. *Yeah, no thanks.* I kept walking toward the back of the house. Finally, I arrived at a huge room with high ceilings and an ensuite bathroom.

"Perfect."

There was a door that led to the backyard as well. When I glanced out, I saw nothing but a high, stone fence beyond the grass, pool, and hot tub. Private, quiet, safe. I plopped down on the bed. The air conditioning felt amazing, but I was already antsy. There was no sound in this small, Phoenix town the way there was in New York. It almost felt too insanely quiet.

"Get out," Finnian said as he stood in the doorway. "Your room is next door."

I sat up on my elbows. "Like hell it is. This is my room."

"No," he said shortly. "This room isn't in a good, tactical location. You'd be safest in the middle." He nodded toward the door. "Go."

My irritation hit an all time high. I stood up and stared at him. "No," I said firmly. "You've all forced me out here to live in this goddamn, hot, boring place. I'm not going to give up the room I want. Either do your job and protect me or tell my father that you can't."

Finnian's eyes narrowed at me. He opened his mouth before shutting it again. I watched as he stormed off, a smile spreading on my face. I fell back on the bed and stared up at the ceiling. I might not be where I wanted to, but at least I'd won a single, sad battle.

Yeah, I'm a real badass.

The smile fell from my face again. My father's men were right. I *was* a joke.

CHAPTER THREE
CIAN

IT WAS hotter than the devil's taint in bumfuck nowhere Arizona. I'd been sent to a lot of places, but Arizona was just not it for me, especially during the scorching summer.

The blazing sun beat down on my head as I made another lap of the neighborhood. It consisted of fifteen different subdivisions with different names. I made sure to map each of them out on my run. My legs burned as I kept pushing forward. My breath was even as I jogged up a small hill. The house we were staying in was finally visible.

The neighborhood was mostly families and a few elderly couples. On each side of us was a family with a dog. It was normal in every way. It was almost too normal for my comfort. My skin crawled to get out of suburbia. It was plain, no action, no honking horns, or traffic noise.

I liked the quiet as much as the next person, but it was almost too quiet. I opened the side gate and slipped into the backyard. The blinds in the main bedroom were up.

Fucking idiot.

I stopped short as Jack walked out of his bathroom towel ruffling through his dark hair. His slender body was on full display. My displeasure vanished the moment I caught sight of him.

Fuck. It was a little treat every single time I watched him. It didn't matter how often I caught glimpses, I hadn't grown bored yet.

I licked my lips. The princess had a nice body. His nipples were pierced, and I swore his cock was as well.

Jack was none the wiser as he flopped down on the bed and spread his arms and legs. He stared at the ceiling as if it was going to give him answers to his problems. He had a lot of them for someone who was only twenty-two and rich as fuck. Jack had no idea how good he had it, not that I was going to be the one to tell him.

He rolled over and lifted his ass, showing off the firm globes. *Bet they'd look good red.* My cock twitched in the confines of my shorts. I forced myself to keep moving. I'd planned on going through the back sliding doors, but I had a better idea. My normal workout routine tossed in the wind for something more entertaining.

I grabbed the lock-picking kit I kept on me and got to work on the locks on the door. *Maybe after this stunt, Finnian will listen to me when I say all the doors need three more locks and they need to be the ones I choose.* I held back the groan of annoyance just thinking of that man sent through me. He was a pain in my ass on a good day.

The soft click of the lock turning was familiar to my trained ear. I eased the door open slowly, Jack was lost in whatever he was doing. *It should be a crime to be this easy of a target.* His father had been right. Jack wasn't ready for this life. I doubted he ever would be.

"Hey princess."

Jack shot up off the bed twisting around to face me. His hands went up in the air as he tangled with his bedding and crashed to the floor. "Fuck!" His shout of pain was music to my ears. The bedroom door flew open as Ronan and Finnan both ran in guns raised.

I counted each second that passed. Our eyes met and I smiled at them. I didn't need these two here. I could protect Jack by myself. Tie the princess up and make sure to give him food and water. The memory of my very dead house-plant came to mind and I mentally sighed. It was so much easier to kill than to keep something alive.

"He'd be dead waiting on you two to respond." I crossed my arms over my chest staring at the two of them. "It took exactly forty-seven seconds. In that time, a bullet would be in the middle of his forehead and I'd be out of here."

"What?" Jack sat up and he still was stark naked on the ground. His face had gone ashen white. "There is no way."

"Way, princess." I winked at him. "I'm damn good at my job."

"Cian," Ronan groaned out. "Is that necessary?"

I shrugged. "He's defenseless and an open target. What's to say someone won't come shoot him in the face and then move around the house taking us out one by one."

Finnian's hard gaze stayed on me as if he wanted to argue. But he couldn't because we both knew I was right. I wanted to instantly shove it in the man's face. He was the only asshole who got under my skin. Most people were nothing but meat bags or white noise in the background. Finnian was a thorn in my side.

"So, you broke into the house?" Ronan shook his head. "Why?"

"How do you know it wasn't unlocked?"

Ronan's eyes widened and for the first time, he looked over to Jack. If it was possible his eyes widened even more. The slight flare in his nose and the way he went rigid spoke volumes. He marched over to Jack and pulled the blanket off the bed and tossed it over Jack's naked body.

"Aww shielding the princess from our delicate eyes?"

"Who the fuck is a princess?" Jack growled.

"Language," Ronan chastised.

"Yeah, be a good proper princess and shut your mouth."

Jack's face grew red as he glared at me. There was a fight burning in his dark brown eyes. A fight I wanted to engage in. I had no delusions he could take me on, but it would be fun to knock him around a bit. He had some serious authority issues.

"This wasn't necessary," Finnian said. He put his gun away, always in control.

I wanted to see him lose control and be more like Jack.

"He needs to get dressed," Ronan said.

I shrugged and leaned against the back door. "Then let him."

"You can't be fucking serious," Jack asked. He glared at me as if he wanted my head to explode.

"Keep staring, sweetheart."

"Does he always talk this much?" Jack pulled the blanket up around him holding it close. "I liked it better when you were silent and creepy."

I didn't care for talking but teasing Jack came naturally. I couldn't stop even if I wanted to.

"I agree. Cian that's enough. Go finish setting up surveillance, the rest of the cameras are here," Finnian ordered. He looked over at Jack. "Now you see why I didn't want you in this back room."

Jack crossed his arms and the stubborn brat wasn't giving up. "I don't care, I'll be prepared next time."

"Doubt that, princess. I watched you for a full five minutes and you didn't notice a thing."

"What?" Ronan and Jack shouted at the same time.

Finnian groaned. "You're changing rooms. End of discussion."

"The fuck I am. I'm staying in this room," Jack said.

The air in the bedroom went eerily still. A chill raced up my forearms and the need to grab a weapon made my fingers twitch at my side.

"I didn't ask," Finnian said.

Oh, this was getting good. I glanced at Jack as they had a stare-off. He met Finnian's gaze head-on. He held it longer than I'd imagined he would. Jack's eyes dropped away as his shoulders sagged.

"I want to stay in here."

Ronan's shoulders dropped and he pulled Jack against his side. He babied Jack way too much, no wonder he was so damn soft.

"I'm not here to give you what you want. Your father gave me a job and I will see to it that you are protected. Move rooms. Now." Finn glared at me. I expected him to reprimand me but instead, he turned on his heels. "Ronan, help Jack pack his things. He can move to the room in the middle."

"What about me?" I batted my lashes at the other man. Finn's lips thinned and I could tell he wanted nothing more than to put a bullet in my head. I wanted to see him try.

"Are you always like this on a job?" Ronan asked. His dark curls were pushed back and his beard was trimmed close to his face. Being a bodyguard fit him nicely, I always thought he was too good for the work we did.

"I work alone for a reason."

"I can see why," Jack mumbled as he shoved his legs in a pair of sweats. He snatched up his bag. "I hate you."

My cock twitched for a second time, and I was starting to think it wasn't a coincidence.

Ronan sighed. "Jack, he's doing his job. I'm finishing up lunch, it's your·favorite."

Jack smiled and I wanted to punch Ronan. I had been enjoying his anger.

I FINISHED SETTING up the surveillance and added some extra cameras in a certain spoiled brat's room. I had to wait for Finnian to leave before I snuck a few into his. Ronan was easy. The bodyguard was sharp except for when Jack was around. He was a good distraction, especially when he didn't know it.

Heavy footsteps headed my way and I knew instantly it was Jack. The other two were conscious of the sounds they made. It came with the territory of being hyper aware of oneself. Jack didn't have that problem though. The double doors to the back room flew open, and I flipped the video feed on the four screens to the cameras outside.

"You just wanted this room," Jack said.

I glanced up from the screen and met my guest's gaze. "Maybe, what are you going to do about it?"

Jack took a step toward me, his fist balled at his side. I glanced at them and smiled. Ronan was currently doing outside rounds, and Finnian was cooking dinner.

Hit me.

A visible shiver worked its way over Jack. "Fuck you."

My head fell to the side as I looked Jack up and down. Picturing him naked was easy. His dusky pierced nipples, barely there abs, slender waist, plump ass, and that pierced cock. I wanted to play with every inch of him for fun of course.

"Sure."

"Wait, what?" Jack blinked at me rapidly as if he hadn't heard me right.

I pushed off the bedpost and moved closer to him. "Strip down and show me what I'm working with."

"What?" Jack backed away. "Are you crazy?" He shook his head. "Never mind, don't answer that. I didn't mean I want to fuck you. I meant it as in you're an asshole."

"You sure about that?"

I leveled my gaze on him. We'd only been in the house a single day, but I knew what I felt and saw when Jack stared my way. He was shit at hiding what was going on in his head.

"I wouldn't fuck you if you were the last dick on earth."

I cocked a brow up at him. "You came all the way over here for what then?" I took hold of Jack's chin and tilted it back until he was forced to stare into my eyes. "What's that look for? You going to run home and tell daddy?"

Jack wrenched his face free, and I let him.

"You're a dick."

"You want to see it that badly huh?" I hooked my thumbs in my waistband crowding further into his space.

"No."

"Then why do you keep looking down?"

Jack's head snapped up and our eyes locked for a single second before he shifted his gaze anywhere but at me. There was a nice tint to his cheeks.

"That's—Fuck."

Laughter bubbled freely from me before I knew what was happening. My reactions to Jack were odd but interesting to say the least.

"I already said yes to that. Need me to take the lead, princess?"

Jack sucked in a breath the moment my hand moved to his neck. I felt every single movement against the palm of my hand. His heartbeat raced, drawing out parts of me that wanted so badly to hurt Jack. *Wonder what his crying face looks like.*

"Jack." Ronan's voice was like a needle to the bubble that had formed around us.

"Get the fuck away from me."

"Sorry about that, princess."

I dropped my hand and took a few steps back. Jack was gone before I'd gotten more than three steps back. Shit. I was fine with teasing, and thinking about fucking Jack was fine but that had felt too close. I doubted my perfect record would keep the boss from killing me if I ended up fucking his son.

CHAPTER FOUR

JACK

RONAN SAT my plate on the table. A big, steaming portion of Shepherd's pie that made my stomach growl. I picked up my fork and sliced into it as I tried to ignore everything that had just happened between me and Cian. My body still buzzed even after being far away from the man with piercing blue eyes and a challenging grin. Every time I saw it, I wanted to punch him in the face or drop to my knees, there was no in between.

"Are you going to eat?"

I blinked at Ronan. The concerned look on his face drew me right back into reality. I stabbed at my food, shoveled some into my mouth, and continued to stare at my plate. *Cian isn't what I'm supposed to be focused on. How am I going to prove to my father that I can handle this life? What do I have to do to show that I can do this on my own?*

My head ached as I thought about it. Honestly, it felt like an impossible feat. My father had treated me like a child my whole life, why should that stop now? I pushed my plate away from me before I stood up.

"I'm going to bed."

"Are you sure?" Ronan frowned as he looked at me. "I

know how much you love Shepherd's pie. I asked Finnian to make it exactly the way you liked." His frown deepened as he glanced into his plate. "Did I give the wrong instructions?" He muttered to himself.

My heart threatened to jump right out of my chest. Ronan. Out of everyone in my world, he was the soft, sweet side that I had gravitated towards. Even when I was young I listened to him because he wasn't like my father's other men. They were all rough, short, silent. Ronan had come in right away annoying me with his questions and asking me about myself until I felt like I was going to scream. I'd hated it back then, but now? I loved that he was so interested in me. Especially because he showed it; every gift, concern, and small gesture was real. I loved that about him.

"The food is fine," I said quickly. "It's not that. I'm just tired, especially after having to move my room," I said, my words clipped as I glared at Finnian.

Finnian raised a brow and went back to eating as if I'd said nothing at all. I wasn't sure what to do with him. The man did and said whatever he wanted, and it seemed like no one questioned him about it either.

"Where you going?" Cian asked as he joined us in the kitchen. "Not hungry?"

I looked him up and down trying to show him my disdain. Instead, my cheeks grew hot as I watched the smile spread on his lips. Heat swept over my body. I opened my mouth to tell Cian exactly where he could fuck off to, but nothing came out. His smirk grew. I turned on my heels and stormed to my room. The door slammed, and I threw the lock as well.

"Fuck him."

Cian had worked his way under my skin so quickly it was insane. I should hate him, and I did, but he was hot.

Too hot. No one should look that fucking good. I pushed my fingers through my hair as I stared in the mirror on my wall.

I was already climbing up the walls and we hadn't even been in Arizona that long. The heat, the sun, the constant surveillance, it was making me irritated. What I needed was some time away from the house. My father and the men he'd sent me with were all paranoid. No one was coming after me. There were bigger fish to fry than someone trying to get to me. In the grand scheme of things, I was basically a no one. My father kept me separated from the life, so why would anyone give a shit about me?

Turning from the mirror, I walked over to the closet. I didn't have a door to slip out of anymore, but there was a window. Good enough. I changed my clothes opting for all black. Dark jeans, a t-shirt, and a hoodie to hide my face. I dug around in my suitcase and pulled out the burner phone I'd smuggled into my stuff. Carefully I turned it on and texted Sayge. We'd met a few months ago when he came up to dance in one of the clubs and hit it off right away. He was a huge flirt and funny as hell. The awesome thing was that he lived in Phoenix with his friends Calvin and Dar. They also stayed with their Daddy, but I hadn't met him yet. I just knew he worked for the mafia as well.

"Jack?"

Ronan's voice made me shoot straight up. I quickly made sure the phone was on silent before I tucked it down the front of my pants, into my underwear. When I opened the door, he frowned.

"Why is it locked?" He asked.

I frowned. "I'm not allowed to have any privacy?"

"I never said that."

"That's how everyone acts," I muttered. "Can I go to sleep now?"

Ronan looked me up and down. "You're fully dressed."

Shit. I glanced down at my clothes before I looked up and shrugged.

"Yeah, so what?"

"You're going to sleep? Fully clothed?" He asked as his eyebrow shot up.

"Is that a problem?"

"You only sleep in your shorts or naked."

I bristled. The fact that Ronan knew that about me tickled something inside of me. I closed my mouth before I leaned forward, resting a hand on his chest.

"Do you look at me in my shorts? Or when I'm naked?" I asked. I licked my lips. "Or do you just want to?"

The look on Ronan's face made me grin. He cleared his throat twice looking anywhere but at me. I loved when he looked like that; embarrassed and anxious like he wanted to run away from me. As my hand traveled down his body, he shivered and stepped back.

"Goodnight," he said shortly.

"Night," I called as he fled down the hallway.

I chuckled to myself after shutting the door. Ronan was nothing if not predictable. I'd been getting under his skin for five years now and he still couldn't handle it. I threw the lock on the door, climbed into bed, and waited. Minutes ticked by until an hour and then another passed, I kept an ear out for the others. They moved around the house, talking to each other here and there, but mostly making rounds, cleaning the kitchen, watching TV. I pulled my phone out.

Sayge: You're in AZ! Fuck yesssss. Wanna come out tonight?

Jack: Fuck yes I'm going nuts. Can you pick me up?

Sayge: Cal can. We were going out dancing anyway. Where you at?

I shot him the address as my heart raced in my chest.

The thought of slipping out the house so I could go hang out made every bit of me tingle with excitement. I wasn't used to being locked in the house. Going out, partying, having fun; that was my regular weekend routine. I worked hard during the week, so why not have a little fun on the weekend? Now, I was trapped in a house with three men who wouldn't know fun if it bit them in the asshole.

Jack: Don't come to the house. Meet me around the corner.

Sayge: Oooh someone's sneaking out. Naughty! Sure you can do that?

Jack: I don't give a fuck. Come get me.

Sayge: Lol on the way now. ;)

I nearly hopped out of bed until I remembered I had to be careful. Slowly, I climbed out and glanced around. My lights were already out and had been for a while. I made sure my TV would stay on, the sound low, before I moved over to the window. Every movement I made felt like it was louder than the last. I finally popped the screen out, catching it before it could hit the ground.

"Fuck yeah!" I whispered. I groaned. "What the hell am I going to do without money?"

Finnian. He'd taken a huge amount of cash my father had given him. Even a handful would be more than enough to have some fun for the night. I stood at my door for what felt like ages. I carefully wiped the sweat from my palm onto my jeans. As soon as I was sure no one was out there, I slipped out. Slowly, I walked toward Finnian's room. His door was slightly open, the TV playing. I pushed it open more, but he was nowhere to be seen.

"Cian, we don't need landmines in the front yard," Finnian said.

"That's stupid."

"You're going to blow one of us up!" Finnian snapped.

I peeked toward the front door. They were outside, walking around the front yard with a flashlight as Cian mapped out where landmines could go. I shook my head.

"Psycho."

I moved back into Finnian's room. Going through his things made every hair on the back of my neck stand on end, like he would catch me at any moment. I forced myself to move faster, not to stop, as I dug through his things. The money wasn't in his closet or in the dresser. I moved to the bed and dropped to my knees. I grinned as I spotted the duffel bag. Carefully, I tugged it out and ripped it open. Stacks of cash greeted me. I took a handful, then thought better of it and grabbed another. I shoved the bag back beneath the bed.

As I stepped out of Finnian's room, I made sure the door stayed cracked open. I waited, listening for Cian and Finnian. They were still outside arguing. That was good enough for me. I ran toward my room, slipped inside, and shut the door as quietly as possible before I threw the lock. My heart raced in my chest as I leaned against the door.

I checked my phone.

Sayge: We're almost at your place. You still coming?

Jack: Give me fifteen and I should be there.

Sayge: Don't keep us waiting ;)

I laughed, shaking my head as I read his message. Sayge and his never ending flirting. He always said his Daddy would kill him if he knew he was doing it, but he still did it either way. Sayge was kind of insane. I liked that about him.

Jack: I won't. Be right there.

I patiently waited until I heard Cian and Finnian come back inside. They each went their separate ways leaving me alone. Excitement made my stomach knot. I shoved a leg out of the window and carefully made my way out. It took only a few moments to lower the window, replace the screen, and leave it a bit cracked so I could get back in without having to use the door.

I listened, trying to make sure I couldn't hear Cian lurking around somewhere. Apparently, even psychos needed to sleep, or take a shower, or whatever he was doing because no one came after me. I rounded the house and carefully moved the door to the gate. The moment my feet hit the driveway, I felt like I was free. I could have whooped, danced, and hollered. Instead, I forced myself to get moving.

Around the corner, three blocks down, lights flashed at me. I grinned as I raced toward the car.

"Finally!" Sayge yelled. "Get in already!"

I laughed as I opened the door to the backseat. Sayge scooted over and I took the seat behind Calvin. He smiled at me, but was quiet otherwise. Dar on the other hand twisted around and looked me up and down.

"Hey, Jack!" he yelled. "Ready to get fucked up?"

"You know it," I said.

Sayge laid a hand over my shoulders. "That's what we love to hear."

"Get out of here," I said as I nodded for him to drive. "If I get caught, I'm dead."

Cal took off and I was finally able to blow out a breath. Just for a few hours. I needed to blow off some steam.

CHAPTER FIVE

JACK

LOUD MUSIC THUMPED through the stereos echoing in my ears and through my veins. As soon as I hit the darkened room, the lights flashing, bodies pressed together, and the heat that surrounded us, I felt like I was right at home. I ditched my hoodie back in the car and I was glad I did now. At least I wasn't going to melt to death in the heat.

"Want a drink?" Sayge called over the noise.

"Yeah! A screwdriver!" I yelled.

Sayge shoved a thumbs up in my direction. "Be right back!"

He wove through the crowd expertly as if he was born to move through it. Everyone that looked his way either moved out of the way or admired him and then moved out of the way. I grinned, shaking my head as he half walked, half danced his way to the bar. Sayge never failed to be entertaining. I glanced around. Cal was chasing after Sayge, muttering something in his ear. And Dar? He was either dancing or possessed by a demon. I couldn't tell which.

At least he's enjoying himself.

I had to admit, the beat made me move too. Finally, I could relax and unleash the pent up irritation that had been growing in my body since I'd returned from college. Even after I came back, after doing what my father wanted, he insisted that I didn't need to lead. That I didn't need to take his place when he was done. I'd done my part, going off to school to get the education he demanded I get, now that I was back, I wanted things to go my way.

But that wasn't happening.

"Here you go!" Sayge yelled over the crowd as he passed me my drink.

I took it, thanked him, and drank it all down in one go. The warmth that filled me immediately made me feel like a brick was lifted from my chest. Sayge whistled.

"Either you were thirsty or you're really stressed out."

I shrugged. "Fuck it, let's dance. I don't want to talk."

Sayge grinned. "I communicate better with my body anyway," he said as he winked. "Want to dance with me?"

I shook my head at Sayge's flirting. "Yes, but don't be all up on me. Isn't your boyfriend super dangerous?"

"My Daddy would kill us both," he purred. "But that's part of the fun, you know?"

"For who!" I exclaimed. "I don't want to die, thanks."

Sayge laughed as he took my hand and led me to the dance floor. Cal and Dar joined us. While Cal was more reserved, Dar's dancing was a mix of grinding and karate moves that I steered clear of so I wouldn't get hit in the face. Sayge and I danced together the most. Even with all his flirting, he was a good friend. We danced until I started to sweat. A quick trip to the bar, a refill on our drinks, and we went right back to it.

By the time we were all worn out, I panted and slumped onto a black leather sofa. I was glad I was wearing jeans because the material stuck to the back of Sayge's bare thighs. His shorts were insanely small, so small I wondered if I could pull it off and if I would be able to feel my nuts after they went numb from lack of circulation.

"So," Sayge said as he flagged down a girl. "What's so bad that you needed to escape the house tonight?" He turned to the girl. "Can we get more drinks please?"

"Right away," she said after he relayed our orders.

I waited until she was gone. "My father had me sent out here. This is our go to place when things get really bad back home, but I haven't had to come out in ages." I groaned. "And he sent me with the three most annoying men ever. Finnian's always on my ass. Ronan babies me. And Cian is a psychopath."

"So? Kick their asses," Dar said.

I rolled my eyes. "Yeah, that'll really work. All three of them are Irish mobsters. I'm sure I can just kick their asses and go about my day." I shook my head. "I mean it's not all bad. At least they're all hot."

Dar whistled. "So you want to fuck them?" He slapped me on the back. "Hop on some dick and ride!"

Sayge nodded along. "I have to agree. If you want to screw them, do it. One, it'll be fun. Two, you'll probably have more control over them once they feel how tight your ass is. I mean, I'm assuming it's hot and tight..." He grinned.

I groaned. "Sayge!"

"Just saying!"

I turned to Calvin. "What do you think?"

Calvin shrugged. "I thought Elio was a bad idea but it turned out to be the best decision we ever made. I say go with what feels right."

All three of them were nuts. I thought at least one of them would tell me that was insane, but they all stared at me as if I was the one off my rocker for not getting it sooner. I couldn't lie... I wanted their dicks. As long as two out of three of them didn't speak.

"No way," I scoffed. "They're hot, but annoying. Anyone who's on my father's side isn't going to be a good lay." I slumped in my seat after grabbing my drink. "Besides, I want a good Daddy. Like the ones I've read about online."

"You've never had one?" Cal asked.

I shook my head. "Well yes. A few online, nothing in person. Some of them were fun, some of them just wanted naked pictures. None of them were what I needed." I thought about Ronan. "There's one guy back at the house though that I think would be really good at it. He's been my bodyguard since I was sixteen. All he does is look out for me."

"Oooh potential!" Sayge exclaimed. "What's his name?"

I grinned to myself. "Ronan. He's hot, nice, and he always knows what I need before I even know it. I can't even stand yelling at him because he's so nice to me." I sighed. "But whenever I try to move things forward, he runs. Ronan's like... the most boring of boring men when it comes to sex. Or anything. He wants me to be safe, but safe can be—."

"Boring?" Dar asked. "Yeah, it's a fucking drag."

"That," I nodded. "I need a little freedom or I'm going to go insane!" I looked at them. "Any advice?"

"Hop on one of their dicks!" Dar yelled.

I pinched the bridge of my nose. "That can not be your answer for everything."

"It really is," Cal sighed. "It's all he knows."

"Hey!" Dar growled. "Don't be a dick!"

Sayge patted Dar's head. "Yes, yes we hear you." When Dar settled down, he smiled at me. "He's right though; if you want something, go get it. Why should you have to suffer? Besides, you know what's better than one Daddy?"

"Three Daddies?" I sighed.

"Exactly!"

I shook my head, but couldn't stop laughing. Sayge was out of his mind. Ronan avoided me at all costs. Cian was a psycho who I was pretty sure couldn't even begin to understand what being a daddy was. And Finnian? He was a major pain in my ass. There was no way in hell he was a good Daddy.

"Look at him," Dar whispered so loudly I could hear him over the music. "He's thinking about it."

I took my straw from my drink, sucked in the tangy cocktail, and tossed the straw at Dar. He laughed, trying to dodge it while Sayge giggled and Calvin grinned. I settled back into my seat, sipping my drink. *At least I have friends here. This could be a lot worse.* As long as I got back before morning, my three prison guards wouldn't even know I'd left. I could go on having a break from the house and they could pretend I needed watching over.

Win win.

"Enough about that," I said, waving a hand. "Let's have more drinks and get back to dancing." I pulled out some money. "Let's go!"

All three of them whooped right along with me. We slammed our drinks, paid for more, and before long we were back on the dance floor. I forgot every last one of my troubles as I fooled around with them. Sayge showed me how to dance like him, and I completely gave into the fun.

"What are you three doing?" A voice growled.

All of us stopped at the same time. Sayge, Dar, and Calvin looked sheepish as they stared at the man who looked at them with a raised eyebrow. From the look on their faces, I could tell who it was.

"Jack," Sayge said, waving a hand toward him, "this is Elio. Our Daddy," he said, shoving his chest out proudly. "And we're probably in trouble, huh?"

"Did you ignore my texts?" Elio asked.

"Yeah," Dar grinned. "Sayge said it would probably be a lot more fun if we-."

Sayge elbowed Dar. "Shut up," he hissed. "Sorry, Daddy." He said as he blinked up at Elio. "We just wanted to have some fun."

"Uh huh." Elio's eyes traveled over me making a shiver run up my spine. "Jack," he said. "Have you been drinking like the three of them?"

"Yes," I muttered, shifting from one foot to the other.

"Do you have a way home?"

I shook my head. "I guess I really didn't think about it..."

"Come along," Elio sighed. "Let's get you back to your parents."

Sayge cackled. "Not his parents. His Daddies," he teased.

"They're not!"

"Yeah they are," Dar said as he draped an arm over my shoulders.

"Dar, remove your arm," Elio growled.

He tightened his hold. "Why?"

I wriggled out of his arm. Nope, that man had a look on his face that made my stomach tighten into a thousand knots. Dar could play with him all he wanted, but I valued being in one piece above anything else.

"I'll deal with you later," Elio said to Dar before he waved a hand. "Let's go."

I downed the last of my drink before I tossed the cup in the trash. We exited the club into what was now the freezing cold. I wrapped my arms around myself.

"Shit," I swore. "It's cold as fuck."

"Yep, that's the desert," Calvin said with a nod. "Where's your hoodie?"

I genuinely had no idea. My head was swimming, my body running between hot and cold as the liquor made my bladder feel like it was going to burst. I shrugged at Calvin.

"No idea. Gotta pee!"

I made a beeline around the building and unzipped. As soon as I started peeing, relief blanketed me. *Where the hell did I put that hoodie?* I really had no clue. I was too drunk. *Shit, I should have paid attention.*

I zipped up my pants and froze. The back of my neck tingled like someone was staring at me. I turned on my heels. The alley was empty, no one in sight. My eyes swept over it, every hair on the back of my neck on edge.

"You finished?"

I nearly jumped out of my skin. Sayge stared at me down the alley, waiting. I glanced around before I nodded.

"Just about."

Sayge nodded. "Elio's impatient. As always."

Quickly, I adjusted my clothes and headed toward them. I turned back, but no one was around. *Shit I'm drunk. What's wrong with me?*

I jogged down the alley to the car. All three of them were in the back, so I took the passenger seat even if it put me on edge. I tucked myself against the door as best I could and stared out the window. Something caught my eye and I quickly turned to look back at the alley.

Who is that?

I could just make out a shadow, but as the car moved I lost it. Sighing, I leaned back against the seat and forced myself to get it together. I had to climb back into my window, get into bed, and probably hide a massive hangover the next day. I steered Elio in the right direction until we pulled up near my house.

"This is close enough," I said.

"No, I'm taking you all the way home," Elio said as he glanced around. "Where is it?"

I shivered. "No, I really will get yelled at if a strange car is outside our place. I better just--."

"Jack!"

I winced as I heard that familiar voice. Ronan. He marched over to the car, wrenched open the door, and yanked me out by my elbow.

"What the hell were you thinking?" he snapped.

"Ow, I'm fine," I said as I tried to get free, but he refused to let me go. "I'm home, so chill!"

"Chill? Chill!" He snapped. "Is that all you have to say for yourself? I nearly had a heart attack when we found your room empty! Thank God Cian reviewed the footage and saw you sneaking out, but I thought—." He shook his head as if he didn't want to say what he'd thought. "We're going home. Now."

"I can walk by myself!" I protested.

"No, you clearly can't. Finnian is going to kill us both," he muttered. He froze and gazed into the car. "Who are these people?"

"Those are my friends," I said as I jerked a thumb toward the backseat. "And that's their... boyfriend."

"Daddy," Sayge said helpfully as he climbed into the front seat with a grin on his face. "Hey. You must be one of Jack's Daddies. I'd know that bossy tone anywhere."

Elio clicked his tongue at Sayge. "Stop flirting before we don't even make it home."

Sayge pouted. "Bye Jack," he winked. "I'll talk to you real soon."

"That's it," Elio snapped.

I watched as the car peeled off. No doubt all three of them were going to get fucked stupid. Me? I was just going to get fucked.

"Come on," Ronan bit out.

I groaned. "I'm coming! It's not even that big of a deal," I muttered.

Ronan sucked in a sharp breath. "Anything could have happened to you. Do you know how worried I was?" When I didn't respond, he glanced back at me. "Jack... Don't you give a damn that we were all concerned?"

My chest tightened. No. I didn't give a fuck what Finnian or Cian thought, but I didn't like the look on Ronan's face. I stopped fighting as he dragged me back to the house. As soon as I was pushed inside Finnian stood in the hallway, arms crossed over his chest. Cian was right behind him.

I'm so screwed.

CHAPTER SIX
RONAN

My MIND WAS CLOUDED with hurt and confusion. I stood outside Jack's door frame. The actual wood door was gone; Finnian had stripped it off before he left. There was no longer any privacy for Jack, but he'd done it to himself. One of us needed to be with Jack at all times and another on watch for anyone around which meant our new rotation was two men on, one man off.

"Guarding his door huh? Like a dragon to a princess?" Cian sipped his coffee staring at Jack's curled form on the bed.

I couldn't argue with him. No matter how upset I was with Jack, I wasn't going to leave his side.

"Finnian stepped out."

Cian nodded. "Saw on the camera. Should have let me plant the bombs in the front yard. Princess wouldn't have gotten far."

"He would have gotten hurt."

Cian shrugged. "What's worse? A missing leg or death?"

"Neither is a good option." Arguing with Cian was like arguing with a wild animal. He never saw reason in something as mundane as compassion or concern. He was the

49

best attack dog Declan had and it showed why he excelled at it.

"Princess is waking up," Cian said, jerking his head toward Jack's bed.

"Stop calling him that. He doesn't like it."

"I don't tell you how to baby him."

I don't baby Jack, right? Thinking back on it there had been plenty of times I'd been known to cater to Jack's whims. It was hard not to. I enjoyed watching him smile or get lost in a drawing. He was especially breathtaking when he was excited about something. Then I couldn't help but give him whatever he wanted.

"Would you two stop shouting?" Jack pulled the blanket over his face hiding away from us.

"Rise and shine princess!" Cian marched into the room and snatched the blanket off Jack.

I mentally sighed. Jack probably had a hangover if the state he was in last night was any indication to go off of.

Jack groaned as he slipped from the bed. He wore tight shorts that left nothing to the imagination. They hung low on his hips, but what caught my attention were the piercings on his dusky-colored nipples. Silver bars with pink jewels decorated each side of his nipple and my fingers tingled. I wanted to play with them, to watch Jack's face shift with ecstasy. My gaze was instantly drawn to them and had been since Jack had secretly gotten them on his 19th birthday. His thick lashes hid his dark brown eyes as he kept his lids low.

"Fuck off, Cian. It's too early in the morning for your shit."

"Language Jack," I chastised.

He sighed. "Really? You don't get on Cian or Finnian when they curse, why me?"

Because you're important to me.

Because you're mine.

None of those reasons were allowed to be said. Jack was my boss's son, that was all it could be. "Jack, you shouldn't talk that way."

He tossed his arms up but he didn't curse. The good boy weighed heavily on my tongue, but I kept it to myself.

"Yeah, princess, a dirty mouth like yours only exists for one purpose, better learn to clean it up." Cian couldn't leave well enough alone.

Jack's cheeks went red as he stared at Cian. "I—fuck you."

Cian moved toward Jack with a smirk on his face. "Yeah, we've been over this, stop teasing and bend over princess."

"Cian," I called out.

Jack on the other hand looked equally angry and intrigued. Was that what he was interested in? I'd seen and ran off plenty of men that Jack had tried to entertain. None of them had been like Cian. I wasn't sure I'd be able to run someone like Cian off. He seemed like the type to lick something and call it his.

I don't want to lose Jack to anyone.

"Shut up. Ronan, help," Jack whined. He pressed his fingers against his temples as he winced. He moved around the both of us and made a beeline for the kitchen. The coffee maker on the counter was already filled with fresh coffee. Jack sighed in relief as he grabbed a mug from the cabinet.

"Don't call your guard dog out now. Not after the shit you pulled last night."

Jack glared at him. "You act like you never went out before. I was going crazy in here, stuck with the three of you."

"That doesn't excuse you sneaking out and stealing money." I couldn't believe he'd snuck out.

Jack had disregarded everything we said. The entire reason we were in Arizona was to protect him and he snuck out as if it wasn't a big deal. As if we weren't important. *I* wasn't important. My chest burned in the most uncomfortable way. The sensation started slow until it encompassed the entire area and set it on fire.

"Looks like you fucked up," Cian teased.

Jack glared at him before glancing my way. His mouth dropped down in a frown, and he took a step toward me. As much as I always wanted him near me, I didn't trust myself with him right now. I was so angry and hurt I was liable to say or do something to hurt Jack. I stepped back and the crestfallen expression that overtook Jack's face nearly had me going to him and comforting him.

"Ronan." Jack's voice was soft and lost.

"If you'd come to me, we could have figured something out. I asked what was wrong—"

The front door slammed and all three of them turned to see Finn walking in. His glare cut right to Jack. I knew that look. I straightened up instantly ready to defend Jack even if I was upset with him.

"You spoiled rotten sh—"

I moved in Finnian's path, and he stopped short. "Ronan, move."

He was technically in charge of me now. I took orders from him when they didn't come directly from Declan, but Jack was my priority. Always.

"Move or I will move you," Finn threatened.

Cian whistled. "Look what you started princess."

"Wait, I didn't start shit. Look, I just needed a break. Nothing happened. I made it back in one piece."

Finn glanced over my shoulder. "You made it in one piece thanks to the Laureati family. I had to go pay respects."

I turned on my heels and stared at Jack. "You said you went out with friends."

"I did."

"From another family and an Italian one at that?" Cian asked. He shook his head, his coffee forgotten as we all stared at Jack as if he lost his fucking mind.

"What part of no one is supposed to know we're here did you not pick up on?" Finnian asked.

"It's not that big of a deal," Jack stressed.

Finnian pinched the bridge of his nose. His brows were drawn together and his frown was deeper. "Are you that naive?"

"Jack, this is a big deal. Your father hasn't picked a side and you're basically making it seem like we are siding with the Italians." I stared at him imploring him to understand what he'd done.

"All I did was go out and have drinks with friends. Their daddy came to pick them up and drove me back home, that was all," Jack said.

Finnian stepped around me and marched over to Jack. I was right behind him.

"Ronan, if you stop me, know that I will put you through the floor. You are to stand by, am I clear?"

Finnian's voice brokered no argument. I looked at Jack and still, the boy didn't seem to understand the problems he'd caused.

"Yes sir."

Cian moved silently, slipping behind Jack as he attempted to step back from Finnian.

"Where do you think you're going princess?" Cian teased.

Jack visibly shuddered. "What are you two doing?" He looked to me, his eyes pleading with me for help. "Ronan."

"I'm done catering to you. Nothing we say gets through

your head. We've repeatedly explained the dire situation we are in," Finnian said.

"I told you and my dad that I could handle myself. If he'd let me stay in New York—."

"Enough." Finnian grabbed Jack and pulled him over to the open living room right off the kitchen. The sliding glass doors' curtains were drawn keeping most of the morning light at bay.

Finnian sat on the emerald green sofa and tossed Jack over his lap.

"What the fuck?" Jack moved to get up, but Finnian pressed down on the middle of his back keeping him pinned.

"You can either take it gracefully or make this worse."

"Let me go. Do anything and I will—"

Finnian smacked Jack's ass effectively shutting him up. My heart rate picked up instantly. He wasn't going to do what I thought he was right? *Why in the hell am I excited?* I should dread anyone touching Jack even if he did deserve a spanking.

Jack recuperated and glanced over his shoulder, our eyes locked for what felt like an eternity. I stepped toward them, and Finnian's voice broke the momentary bubble.

"Ronan, don't even think about saving him."

Cian snickered and tugged me back. I let him. Maybe this would help Jack understand and grasp just how worried I was.

"You can't do anything to me," Jack argued.

"Or what? You're going to cry to daddy?" Cian asked.

Jack gritted his teeth, his fist balled up on the couch. "I didn't do anything wrong. You guys were keeping me locked up like some prisoner."

Finnian shook his head, "You just aren't getting it through your head." He hooked his fingers in Jack's sleeper shorts and shoved them down baring Jack's creamy ass. Freckles tantalizingly decorated his flesh.

"What the fuck is happening?" Jack asked. He squirmed over Finnian's lap. His head was nearly to the floor as he was forced on his tippy toes.

"This isn't fair. We're each pissed off that you're the only one who gets to punish him." Cian leaned against the wall, his eyes zeroed in on Jack's bare ass.

I wanted to cover him up instantly. No one got to see him. No one but me. I forced myself to stay glued to the wall even as my stomach tightened, and the base of my spine tingled. Jack was a squirming mess over Fin's thighs.

"You're pissed that he escaped?" Finn asked.

Cian shrugged. "Fuck yeah. The princess got past my security. You can't be the only one who gets to have fun."

"I'm not some toy," Jack interjected.

None of us were listening. I looked between each of the other men. I could tell there was no way around it. Finnian was going to spank Jack regardless of what I or Cian said.

"I agree."

"Ronan!" Jack tried again to get up.

Finnian shoved him back down and pinned him in place. "Stop moving, I haven't started yet."

"This is embarrassing! I'm a grown ass man."

"Then shut your mouth and take it like one," Finnian shot back.

Jack went momentarily still, his mouth clamping shut as he glared at the floor.

Finnian looked at both Cian and I. His emerald green eyes bore into us. "Nothing permanent."

Cian groaned. "Take all the fun out of it."

I took another peek at Jack, my stomach clenched. "Maybe—"

Cian elbowed me. "You can't say you don't want to

punish him after last night." He gave me a knowing look. The man was insane, and I was sure whatever was going on in his head was a mess, but he wasn't wrong. Cian smiled, his blue eyes sparking with mischief.

"Then it's settled. Jack will take all three punishments," Finnian said.

"What? I didn't agree to shit. What about what I want?" Jack argued. He wiggled around on Finnian's thighs.

Fin's hand came down with an audible smack. The sound resonated through the room. My stomach coiled and heat blossomed in its wake. Jack went still as his mouth was left open and his eyes widened to saucers.

"We are over your entitled behavior. Until you can learn to respect us and follow the rules, you have no say," Finnian said. He brought his hand down. "Do you understand?"

Another smack. Jack jerked and his mouth snapped shut as a yelp escaped him.

"I need an answer," Finnian said. His hand came down again pulling a scream that tapered off to a moan from Jack.

I shouldn't. I knew I shouldn't and yet I couldn't help myself. I glanced further down Jack's body, his ass was turning bright red as Finnian brought his hand down repeatedly. But what stole my breath was the fact Jack was hard. His cock was an angry red between his legs even as he shouted protest and tried getting away from Finnian.

Jack's breathing changed the more Finnian spanked him. His ass got redder by the second. His legs trembled as he fought to stay up on his tippy toes.

"You still haven't replied," Finnian said.

Jack shook his head, earning him another smack. My cock jumped. I couldn't believe I was getting turned on by another man spanking Jack. I would have never imagined it.

"I—I okay," Jack said.

Finnian smacked his ass again. "Not good enough."

Jack wiggled on his lap, his hips moving as he sought out friction against his leaking cock. I wanted to step over to them and wrap my hand around Jack's length and stroke him. Drive him crazy as Finnian spanked him. Butterflies erupted in the pit of my stomach at the vivid imagery taking over my brain. My cock pressed heavily against the seam of my jeans. This felt like we were stepping over the line I'd made sure to tip-toe along for so long. Something achingly close to relief and excitement settled in the middle of my chest.

Did this mean I can make Jack mine even for a short while?

"Yes, I under—stand." Jack sniffled.

I expected Finnian to smack his raw ass again but instead, he rubbed firm circles over the red globes. "Will you listen to what we say?"

Jack nodded and Finnian tapped his ass pulling out a moan.

"Yes," Jack half moaned and shouted.

"Good boy," Finnian said.

Jack visibly sagged, his soft cries were unmistakable but what caught my eye even more was how Finnian treated him after. He could have made it far more humiliating for Jack. Instead, he'd been focused solely on Jack and his spanking. Even now as he rubbed Jack's ass it was clear to see he was giving him comfort.

"Ronan," Finnian called.

I pushed off the wall and moved toward them and unclenched my fist. It had taken everything in me not to move toward them. Finnian looked up at me and then back down at Jack. Something passed over his face before it disappeared. It was impossible to decipher exactly what it was.

"Take him."

I grabbed the yellow throw blanket off the back of the couch and draped it over Jack before I scooped him up. His arms went around my neck instantly and he pressed his tear-streaked face against the crook of my neck. My arms tightened around him at the same time my heart skipped a beat. Finnian stared at us for a long while before getting up. "I'm going to get some rest. Cian, you're on watch."

"You can have him." Cian pushed off the wall and moved toward us. He smiled at Jack. "What I have in mind would break him right now."

I pressed Jack against my chest and nodded, not sure what to say to that. Cian was crazy and there was no telling what Jack would have to endure from him. He snuggled up closer to me. Tears wetted his eyelashes making him seem even more innocent than he was. My heartbeat was still racing as I made my way to Jack's bedroom.

"Does your head still hurt?"

Jack sniffled and nodded his head. "Yes."

There were already pain meds and a bottle of water waiting for us on the bed. Finnian must have gone ahead and got it for Jack. The man was a hard ass, but I was starting to see the softer parts of him, or at least I hoped I was. I sat down with Jack in my arms and the boy clung to me even tighter. His blunt nails dug into my flesh leaving little bites of pain. It did nothing to combat the smoldering desire rocking in the pit of my stomach.

"Jack, I need you to pull back a little and take this pill."

Two glossy brown eyes looked up at me.

"Open up."

Jack didn't argue or ignore me. His mouth opened up and he stuck out his tongue. I placed the pain pill in his mouth and held the water bottle up to his lips. Jack swallowed the pill.

"Keep drinking," I said.

Jack looked at me through his wet lashes as he continued to drink the water. He didn't stop until I pulled it back.

"It will kick in soon, anywhere else hurt?"

Jack's cheeks reddened further. "My butt."

I couldn't help the tilt of my lips. I didn't think as instinct took over and I pressed a kiss to each eye. "Good boy."

Jack squirmed in my hold as a shy smile that took my breath away came over his face.

He's gorgeous.

"Da—Ronan," Jack called. He put out his bottom lip and I fell prey to it this one time.

I pressed the faintest kiss to Jack's forehead. "You did good taking your punishment, but you know it's not over, right?"

Jack whimpered and it tugged at something in my soul. I wanted to give him the world to hold and kiss him for the rest of our lives. It was a feeble dream, but for now, I could pretend and cave into it. Just for a little bit, I'd have Jack O'Brien.

"But—"

I pulled back and looked down at Jack. "Are you trying to argue with me?"

He looked away instantly and stared down at his hands. "No—"

There was more to it, and I was desperate to hear what Jack wanted to tack onto his response. Instead of demanding like my heart wanted, I moved on to my punishment. I laid Jack down on his stomach and checked his ass. It was red and as I laid my hand on it, I could feel the heat radiating off his flesh.

"Here." I grabbed his loose-fitted joggers and helped him slip them on.

Jack whimpered and looked back. "Can I have french toast and sunny side up eggs?"

Yes, was my immediate answer but I swallowed it down. "Not till you're done with my punishment. Be a good boy and maybe Finnian will make it."

Out of all of us, he had the best skills in the kitchen. None of us trusted Cian in there. There was no telling what he'd feed us. Might even poison us just for shits and giggles.

Jack bit his bottom lip and I pulled it free instantly. I ran my thumb over his plump bottom lip hypnotized by how soft it was.

"You're going to kneel in the corner and think about what you did wrong."

Jack glanced at the corner and then back at me. "Yes Da—"

Again, with that slip up. I wanted to hear him finish it more than anything. If he kept it up, I was going to end up shaking it out of him. I helped him off the bed and over to the corner. Jack sank on his knees, moving to get as comfortable as he could. His face was tight as he was forced to stay perfectly upright.

"And no dessert for the next week."

Jack groaned. "But—"

I cocked a single brow at him waiting to hear his argument. Jack could be difficult if he wanted to be.

"Would you like to go for two?"

Jack shook his head. "No. Sorry, I'll be good."

My chest tightened at his words. *You want to be my good boy, don't you?*

"I'm very disappointed in you Jack. I understand you don't like being locked up, but this was for your safety." I pushed my fingers through his soft brown hair. "Thirty minutes. And after you've thought about your actions you can get up. You then need to properly apologize to Cian and Finnian. Once you're done, come find me."

Jack looked up at me. He nodded, still pushing his head into my caress.

"Till then I won't touch or speak to you."

Jack's eyes widened. "What?"

My hand dropped and I took a few steps back. The idea of walking away from Jack was my least favorite but I did it all the same.

"Ronan."

I shook my head. A whimper fell from between Jack's pouty lips.

"I'm so—"

I pressed a finger against his lips. I didn't want to hear a half-ass apology. Jack attempted to sit back on his calves and instantly shot back up. His ass was probably on fire. I grabbed a pillow off the bed and handed it to him. I left him in his room to think about what he'd done. I just hoped he came to his senses soon. We couldn't afford for him to be reckless. One slip up and I'd lose the boy I was secretly falling in love with.

Who was I kidding? I've been in love with Jack O'Brien for a while now.

CHAPTER SEVEN
JACK

My calves burned as I balanced myself so I wouldn't fall.
Ronan had given me a pillow, but my ass still burned when
I tried to use it. I rubbed at my eyes. My tears had dried, but
the embarrassment of being draped over Finnian's lap and
spanked stayed with me. Every time I remembered, my face
burned. I buried my face in my hands.

"What the fuck is happening?"

Even as I muttered the question to the empty room, I
squirmed. My cock was so hard it hurt. I had liked Finnian
spanking me. His sure, steady hands, firm strokes, stern
voice; it did it for me in ways other men couldn't. I almost
wanted to hear that Irish brogue scold me again while the
heat of his hand rested on my back. More than that, I
wanted Ronan back.

I glanced over my shoulder. He was nowhere to be
found. I stared at the ceiling, at the floor, at my cock that
refused to go down. I poked at it.

"Come on," I muttered. "Go away!"

I'd almost called Ronan daddy more than once! It had
felt so right though, the words on the tip of my tongue as he
wiped my tears and held me gently. Those moments always

felt as if the rest of the world fell away and I had nothing but support and comfort. I felt younger than I was, like I'd gone back in time and was small and needy. That side of me was rare. I never let it out, not when someone could find out about it and use it against me. I had enough working against my desire to run our territory in New York. No one needed to see that fleeting small side that desired to be loved, held, and babied.

"How much longer?" I called.

"If you're asking that, then you're not thinking about what you've done," Ronan said as he appeared in the doorway. "The timer will go off on the microwave when your time is up. I'm adding ten minutes."

"What?" I asked. "Come on," I whined.

"I can double it."

My lips sealed together. Ronan examined my face before he turned on his heels and walked away. My heart skipped a beat. I both loved and hated this. I wasn't used to Ronan walking away from me. Part of me wanted to throw a fit, but I remembered the disappointed look on his face. Sighing, I stared at the boring wall. Minute after minute ticked by, every second reminding me that my ass was sore and my calves hurt. Thank god the pain pills kicked in. At least my headache was gone.

The microwave chimed a jingle and I sighed. Slowly, I moved away from the corner, taking my time to get to my feet. I stretched, rolling my shoulders back as I chewed my bottom lip. *Do I really have to go say sorry to Finnian and Cian?*

Ronan's punishment was by far the least fun. Corner time was bad enough, but having to say sorry to those two? How could I stare at Finnian without getting hard all over again? And how could I say sorry to Cian when I wanted to punch him in his smug mouth? I shifted from one foot to the other.

I can do it. Just go out there, say sorry, and keep it moving.

The problem was that it was easier said than done. Sitting in the corner really had made me think about how worried they'd been for me. Not to mention the fact that if I ended up dead, they'd be dead too. My father didn't joke around when it came to my security. If I was gone, they didn't stand a chance.

Slowly, I shuffled out of my now open bedroom. I didn't even get a door anymore. I glanced around. Ronan sat on the couch, a book in his hand. He didn't look up when I came out, didn't come rushing over to me. My stomach twisted, nausea rising in my chest. I hated that.

I turned on my heels and walked to Finnian's room first. After knocking, I heard him call to come in. Finnian laid back in bed, his legs crossed at the ankles as he watched TV. I chewed my lip until he finally glanced up at me.

"Yes, Jack?"

I toyed with the doorknob. "I'm..." I swallowed thickly before I glanced away from him.

"You're what?"

"Sorry," I muttered.

"Jack, look at me."

How could I? All I could imagine was lying over his lap while he spanked me. My face burned.

"Look at me, now," Finnian growled, making my head snap up without my consent. "If you're going to say it then say it while you look at me."

I swallowed thickly. My mouth opened, but then shut as I let out the most pathetic sounding whimper. It was hard to say anything when he stared at me with those green eyes. I licked my lips before I forced myself to move forward.

"I'm sorry," I whispered before I cleared my throat. "I'm sorry I didn't listen and made you guys worry. I get it... what I did was stupid. I just didn't want to stay in the house all locked up."

"We all have to do things we don't want to do," he said steadily.

I frowned. "Yeah. I know you don't want to be here watching me. I get it."

Finnian opened his mouth before he shut it again. He shook his head. "Apology accepted. Next time you slip out of this house, I'll track you down and drag you back by your throat."

I shivered. "That's extreme," I muttered.

"Do you need another spanking? What did I say about respect in this house?"

"No," I said as I shook my head. "Sorry."

"That's better," Finnian said before he nodded toward the door. "Go on. You're alright with me, boy."

I lingered, waiting. *Where's the good boy?* I wanted to hear Finnian say it in that thick accent of his. When he turned toward me, I quickly skittered away. These three men would ruin my brain; that was clear. One after the other, they were turning me into something I tried to hide about myself. It wasn't fair.

"You paying attention?" Cian asked as I crashed into him. He moved back, rubbing his massive chest as he grinned down at me. "Where are you going?"

Cian. I wasn't sure if I wanted to fight him or get on my knees and slide his cock into my mouth. Both options would be fun if he didn't break me first. I glanced over toward the couch. Ronan was still reading, but I could tell he was more than aware of me. I couldn't screw up.

"I was going to talk to you," I muttered.

"About what, princess?" He asked. When I glanced

away, he grabbed my chin, forcing me to look at him. "Open that pretty mouth and speak."

A shiver ran down my spine. Heat swept over me from head to toe. A few short words from Cian and I lost my sanity. As I stared up at his tall frame, even taller than my six foot one height, I swallowed hard. He grinned like a shark watching its prey. I wanted to turn tail and run, but I stayed my ground. I was an O'Brien. I couldn't let Cian scare me.

"I'm sorry for leaving the house," I said. "But not for being disrespectful. Not to you. You're an asshole."

Cian's hand went in my hair before I could think straight. His nails dug into my scalp. As he shoved me down, I fought until I was forced onto my knees.

"Ronan!" I called.

"Don't call him," Cian laughed. "He can't help you." He tilted his head at me. "You haven't eaten yet, have you?"

I blinked at him. "N... no."

"Sit right here."

I grunted as he pushed me down. He walked around the island. I couldn't see anymore, and that just made me more nervous. I watched as he came back into view, pushed food into the microwave, and heated it up. Cian whistled under his breath.

What the hell is he doing?

It felt like ages until he came around to the kitchen table and sat down. I watched as he took the bowl of shepherd's pie from the night before and set it on the table. He undid his pants, my eyes going wide as I watched his cock pop free. Cian was already hard, his purple cockhead calling to my starving tongue. I wanted to taste it and the bead of precum that had formed on the slit.

"You're such a slut," he grinned. "I knew it. One look and I could see it on your face."

"I'm not!" I snapped.

Cian spit in his palm. "That's a lie," he said evenly. "Tell me you don't want to stare at my big, fat cock while I jerk off."

"I—I don't," I muttered.

He groaned as his hand wrapped around his dick. Cian shifted down further, spreading his legs more. Ronan walked over to us and paused. When I looked up at him, the look on his face was something I had only seen briefly when I teased him. Desire fluttered away as quickly as it had come.

"What are you doing?" Ronan asked.

"My punishment," he said as he grinned. "Since he wanted to be a little smart ass, I decided to do it now."

I groaned. "Don't talk about me like I'm not here!"

"Sluts should learn to be quiet," Cian said as he turned his blue eyes on me. "Take your cock out."

I stared at him. "What?"

"You heard me." When I didn't move, he gazed at Ronan. "Either you take his cock out or I will. And I won't be nice about it."

Ronan looked as if he was weighing his options. My mouth fell open as he walked toward me. I moved back on instinct, shocked that he was actually about to go through with this.

"Hey!" I snapped. "Are you really listening to him?"

"I told you to apologize properly. You decided not to do it." Ronan crouched and lifted me to my knees. His finger hooked in my pants. In seconds he yanked them down, exposing my hardened cock. He gasped. "When did you pierce *that*?"

"Fuck, that's good," Cian moaned. "I bet it tastes even better. I knew you had a wild side."

My face was on fire. I wanted to run to my room, shut

my now non-existent door, and hide. Cian grinned as if he knew exactly what I was feeling, and he loved every minute of it. He pumped his cock harder, faster as he stared at me.

"Touch yourself. Come on."

My heart picked up speed. I squirmed on the spot, looking from him to Ronan and back again. *Is he serious? He wants me to touch myself?*

"If you're not comfortable going that far, you don't have to," Ronan said softly. "Cian's probably going too far," he added as he glared at the man.

Cian chuckled. "What? You too much of a pussy to take my punishment, princess?"

I stuck out my chest. "I'm not a pussy," I snapped.

My hand wrapped around my cock. Big mistake. Pleasure assaulted me as I tried to stay on my knees. I leaned against Ronan. He kept me upright as I shivered and stared up at Cian, who's smile had only grown. He picked up speed, pleasuring himself as he watched me slowly touch my cock.

"Fuck," Cian groaned. "You touch yourself like you're new at it. Come on, show me how you do it when you're alone, baby."

My tongue swiped over my lips as I tightened my grip. I bucked forward, moaning as I fucked my fist. My cheeks clenched as my ass throbbed in protest. I licked my palm, wrapped my hand around my cock again, and groaned as Cian matched me stroke for stroke. He stared right at me, holding me enthralled as he jerked off.

"Move closer," Cian groaned.

"Cian," Ronan said.

"He wants to. Look at him. Hypnotized by my dick."

I shuffled forward and Cian laughed. The sound made me want to fight him and cum all at once. Instead, I simply stared as Cian's head fell back. My eyes were drawn to his dick. I wanted a taste so bad it hurt.

"You don't get to cum," Cian said.

"What?" I asked, my hand stuttering as I stared at him.

"I said you can't cum," he reiterated as he sat up and grinned at me. "It's a punishment. Not fun for you." He lifted his hips as he panted. "Fuck, fuck!" Cian called. He snatched the bowl from the table and stroked himself through his climax. Ropes of cum decorated the food. When he was done, he sat back as his cock went soft. "Eat. I can't play with you properly if you don't have any food in your stomach."

I stared at him in shock. "You can't be serious."

"Do it," he snapped as he sat the bowl on the floor. "And only eat with your mouth. You don't deserve any utensils." He gazed at Ronan. "Don't glare at me. He wanted to step to me and run his fuckin' mouth? He'll get the punishment he was craving."

Why was it so easy for Cian to embarrass me? One word, one order, and I was putty in his hands. I stared at the food on the ground, and my stomach twisted with need. Skipping dinner, drinking, and then going straight to bed had been a mistake. I was starved.

"Eat, princess," Cian said as he reached out and grabbed a handful of my hair. "Come on, before it gets cold."

He shoved my head toward the bowl. I sucked in a breath as I inhaled the scent of the food decorated with his creamy cum. Tentatively, I stuck out my tongue. Cian's cum assaulted my tastebuds, all salty and warm. I should have hated it, but my cock betrayed me again. It twitched hard, my pulse ramping up as I lapped at the food. Despite how much I wanted to tell him to go fuck himself, I couldn't. Instead, I started to devour what I'd been given.

"Told you he was a good little slut." Cian laughed. "See? You've been babying him too hard."

"I don't baby him."

"You do," Cian argued. "You should get him some water so he doesn't choke. I need to check the perimeter." His fingers tangled in my hair. "Next time, I'll feed you my cock directly."

I groaned despite myself. My pants were still around my ankles, my heart racing as I forced myself not to crawl after him and beg for more. I'd clearly lost my mind, but I didn't want to stop.

I wanted them to own me. Even if I hated them for it.

CHAPTER EIGHT

FINNIAN

I STARED into the bedroom as Jack slept. He'd spent the day before mostly confined to his room after his run-in with Cian. Of course Cian had to be the one to take it too damn far. I'd already crossed a line, but he jumped right over it and danced. I wanted to strangle him. Jack hadn't seemed to hate it too much, but still. I wanted to get Jack in line, not turn it into something sexual.

Even if I did have a hard on when I spanked him yesterday.

My cock had a mind of its own. I'd always had a thing for discipline, for order, and good behavior. Seeing Jack over my knee had brought up all of those wants and desires. Even if I thought he was a little shit, knowing that I could train him to behave made me eager. Until he said he knew I didn't want to be there watching him. Now that had made me feel like shit.

"Pervert."

I turned on my heels, my hand wrapped around a muscular throat. Cian grinned at me, but there was fire behind his eyes. A dare.

"What are you doing?" I muttered.

73

"Watching you watch Jack." His grin grew. "Don't you just want to go in there, rip off those shorts, and shove your cock up his ass? I know I do," he said as he reached down to adjust himself through his jeans.

I shoved Cian back. "Get the fuck out of here," I said as I advanced on him. "He's already going through enough shit."

"You mean the way he gave you big old puppy eyes about you having to watch over him? Admit it. You felt bad about that."

I narrowed my eyes at Cian, trying to push away the reality of his words. Maybe I had felt a little bad. Maybe I was...harsh. I hadn't meant to drag him over my knee yesterday and punish him, but it was part of me. Something that worked its way up as I stared at his smug face and nonchalant attitude. Now I had to live with that.

"Enough," I snapped at Cian. "What I did was stupid."

"Or fun," Cian said. "Loosen up, why don't you?"

I shoved a hand against his chest as he tried to advance on me. "Fuck off. I don't need to have fun. I need to do my goddamn job."

"You're so boring. Is that why you've been alone for so long?"

I turned on my heels to glare at him. "What did you say?"

"I said, are you alone because you're boring as fuck? Or maybe you've got a dick problem or something," he said, contemplating it. "I'm thinking probably both."

My body slammed into his, and we both hit the floor. Cian grunted, and I almost laughed as the air was knocked from his lungs. I saw the panicked look on his face morph into anger, but I didn't stop. I straddled his lap, my hands around his throat as he lifted his hips trying to buck me. The back of my hand connected with Cian's cheek. His head turned to the side before he turned back to stare at me, a trickle of blood sliding over his bottom lip.

"You want to try that shit again?" I asked.

Cian licked the blood away. "If I do, will you hit harder than a little bitch? That was pretty fucking weak."

"What are you two doing?" Ronan hissed as he stood beside us. "You're going to wake up Jack."

I quickly climbed off of Cian. "We were just having a conversation," I said.

"A conversation with your fists?" Ronan asked.

I didn't have an answer to that. Cian slowly pulled himself to his feet, still panting as he tried to regulate his breathing. All the while, that grin stayed in place. I wanted to knock it off of his face. Cian stepped forward and slapped my shoulder.

"Don't worry. I know you only acted that severely because it was true."

I wanted to wring his neck. Every bit of my composure was stolen away as I thought about kicking Cian's ass. A hand pressed against my chest and pushed me back. I glanced at Ronan as he shook his head.

"He's just trying to rile you up. Ignore him," he said. "What are you two fighting about anyway?"

"Nothing," I said as I pinched the bridge of my nose. "We've only been here a few days and everyone is climbing up the walls. I don't know how we're going to last."

"We'll be fine," Ronan said as he gazed toward Jack's room. "Mostly fine. What we started with Jack..." He trailed off.

"It's wrong," I answered.

Ronan half nodded, half shrugged. "Yes, that," he muttered. "Declan will have our heads if he finds out."

Cian laughed. "Yeah, right." When we both turned to stare at him, he grinned. "You two really think Jack is going to say anything? He loves this shit. I've never seen anyone who wanted to be fucked into submission so badly. You two are just soft."

"You're just a pervert," I snapped. "Keep your hands off of him. I'm trying to make sure he stays in this house and stays alive. You're trying to make sure he ends up on your cock."

"Guilty," Cian chuckled.

I stepped closer to him, invading his space. "If you put your dick anywhere near him, I'll handle you."

"Oh yeah?" He stepped closer until our chests touched. "How?"

Even with three inches of height on me, I didn't give a fuck. Cian was a big man. One that needed to be taken down a peg.

"Trust me, you don't want me to give you the same treatment," I answered. "My cock will go so deep in your ass it'll reset your psychotic brain."

"Okay," Ronan said as he stuck a hand between the two of us. "Enough. We haven't even been here this long and we're falling apart? It's ridiculous." He turned to me. "Can you please make Jack breakfast? He'll be up soon. I can do it, but you cook better than I do, and he deserves it after yesterday."

I sighed. "What does he want?"

"French toast and eggs sunny side up. I didn't let him have it yesterday because he started problems with Cian."

Cian whistled. "Look at you growing a set of balls."

Ronan ignored him. "I'll get started on coffee."

"Yeah, thanks," I grunted.

I stepped away from Cian before I took him to the ground and showed him why I was in control and he wasn't. Cian was our reaper, an elite assassin, but that didn't mean I would back down and let him run all over me. Sure, he could kill. But I had fought my entire life. I'd fought through my childhood, as an adult, through the ranks until I took up residence on Declan's right hand side. I had to keep that position. After yesterday, if Jack ever decided to say anything, I'd be screwed. Either I would be on my own or dead.

Jack staggered out of the bedroom as I flipped out slices of cinnamon French toast onto a plate. He rubbed his eyes only dressed in those tight little shorts. His bare chest boasted pierced nipples. I wanted to pop one after the other into my mouth and suck until he fell apart. Instead, I cleared my throat and cracked an egg into the pan.

"Sit down. I'm making breakfast," I told Jack. I glanced over my shoulder as he took a seat. "Once breakfast is done you have chores."

"What?" Jack muttered. "Chores? I've never done a chore in my life."

"You're going to learn," I said evenly. "Everyone needs to pull their weight here, not just us."

Jack pouted. "Come on, man. I've already done enough! I want to lay in bed and do nothing."

I froze before I slowly turned to face him. "Did I ask for your attitude?"

Jack's eyes cut away from mine. "No."

"Look at me."

As our eyes met, I almost walked toward him and dragged him over the island. He was as feisty as Cian. I stood in front of him.

"I said you're going to be cleaning today. Do you understand me?"

Jack tried to look away, but I snapped my fingers, dragging his attention toward me. "Don't make me ask again, boy."

"I- I understand," he muttered.

"You speak louder than that on a daily basis."

"I understand!" He snapped before he shrank away, slapping a hand over his mouth. "Shit, sorry."

Nodding, I moved over to the stove to complete the eggs while I hid the stupid grin that had decided to stretch my lips. Why was Jack freaking out so funny to me?

Focus. My job isn't to play with Jack. I'm supposed to be keeping him safe and setting him straight so he's not such a little brat.

I tried to remind myself of that and wiped the smile from my face. When I moved back to him, I sat his plate down and put syrup beside it. As I went in search of utensils, Ronan's voice made me glance over my shoulder.

"Do you want me to pour your syrup?" He asked.

"I can do it," Jack muttered.

"Are you sure? You don't like when your hands get sticky."

Jack groaned. "Da- Ronan, come on," he said. "Don't tell people that! They'll think I'm weak."

"There's nothing weak about needing a little help," Ronan said as he uncapped the syrup and started to pour. "Let me do it for you."

Jack sighed. "Fine," he muttered.

He slumped, but I saw the smile on his face. I'd always assumed he hated it when Ronan babied him, but from the look on his face, he loved it more than he let on. I laid a fork and knife on his plate. Ronan picked it up, cutting Jack's food into tiny bite sized squares. I raised a brow as I tried to ignore the jealousy that crawled through me. I didn't want anyone else so close to Jack. He was mine to deal with, mine to mold.

"What?" Ronan asked. "He likes it."

I looked at Jack. "Is that true? Do you like it when Ronan cuts up your food?"

He fidgeted. "I don't know."

"Is that what... your friends Daddy does for them?"

Jack's face went bright red. He'd brought up his friends having a Daddy the day before, but I hadn't gone into it at that moment. Not when I needed him to see the seriousness of what he'd done.

"I don't know," Jack shrugged. "Not really I guess? They're different."

"Different how?" Ronan asked, a frown on his face.

"Just different!" Jack huffed as he pulled his plate toward him. "I don't know how to describe it."

"Watch your tone," I growled.

Jack glanced away before he looked back at us. "I just know they have a Daddy. They don't go into details or anything. Sometimes Sayge talks about them being in trouble or..." His face flushed.

"Or what?" Ronan asked.

"Or Dar talks about how good the sex is," he muttered.

Ronan and I exchanged a look. We were around the same age. I wasn't totally sure Ronan wasn't a virgin by the way he acted, but I'd definitely been around the block a few times. I'd seen my share of Daddy stuff, but I had never indulged in it. I was nothing like those soft men that cradled their boys and told them they were perfect even while they ran their mouths and misbehaved. I much preferred a well-behaved boy, even if I had to break a brat to get to that side of him. The thought of taming Jack made me heated all over again.

"Hey," I said as I placed a water bottle beside Jack's plate. "Eat up."

"Okay."

Yes, Daddy. That's what I want. I want you to say it while you look up at me with those big, brown eyes.

Jack stopped with a forkful of food halfway to his mouth. Slowly, he put it down.

"What?" He asked.

"About yesterday," I said, trying not to think about how cute he looked with his head tilted to the right. "It's not that I don't want to be here, watching over you," I said slowly. "I just want all of us to stay here, for things to be quiet, and then to go back home when we're done. Okay? It has nothing to do with you specifically."

Jack frowned. "Are you sure you don't just fucking hate me?"

"Language, Jack," Ronan groaned.

I let out a laugh by mistake and swallowed it. "No, I don't hate you. I think you're a brat that needs to be taught how to behave, but hate is a strong word. If I hate anyone, it's Cian."

"I heard that!" He called.

"Where even are you?"

"In the bathroom!" He yelled back. "But I have my phone and cameras everywhere."

I stiffened. "Isn't there a bathroom in your room?"

"Yep, but I like messing up yours!"

Jack burst out laughing and quickly covered his mouth. Even Ronan glanced away trying to hide the grin on his lips.

I was going to kill all of them.

CHAPTER NINE

CIAN

THE SUN WAS out cooking anything dumb enough to be outside. I sucked in a breath and regretted it instantly. The dryness in the air made it so much worse. I fucking hated Arizona; it was official. Ronan and Finnian only left a little while ago. I made my way inside, needing water and something to fix my shit mood. Sweat dripped down my back and sides. My shirt soaked up and clung to me like a second skin. The moment the air conditioning hit my overheated flesh, a chill raced down my spine. It wasn't enough to erase my shit mood.

Music played from the living room television, filling the house with the latest pop music. I headed for the kitchen needing some water. The moment I saw Jack, I stopped dead in my tracks. The sight of Jack swinging his hips back and forth as he washed dishes was mouth-watering. His slender waist dipped as he shook his ass to a sped-up part of the song. *Now I'm hot, tired, thirsty, angry, and hard.* I licked my lips as I pulled open the fridge. I didn't take my eyes off of him for a single second as I grabbed a bottle of water. I downed half of it without realizing it. I was too busy watching Jack.

He was unaware of me still even as the song changed. His dance movements changed but he didn't once turn around. If I was there to kill him, it would be so easy to get behind him and drag my knife over his throat. What would he do? Cling to life or cry out in anger? So many possibilities, but I couldn't kill the boss's son. Even I wasn't that crazy.

I moved behind him more. His movements slowed a little. My lips tilted up in a smile. Maybe he wasn't hopeless. I pressed two fingers against the back of his head.

"Bam! You're dead, princess."

Jack jumped. The glass he'd been washing went flying. It shattered upon impact. He whirled around and threw his elbow toward my face. I leaned back, letting his hit graze me over my nose.

"You have to be quicker than that. I could have killed you at least ten different ways."

"What the fuck, Cian!" Jack glared at me. "Why are you fucking like this?"

I tsked. "Your guard dog would be sad to hear you speak like that."

Jack looked around as if waiting for Ronan to come to chastise him. "He isn't here."

I couldn't help but laugh, messing with Jack was too much fun. "Shouldn't you be more alert?"

"I'm not good at hand-to-hand. Give me a gun and I'll show you what I can do."

The confidence that shimmered in his brown eyes was something to behold. For some reason, I didn't doubt his words.

"Maybe I'll take you up on that offer."

Jack stood up taller. "Really?"

"Yeah, when pigs fly."

Jack groaned and turned away from me. "You're a

fucking asshole. Don't you have something to do besides make my life a living hell?"

"Nope." I leaned in close and blew over Jack's ear. "I'm all yours, princess."

"Fuck." Jack jumped away, another glass slipping between his fingers. "Now I have to clean that up," Jack complained.

My hand curled around his upper arm, stopping him from walking away from me. "Where do you think you're going?"

"I have to clean up the broken glass. Finnian is going to be pissed. That's like the fifth one I've broken."

Jack was shit at cleaning up, but it was still fun to watch him fumble about. An idea came to mind, and I smiled.

"What the fuck, let me go," Jack said as he attempted to pull his arm free.

I reflectively tightened my hold on his arm and tugged him against me. "No."

"I want nothing to do with that creepy fucking smile."

"Awe, thanks princess."

"It wasn't a compliment." Jack groaned as I dragged him out of the kitchen and to the backroom. "You already had your punishment."

"Who said I was done?"

Jack visibly shivered in my hold. I liked the fear and desire swimming in his brown eyes.

"That's not fair."

"Are you really complaining? Not to mention I was certain I told you that you weren't allowed to cum."

"I didn't."

I stopped in the middle of my room and grabbed one of the remotes. After a quick few changes, the footage from a few nights prior came on the screen. Jack was sprawled out in bed, his gaze flickering over to the door as he palmed his hard cock. We both watched as he sank two saliva-slicked fingers in his greedy hole and pumped his cock furiously. His teeth sank into his bottom lip as he strained not to make too much sound.

"You recorded me?" Jack lunged for the remote in my hand.

I moved backward, grabbed the back of his neck, and shoved him down on the bed. I pressed against his backside and groaned.

"Who were you thinking about as you stuffed your ass with your fingers?" I rocked forward, loving the way Jack felt against me. "Was it really enough?"

"No one. And yes it was."

"You're a shit liar."

I pulled back slightly, and Jack followed, pressing his firm ass against me. I laughed.

"I'm not." Jack glared over his shoulder, his face flush as he tried to convince me he wasn't a pretty little whore.

"What would you say if I told you I jerked off while you did and imagined instead of your fingers that it was my cock inside of you?"

Jack moaned as he quickly looked away from me. "I'd say you're a crazy, delusional bastard."

"Maybe," I said as I chuckled.

I took a few steps back and released Jack. If I kept going, I was going to fuck him and once I started, there was no way in hell I was going to stop.

Jack scrambled up, moving as far away from the bed as he could without leaving the room. Him running only made me want to hunt him down all the more.

I went to the closet, grabbed what I needed, and brought it back to him. I laid out the pink skirt and matching bra and panties.

"Here."

"I don't know if I want to ask why you have that. More importantly, I'm not wearing it." Jack crossed his arms staring at the clothing items on my bed.

No one should be this tempting.

"Put the clothes on, princess."

Jack shook his head. "Finnian said I had to clean, he didn't say I had to wear that while doing it."

The mention of Finnian made my blood boil. He was another temptation in this damn house. I couldn't help but want to see him angry. Ronan was the only one I seemed to be unable to rile up.

"I want you to wear it."

Jack looked at the clothes again. "No way. You're a pervert."

I smirked at Jack. "Like you're one to talk. Which one of us was hard and shaking his hips as he ate my cum?"

Jack's cheeks reddened as he looked away. That wouldn't do. Having his big brown eyes on me felt too good. I closed the gap between us and grabbed his chin.

"Don't you want to be a good whore for me?"

"No." Jack's breath hitched and although his mouth said one thing, his body leaned toward me as if he was seeking me out.

"You sure?" I walked him back until his back hit the wall. His eyes widened only for a moment as I pushed his shirt up. My fingers traveled up his torso to his pecs. The warm metal of his piercing grazed my fingertips pulling a groan from the both of us.

"I'm sure you're an as—"

"Finish that sentence and I *will* punish you. It's been a few days. Your ass is probably good to go for another spanking." I leaned in even more. My lips brushed over the side of Jack's face. "I won't be as gentle as Finnian." I flicked my tongue against his earlobe before biting it. The sharp gasp from Jack was music to my ears. "I want to hear you scream and beg for me to stop." A laugh escaped me as I moved in closer until we were flush against one another. "Or will you beg me to keep going? You're such a good slut."

Jack's mouth fell open as he moaned. His lashes lowered, hiding his gorgeous eyes away from me.

"Was that a yes?"

Jack's tongue swiped over his lips leaving behind a glistening streak that drew my attention. An idea came to mind instantly.

"Wear it and I will reward you."

Jack's eyes opened instantly, and he stared at me. "With what?"

"My cock."

Jack audibly swallowed. He stared at me intently before blowing out a breath. "That's not a reward."

The hungry look in his eyes said otherwise.

I tweaked his nipple pulling on it until Jack's body lifted off the wall. He hissed but didn't tell me to stop once. His hips moved, rubbing his clothed cock against my leg.

"Slut."

Jack shook his head. "I'm not."

I twisted his nipple, earning another moan from him.

"What do you want besides my cock?" I wasn't sure why I was willing to negotiate with Jack, but it was fun and I did anything that entertained me.

"Teach me how to fight."

I pulled away, taken aback by his answer. "I'm not a teacher kind of guy. Why not ask Ronan or even Finnian?"

Jack shook his head. "Has to be you."

Why me? Jack probably knew nothing about me, and yet he wanted me to teach him?

"Okay."

"And—"

"Someone's greedy."

I waved my hand for him to go ahead and ask. There was no guarantee I'd give him anything else, regardless of how badly I wanted to see him dressed up.

"Your cock." His reply was barely over a whisper and if I wasn't so close, I might have missed it.

I slammed Jack up against the wall before the thought had been processed. My brain had short-circuited leaving me with nothing but primal instinct. Fuck everything else, I wanted to bend Jack over and fuck him stupid. I pulled at both of his nipples making him cry out. The sounds that came from him filled me to the brim with need. How was I the one toying with his body, and yet he had me on the edge of losing control?

"You'll put on the outfit for me right?"

Jack whimpered as he nodded. I teased his nipples playing with the piercing until he made the same whimpering noise as before. I wanted to tease him even more. I grabbed the clothes and handed them over to Jack once more. He took them this time, chewing on his bottom lip as he stared down at them.

"Get out," Jack said.

"Not happening. Not after you snuck out."

"Wait, there were cameras in my room... Did you know I was sneaking out?"

I shrugged. "Who's to say? The cameras in the house might not have been working that day."

"Did you let me —"

"Princess, get dressed and stop talking before I put your mouth to good use."

Jack stripped down and his hard-pierced cock between his thighs had my hand itching to touch him again. I restrained myself just barely as Jack got dressed. The pink panties barely confined his hard cock and the mini skirt rested in the middle of his ass. There wasn't even a need for him to bend over.

"Do I have to put this on too?" Jack asked as he held the pink matching bra up.

"Yes." I snapped my fingers hurrying him along. I wanted to see the full get-up.

Jack put the straps of the bra over his arms. He reached behind him flailing about trying to grasp them and hook them together. I leaned against the wall enjoying his suffering immensely. It was the little things with Jack that seemed to entertain me.

"Can you help?"

"I can." I didn't budge from my spot.

"Motherfucker." Jack grumbled a few more curses my way as he struggled with the bra. He whooped in victory when he finally succeeded in getting the bra to clasp.

"Hope you're not tired, you still have to go clean up the mess you made in the kitchen."

Jack flipped me off as he tried to tug the skirt down a bit more. It was pointless, it wasn't going to hide anything. I laughed as I followed him out of my room and toward the kitchen. I took up a spot on the table and watched as Jack went back to work. I made sure to turn on his music. The song bumped through the speakers filling the entire house.

"Clean how you were before."

Jack glared at me over his shoulder as he swept up the glass that had broken. I could tell he wanted to argue with me but he couldn't be taken seriously while wearing a mini skirt. Then again he could probably convince me to hand over my wallet while dressed like that. I was transfixed as Jack finally started losing himself in his chores. He wasn't the best at cleaning, but fuck he had my full support as long as he wore the outfit while he did it. I'd say he did a fantastic job, even if he left dirt behind.

"The floor needs to be cleaned." I pointed down to the scuffed-up granite flooring.

Jack headed toward the front hall, and I whistled for him to stop.

"Where do you think you're going?"

"To get the mop."

I shook my head and got off the table. I grabbed a sponge and a bowl.

"You have got to be shitting me."

"I want to see my reflection." As Jack made no move to do what I asked, I stepped toward him. "Are you wanting that punishment instead?"

Jack's pupils dilated. "Would I still get my rewards?"

Man is this boy made for me.

"Depends how I feel later."

Jack smirked at me and dropped down to his knees. "I really want to learn how to fight."

"And here I thought you were most excited about having my cock."

"That depends."

Fucking tease. I sat back on the table, my finger curled around the thick wood as I physically held myself back from attacking the princess of the house.

Jack's ass rocked from side to side as he scrubbed the floor. The alarm went off on my phone and I glanced over at the screen to see Finnian and Ronan had come back. The sound of the locks clicking didn't escape Jack's notice. He lifted his head.

"Don't stop, princess." I held the remote up and waved it at him. "You missed a spot there."

Jack went to stand and I tsked at him.

"Crawl like the bitch you are."

Jack whimpered as he followed my order. My cock ached to be inside of his firm ass. Fuck. I thought I was torturing him, but I was doing more harm to myself. His ass encased in pink panties was my new favorite sight.

"Jack, I got you your favorite snacks. And I picked up a gaming—"

Ronan stopped dead in his tracks as he entered the kitchen, his gaze instantly drawn to Jack on the floor wearing nothing but the skirt, panties and bra I'd given him.

"Fuck."

"Look at that princess, you got your guard dog to swear."

Jack looked up at Ronan. As long as none of them stopped me from playing with Jack, I didn't seem to mind them looking at my plaything.

"Ronan, why are you blocking the hallway?" Finnian asked. He slipped past Ronan and our eyes met briefly before he too noticed Jack on the floor. "What is the meaning of this?"

"He's cleaning like you ordered," I pointed out.

"I didn't—fuck...Jack, get up," Finnian ordered.

"Hey, I'm enjoying the view."

He pointed at me, a glare on his face. His thick auburn brow furrowed. "You fuck off. Cian you're left to watch Jack for less than two hours and we come home to this? Have you lost your mind?" He shook his hand. "Don't bother answering that."

Jack stood up and the tent beneath the skirt was unmistakable. His cheeks were flushed as he bounced back and forth on the balls of his feet.

"See, he loves it. Don't you, princess?"

Jack licked his lips, his gaze skirting over each of us. His mouth opened and closed as he tried to talk.

"Look at me, Jack," Ronan said. His voice was strained. "Did he force you to do this?"

I rolled my eyes as we each waited for Jack's answer.

"No I—I want—"

"Jack, speak clearly," Finnian said.

Jack glanced over at us, his eyes shimmering with unshed tears. Shit, he was sexy when he cried. I wanted to drag him closer and make him cry even more.

"I agreed, he didn't force me."

"See."

Finnian sighed. "I don't know what to do with this situation."

"What do you mean?" I laughed as I moved around Finnian and toward my slut. "Nothing. I'm playing with him right now. He's mine."

Both Finnian and Ronan went still. "What did you just say?" Ronan asked.

"Cian, are you taking the piss?" Finnian asked. He grabbed the front of my shirt. "Declan would have you killed."

"There is no better reaper than me."

"I knew you were psychotic; I didn't think you were stupid."

"Princess, you going to run back to daddy and tell him what's happening?"

Jack fidgeted and shook his head.

"See."

"Don't intimidate him," Ronan argued. "Jack, you can tell me if you don't like it."

Jack's face went stark red as he looked at anything but us. "I don't, *don't* like it."

I huffed out a laugh. "You two can hold back, but why should I?"

Finnian shoved me back. "Because it's common sense. Something you seem to be lacking."

"Fine, why don't you ask him what he wants," I said.

Everyone went still as if it hadn't occurred to any of them. I'd pointed it out already. Jack wanted it. There was no way in hell I was wrong in my observation. I spent my entire life people-watching. I knew what people wanted before they knew at times.

"Okay," Finnian finally said.

I rolled my eyes. I was the crazy one, but I was the only one willing to act on this insane attraction. So what if Jack was the boss's son? There was danger involved, but if anything, I was pretty certain it made Jack more appealing. We moved toward the living room. The moment Jack sat down, Ronan was right next to him. Finnian tossed the blanket at Jack and Ronan fixed it around him. They both were no fun. I wanted to continue to admire his slender body and the way the pink garments clashed with his pale skin. Finnian took the single chair and I leaned against the wall. I hated sitting for long periods of time unless I had to for a job.

"Jack, what do you want?" Ronan asked. He was as gentle as ever, practically holding Jack's hands.

"I—"

"If you want one of us that way, all you have to do is say so," Finnian said. He glared at me over his shoulder. "Everyone else will fuck off."

"Are you hoping he picks you?" I laughed. "Not with that stick up your ass."

"I will kill you."

A shiver raced down my spine, and I pushed off the wall. "Want to play?"

"Would you two stop flirting?" Jack groaned.

Finnian jerked around. "I'm not."

"Felt like flirting to me," I said.

I winked at him as he glared my way. Fuck, someone needed to pull the ten-foot pole out of his ass so he could relax. He'd been like that since we'd met and still, my opinion on Finnian hadn't changed. He was a stickler, a neat freak, controlling, arrogant, and hot. Above all else, he was someone I knew to stay clear of. We were too different. I loved a good fuck and fight, but we were no better than ammonia and bleach; we'd probably kill each other in the end.

"You're a lunatic. Your opinion isn't relevant," Finnian said.

Before I could utter a word Jack shouted his answer. "I want you to be my daddies."

"What now?"

"You mean Ronan?" Finnian asked.

I couldn't exactly disagree. Out of the three of us Ronan probably fit that title the best. Especially with how soft he was with Jack.

"No."

Ronan's lips dipped in a frown. "Oh."

Jack whirled around. The blanket dropped away from him giving us the full view of his body once more. "That's not how I meant it. I want you. Shit—I mean shoot, Ronan, I've been trying to convince you to see me for a while now."

"You've been seducing your guard dog, princess?" I whistled. Ronan was a better man than me. Jack just had to breathe, and I was ready to stick my cock in him without thought, but Ronan had been holding out this entire time?

"What do you mean then, Jack?" Finnian asked.

"I want all three of you."

"Greedy."

"Cian, shut up." Finnian sat up in the chair. "You want all three of us to do what?"

Jack groaned. "Do I have to say it again?"

"Jack." One word from Ronan and the princess was crumbling.

"I want all three of you to be my daddies, okay?"

"Even Cian?" Finnian asked.

"Hey, I'm sexy as fuck. Plenty of people have called me daddy as I fuck them." The only problem was I'd never been anyone's daddy outside of the bedroom.

"We are nothing like Ronan," Finnian said.

Jack's head tilted slightly, and his eyes widened. "Why would you need to be? I only want one Ronan."

"This can't work." Ronan stood up and moved away from Jack as if he'd been touching forbidden fruit.

"Why?" Jack asked. "You always run away. You guys asked me what I wanted, and I want this."

Ronan looked as if he was about to have an aneurysm. On the other hand, I was down for a good time. We could have fun and pass the long as fuck days while camped out in bum fuck nowhere.

"And when this doesn't work out?" Finnian asked.

I groaned. "You two are ruining this. Princess here is practically spreading his legs and begging us to breed him and you two want to twiddle your thumbs."

Jack gawked at me. "I didn't say or do any of that."

I winked at him. "But now you want to. You're a cock hungry whore. It's what makes you cute."

Jack shot up from the couch. "I'm going back to cleaning."

"Keep the outfit on. I want to watch."

He flipped me off. The other two, on the other hand, glared at me.

"You're crude," Ronan said.

"I'm right."

Finnian groaned as he stood up. "We do this; we do it right."

Great, he was going to lay down rules. Didn't he feel stifled by the constant need to have order? My skin itched just thinking about it. Chaos was welcoming; it was where I thrived.

Ronan nodded ever the faithful lap dog. "*Are* we doing this?"

"I am." I wasn't leaving it to them to decide. I wasn't down for a democracy. Jack had given his explicit consent and I planned on making him semi-regret it. The things I had planned for that boy were going to either turn his brain to mush or make him run away screaming. Both options were hot.

CHAPTER TEN

JACK

TRYING to pretend I didn't hear the three of them discussing me while I was only a few feet away was nearly impossible. They'd lowered their voices, nearly whispering now. I glanced over my shoulder. Ronan gazed at me and turned right back around when Finnian grabbed his attention. Cian winked at me.

Oh God, why did I say that? Why did I blurt that shit out?

Yes, it was what I felt. And what I wanted. Especially after the past few days; Ronan's sweetness, Finnian's sternness, Cian's wildness, all of it was so hot I could die and still be happy as fuck. Saying it out loud though? Was I insane? It was one thing to fantasize about stuff, and another to actually run off and do it. My body tried to burst into flames as I stole a glance at them again. *I'm kind of glad I did it.* Being bold around Ronan was easy, it was fun to tease him. Except now all three of them had turned me into some blushing thing that I normally wasn't. I blamed them for getting into my fucking head. I was a much braver person before.

Time to get brave again. I have to. Or I'm not going to get any dick.

I didn't know how long we'd be stuck in Arizona. What if we were here for months? For a year? The thought of living here that long without being touched made my skin crawl. I hadn't gotten laid in ages, not since I was back at college. Every time I tried, Ronan ran them off. Now I have a chance to get with three hot as fuck men. I really did want them to be my Daddies. Each one made me feel something different than the last. Even Cian who pissed me off. He was hot.

As I turned around to put a glass in the dish drain, the short skirt shifted around my ass. *Seriously, where did he get this?* It was embarrassing but hot. Every time I bent forward, I knew my ass was on display. I wanted to bend over and watch them drool over me. Even Cian had done it. I'd watched as his eyes went wide, and desire consumed his gaze. Fuck, I wanted more. I was so hard I was going to burst.

"Jack."

I glanced up at Finnian's voice. He crooked a finger. I put down the plate I was washing carefully before I picked up a towel and dried my hands. When I moved over to them, they each stared at me. I shifted back and forth.

"Yes?"

"If we're going to do this, there are rules," Finnian said.

"Of course there are," Cian groaned. "So fucking boring."

Finnian punched Cian in the stomach. The man gasped, wheeled back, and glared at him. I watched as he took a step forward, but one glance from Finnian and he paused. *Seriously just fuck already!* I'd never seen two people who wanted to screw each other's brains out as badly as they did. They were playing a stupid game.

"Jack, are you listening?" Ronan asked.

I blinked at him. "Now I am."

Ronan smiled. "Good. We were talking about it and only Finnian and I have experience with this whole Daddy thing."

"You do?" I asked Ronan. "You never told me that."

Ronan shrugged. "It was a long time ago," he said. "In another life."

Now I was curious. However, Ronan glanced away from me as if he didn't want to talk about it. Later. I wanted to know what they were talking about right now.

"What are the rules?" I asked.

"First off, you don't have to do shite you don't want to do, boy," Finnian said. "Is that understood? You have the option to opt out of anything that goes too far. Have you ever done this before?"

I nodded. "Yeah. I've had a few online relationships with Daddies."

Ronan stiffened. "What?"

"Well!" I threw up my arms. "You kept stopping me from having real ones."

"Glad I did," he muttered.

I raised a brow at the vindictive tone in his voice. Heat swirled in the pit of my stomach. Ronan was jealous? Over me? I loved that so much I could hardly sit still. I bounced on my toes grinning as I tried to imagine Ronan being possessive and jealous over me with other guys.

"Focus," Finn snapped.

"Yes, sir." I chewed my lip. "Shit, that just slipped out."

"I think I prefer Daddy Finn," Finnian said, giving me that rare smile that made me want to fly. "You know about safe words then?"

"Yes," I nodded. "Mine has always been red. Easy to remember."

"Then we'll go with that," Finnian said. "If at any time anything goes against what you want, you just say red. We'll stop immediately. Alright?"

"Yes... Daddy Finn," I added, tasting the weight of it on my tongue.

I loved it. Finnian's grin grew and I wanted to say it over and over again if he just looked at me like that a little longer.

"Enough," Cian groaned. "Come on, spit it out. What's the rest of the rules?"

"Jack will have rules to follow. You'll help out around the house, do as you're told, and follow your punishments. Only if you behave will you get rewards. And no, I won't spank you again as punishment. You were hard during the last one."

My face flushed. "You were too!" I pointed out.

Finnian cleared his throat. "Regardless."

"He's got you there, Mr. By the Book," Cian snickered.

"Shut up." Finnian turned back to me. "The other rule is for all of us. Jack will belong to us for the remainder of this... little trip," he said. "All of us. I don't want to see any fucking jealousy. Either we all get along and share, or he's off limits to all of us."

Cian stopped laughing immediately. "What the fuck? Hell no I don't agree to that!"

"Ask me if I give a shit," Finnian growled.

I glanced at Ronan. "What do you think?"

"I think it's the only way to do things," he said as he seemed to think it over. "Either we share or no one gets anything at all. That also means Jack should be shared between us evenly. We each get a day in rotation. That way no one's fighting," he said, as he specifically gazed at Cian.

"This is bullshit," Cian muttered.

"We can stop this now," Finnian said. "And that'll be the end of that."

Cian gave up right away. Instead, he growled as he crossed his arms over his massive chest. The look in his eyes was both terrifying and hot. I wanted him to take out that pent up irritation on me. Particularly my holes.

Shit, is he right? Am I a slut?

"What about you, Jack?" Ronan asked. "Any rules?"

I blinked at them. They all looked at me eagerly. Ronan inquisitively. Finnian examined me, making me feel small. And Cian looked like he wanted to eat me. Yep, I'd decided to throw myself to two sharks and a sweet dolphin. *Wouldn't change it for the world.*

"Just one," I said slowly. "I get my door back in case I want some privacy of my own."

"Never that," Finnian said.

My mouth dropped open. "Come on!"

"I said no," he said sternly. "Not until I'm sure you can be trusted. However, I'll allow you to earn it back. How does that sound?"

I huffed. It was better than nothing.

"Fine," I muttered. "Then I want to do the stuff I've always wanted to do. Spankings, playing video games... sex," I mumbled. "All of it. I've never been able to have a Daddy experience in real life, so if we're going to have this thing before we have to go back home, I really want to enjoy it. You all have to play with me. And..." I glanced at Ronan. "I don't want to be isolated or left alone, ever. *That's* my red. You can all punish me how you see fit, but I don't want to be on my own while it happens. I didn't like that."

Ronan frowned. "Oh, Jack," he whispered. "I'm sorry, I didn't think—."

I shrugged. "It's okay, but I don't want that again. That's all."

Ronan closed the space between us and pulled me into his arms. Like always, I felt the tears gather as he held me close. He was the only one I ever felt like I could be soft around. I had to keep up the hard part of me, the one that would one day run the family if I kept pushing. But when Ronan held me, I melted.

"I'm sorry," he said again. "Do you understand me? That will *never* happen again. I shouldn't have done it."

I clung to him. "It's okay."

"It's not okay," he snapped. "I know better than that. Try to be a hard ass and look where it gets me." He shook his head when we parted. "You should never feel anything but safe with me. That's all I want."

My heart squeezed. I knew Ronan would be the one for me, I always had. He tried to shove me away, but from the day we met I saw softness in him. Clearly, my father saw another side, otherwise he wouldn't have been hired. But I didn't want that side of Ronan. I wanted him exactly the way he was.

"What do you want from the two of us?" Finnian asked.

Ronan slipped his hand into mine. I squeezed his hand as I gazed between Finnian and Cian.

"Well, I want you to be yourself. Stern and bossy," I muttered to Finnian. "I kinda like that?"

"You always complain about it."

"So what?" I asked. "It's hot."

Finnian laughed. "Alright, I get it."

"And what about me? You want me to be your hot dose of dicking everyday, right?" Cian asked as he grabbed his junk. "I can do that."

I rolled my eyes. "I still think you're an asshole, but you can just go on being yourself too. Don't think you'd change even if I asked."

Cian scoffed. "Would you ask?"

I shrugged. "Probably. You're nuts."

"Whatever," Cian waved a hand. "I'm going to go check the perimeter."

"No, we're talking," Finnian said. "You can check it from your phone."

"Last I checked you ain't the boss of shit," Cian said as he walked away. "Fucking up my perfect view. This is bullshit," he muttered until we couldn't hear him anymore.

"Is he okay?" I asked.

Finnian sighed. "I'm sure he's fine. Besides, he really did step over the line with this," he gestured toward me, "little getup he made you wear. I still have an issue with that," he growled.

Not me.

Cian probably wouldn't have forced me into the outfit, but now that I was in it I loved it. Especially because I knew I could control Cian when I wore it. He practically tripped over himself as soon as he saw my ass hanging out of the bottom of the skirt. I hadn't felt something so close to fucking power in ages. I liked it. And I wanted to do it again. I wanted to wear the outfit, bend over, and make him hump against me like a dog in heat until he pegged me with that hard, thick cock.

I shivered. *Okay, so maybe I really am a slut.* I wasn't that ashamed of it. In fact, I wanted to dive into it headfirst. After being punished, given chores, and babied by Ronan, I wanted each one of them to throw me down and stuff me until I couldn't think straight anymore.

"One more rule," Finnian said, dragging my attention back to him. "Whatever one of us puts in place, it can not contradict the others. Cian said you couldn't cum, right?"

I groaned. "I actually have to listen to that!"

"Yes. If we have any problems the three of us will meet up and figure it out. You won't be put in the middle."

Now, that I liked. Sighing, I pushed my fingers through my hair. I gave up. Whatever rules they wanted, even if they said strip naked and stand on my head, I'd probably do. After all, when was I going to get a chance like this ever again?

"Do you agree?" Ronan asked.

"Yes, Daddy Ronan."

I watched my bodyguard visibly shiver. Just like that, it was all worth it. I'd do anything to get underneath Ronan Collins' skin. My heart raced as I leaned toward, desperately wanting to put my hands all over him. Instead, Finnian snapped his fingers.

"Back to work," he said. "I know you've been breaking those dishes. One more and I'll have to train you to do it properly."

I shivered as bad as Ronan had. "Why am I both terrified and turned on by that?"

Finnian grinned. "Because you're a slut, boy."

I groaned. They were all getting to know me a little too well. My cock throbbed, and my hole pulsed. If one of them didn't shove their cocks in me soon, I would lose my mind.

CHAPTER ELEVEN
RONAN

HE WANTED ME AS A DADDY. I was still floored. I knew Jack was interested, but to think that's what he wanted.

"Who gets me first?" Jack asked.

Finnian rubbed at his chin. "Seeing as Cian started this mess, it technically would be his day, but I hate that idea." He looked between us. His gaze stayed on Jack a lot longer. "Why not finish your chores and then you can hang out with Ronan? He bought a game system while we were out anyway."

Jack twisted around with a bright smile on his face. "You did?"

I was flooded with light. I wanted to make him happy all the time. It wasn't possible, but I wanted to try.

"Yes."

"Did you get some of my favorites?"

"He spent most of the trip picking out the ones you liked," Finnian said.

My cheeks felt hot the moment he outed me. I'd scoured the shop until I found every single one I knew Jack loved and then some new ones that were similar.

"Today, he can be free to go to any of us," I said. I didn't want it to seem like I was stealing him away. I was a fair man even if I wanted to wrap Jack up in my arms and never let him go.

"I'll create a schedule that everyone can easily follow, even that psychotic asshole." Finnian headed toward his room mumbling under his breath about Cian no doubt.

The moment Finnian closed his door Jack relaxed in my arms even more. "Why don't they fuck already?"

I cleared my throat as I grabbed Jack's chin and tilted his head back. "Language."

Jack nibbled on his bottom lip, his eyes darted all over my face, watching me closely. I felt as if I was under a microscope.

"Sorry, Daddy Ronan."

It was only the second time and already I was hooked. My mouth went dry. I nearly asked him to say it again. I needed to record it and have it repeat in my ears for moments he wasn't near me.

"Finish up your chores and then we can play the racing game I picked up."

Jack's face lit up and he turned to get back to cleaning.

I grabbed his arm. My fingers tingled where I touched him. "Want to get changed?"

Jack looked down at himself and moved his hips so his too-short skirt fluttered around his waist.

Cian is a demon for putting him in this.

My cock jumped at the sight of him, and I wanted to bend him over the counter and make him cry out Daddy Ronan until he went hoarse.

"No. Unless you don't think I look good in it." Jack pulled free of my hold.

He turned around giving a full view again. He bent over and I nearly swallowed my tongue.

Fuck.

Temptation was the only way to describe Jack. I shook my head and took a step back before I acted on my thoughts. "No, you look good."

Jack stood up and touched his chest. The see-through bra only made his pierced nipples stand out. "Only good?"

Shite. "Jack—" *What did I want to say again?* My brain was useless as Jack touched his nipples.

"Yes, Daddy Ronan?"

Get it together Ronan. You're the daddy here. Stop letting this boy lead you by the cock.

"I'm going to set up the game."

Jack sighed, but I didn't let him pull me back under his spell. I headed for the living room and then remembered we hadn't brought everything in. Jack dressed in a slutty outfit on his hands and knees had stolen every last brain cell I'd possessed. I raced past him forcing my gaze forward as I went to go get everything.

"I brought you a change of clothes," I said. I held up the sweats and one of Jack's favorite shirts.

"Wait, I couldn't find that while I was packing. How did you get it?"

"I went to ask the house cleaner as we were leaving." He took it from my hands and slipped it on over the bra. "Figured you'd want it."

Jack sighed and a soft smile took over his face. "Thank you. I tore up half my room looking for it."

It was a bright blue sweater. There were tears at the seams and around the cuffs of the sleeve. The word on the front was all but gone. Faint letters could be made out if I squinted long enough. It was more than rags but it didn't change the way Jack looked in it. He brought the collar to his nose and took in a big whiff. He sighed as his eyes closed. Instantly he was relaxed. I had no idea what his attachment to the sweater was, but I'd made it a habit to make sure it was packed anytime he had to go somewhere for long periods of time.

"Here, I'll help you with the rest."

"I can dress myself," Jack said, but he made no move to do it.

I attempted to calm my racing heart as I pulled the skirt down. The panties were no better than the bra he was wearing.

"Can I keep them on?" Jack asked softly.

I'm going to die at this rate.

I nodded and held out the loose sweats for him. Jack rested one hand on my shoulder as he stepped into the bottoms. Warmth seeped into my body from our point of contact and threatened to overtake me. His skin was so warm and soft against my fingers as I dragged his shorts up to my waist. I might have taken twice as long to dress him than what was needed.

"Still feel like gaming or are you too tired from cleaning?"

"NoIwanttoplay," Jack rushed out.

I placed the cushions on the floor side by side. The moment I sat down, Jack pushed my legs apart. He took his cushion and moved it between my thighs and plopped down.

"I want to sit here."

Stubborn as always. Normally I'd force him back to my side, but I could have this now. My palms felt sweaty, and I gripped the remote tighter making sure not to let it slip out of my hands.

"Okay."

We started playing the racing game. The first few rounds were on the easy tracks and Jack came in first on every single one of them. He rested against me whooping and shouting every single time he knocked another racer off the track. As we switched to the harder levels that was no longer the case. Fourth and tenth place flashed on the screen.

Jack's shoulders were tense, nearly touching his ears. He had a death grip on the remote and any second now he was going to get pissed off and throw it.

"Another round," Jack growled.

I should probably stop him, but I was enjoying this as well. We started another round on the hard level and sure enough, I got last place, but Jack got second.

"Shit!"

I took the remote out of Jack's hand and turned him around to straddle my lap. His long legs dropped on either side of me as he got comfortable.

"Jack, I know you're frustrated with losing but you shouldn't curse." I cupped his face.

How many times had I thought about doing this to him? How many nights had I spent imagining him in my lap and the sweet innocent look on his face?

"Da—Daddy doesn't like hearing his sweet boy curse. I have a new rule for you to follow. No cursing." I know I always asked it of him, but this felt different with our relationship shifting. "Can you try for Daddy?" I didn't expect him to be perfect. Trying his best is all I asked of him.

"Sorry, Daddy Ronan." Jack blew out a breath. "I was so close to winning."

I nodded. "You were. You did so well."

Jack relaxed in my lap, slipping more into the innocent soft side of him I adored so much.

"Can we play a little more?"

"I don't know, Jack. You got pretty angry with the game, maybe we can switch it out for another?"

Jack looked back at the screen before facing me once more. "Okay. Will you keep playing with me?"

"I'll do my best, but we both know I have no idea what I'm doing."

Jack smiled. "I just like that you're playing with me. It's kind of like when you used to help me relax in college." Jack's gaze softened. "I never thanked you back then. I was really grateful for you."

My chest squeezed, *my sweet boy.* "I'd do anything for you, Jack."

Jack turned around to face the TV once more. We switched the game out for one that was pixelated. There was a lot more to do on it than I'd originally thought. It was some farming game that took a lot more thinking power. There were so many extra characters and helping build a farm took time. The wrong setup and the animals broke free.

Time seemed to pass by and before I knew it the sun was already lowering outside. Jack's head fell back against my chest, his gaze strayed from the television making his character blow up some of the boxes he'd put down.

"Dang it," Jack exclaimed. He sighed and paused the game.

"Are you done?" I asked, already knowing the answer.

Jack nodded and handed over the remote. "But I don't want to be um." Jack fidgeted in between my thighs. I waited patiently for him to tell me what he wanted. "I want to keep spending time with you."

"Did you have any other chores today?"

Jack shook his head. "Fi—Daddy Finnian only told me to do the kitchen."

It was strange hearing Jack call someone else daddy.

Anger is what I expected but instead, I felt confusion. I didn't exactly hate it but I wasn't used to it either. For as long as I could recall I'd always pictured it being only Jack and me, whenever I gave into the delusions. Now that it was happening it wasn't the two of us, but four of us. I wanted all of him but still, we'd agreed to share. Maybe it was for the best. After all, without the other two, I wouldn't be able to cross the line with Jack no matter how strong my feelings were for him.

"What about Cian?"

Jack rolled his eyes but there was a smile on his face that was nothing like the sweet ones he aimed my way.

"That crazy pervert didn't add anything for me to clean."

"You agreed for him to be your daddy."

Jack's shoulders slumped. "I know, and I don't regret saying it, but he is a pervert."

I couldn't exactly argue with him, not when Cian was well Cian. His punishment alone had made me question his sanity. It was already rocky.

"When was the last time you sketched?"

I needed a change in subject. I was bound to ask what Jack saw in Cian. He was good looking but the man was someone anyone with two brain cells would steer clear of. Each of us had dirty hands, we'd taken lives for the family and never looked back on it. Cian on the other hand was different. He bathed in the blood he shed. He was what I never wanted to become, someone so lost to the joy of taking another person's life.

"I haven't been able to." Jack sighed. "Being here has made it hard to draw."

I groaned as I got up on the couch and pulled Jack along with me. The floor was fun and all but my back was starting to hurt. "Want to try?"

Jack shrugged as he stared at his lap. "Why bother? I

suck right now."

That wouldn't do. I wove my fingers through Jack's short wavy brown hair and tugged gently. He lifted his head and stared up at me as if I had some magical answer.

"You do not suck."

"Hard to believe that when I haven't been able to finish a sketch in weeks even before coming here."

Jack could get lost in his head so easily. There had been plenty of times he'd get so stuck on a project trying to reach his idea of perfection. He completely disregarded the work he'd done so far.

"Go get your sketchbook."

Jack shook his head, his bottom lip stuck out slightly. Did he know how cute he was being?

"Please, baby boy."

Jack's mouth fell open, and I helped close it. The pet name had been in my head for a while. It had been hard not to say it in the past but now I could finally call him my sweet baby boy.

"Say—say it again please." Jack licked his lips as he leaned in closer. His big eyes focused on me as he waited on bated breath.

"Please?"

Jack groaned. "No Daddy," he whined. "What, um, what did you call me?"

I tilted my head back and tapped my chin. "Hmm I don't think I remember, wasn't it your name Jack?"

"Daddy Ronan." Jack pushed me lightly and I tipped over dramatically falling on the couch.

"How could you hurt your daddy? I thought you were a sweet boy."

Jack crossed his arms and his cheeks puffed up. He looked like a chipmunk. The urge to pinch his cheeks was hard to suppress. This side of Jack was a rarity. I only got glimpses when we were in private and each time Jack would run away. It was the only time he'd run from me.

"I am good." Jack's lower lip stuck out in an adorable pout.

I sat up nodding. "Yes, you're good."

Jack fidgeted on the couch still pouting as he looked anywhere but at me.

"Baby boy."

The moment the words left my mouth Jack's head jerked toward me. The smile that lit up his face was priceless. I'd kill to keep it there forever.

I hope Declan never chooses a side and we're stuck here with Jack forever.

The moment the thought came across my mind I shoved it away. How was that fair to seclude Jack away from the world? Even if this was the happiest moment of my life, I knew Jack didn't like being locked away. Sooner or later we were going to have to leave.

And who was to say after a month or two Jack wouldn't be bored with us and call the whole daddy thing off? Just imagining it hurt my heart. I rubbed at my chest.

"What's wrong, Daddy Ronan?"

I dropped my hand and cupped Jack's face. "Nothing. Go get your sketchbook and pencils."

Jack sighed as he got off the couch. I knew once he settled into and worked past the creative block, he'd be happier. I smacked his butt on the way past me.

"Daddy!"

"Hurry up."

Jack ran out of the living room and went right to his bedroom. I relaxed back and took in what was happening. I kind of went along with it not questioning it too much, but how could I when I was finally able to hold Jack how I wanted? Finnian walked into the kitchen and our eyes met.

He glanced around me, and without needing to hear it, I knew exactly what he wanted.

"He went to get his sketchbook."

Finnian nodded. "Does he need anything?"

I'd always thought Finnian was a stern man and he was, but it seemed there was more to him especially concerning Jack.

"No, but I did add a rule."

Finnian lifted a single brow my way.

"No cursing."

"Figured as much. I'd already noted it. Anything else?"

I shook my head.

"In order for us to be on the same page I'm also going to make a group message for the three of us." He didn't sound too enthusiastic about it.

The garage door slammed as Cian waltzed into the house. He wiped the sweat from his face as he glared Finnian's way. His blue eyes ran over every inch of the living room.

"Getting his art supplies," I said.

Cian nodded.

"What were you doing out there?" Finnian asked.

"Minding my business."

Those two were going to come to blows soon if they kept clashing. Why in the hell had Declan teamed them up? Jack came out of his room, his arms full of multiple sketchbooks and a few pouches filled with his favorite pencils. He stopped short, seeing Cian. The look of pure mischief overtook his face and my sweet baby boy was gone as another side of Jack came out.

"Hey, pervert Daddy."

"Princess." Cian chuckled and moved toward Jack. "Want to see who's the real pervert?"

My stomach clenched at the thought of Jack not coming

to me. I got that we shared but I was still spending time with him.

Jack shook his head. "Can't, I'm spending time with Daddy Ronan, but I can play with you later."

"Later as on Tuesday," Finnian said.

"You have got to be shitting me. Two days?"

"You already had your fun today." Finnian crossed his arms staring at Cian. "We are doing a schedule, we have to work together on this or it's not happening."

"Fuck that," Cian growled.

"But Daddy Cian, don't you want to see how naughty I can be for you?"

Jack one. Cian none. There was no reason to worry. Jack was innocent with me but he was already learning how to play Cian.

"Fine, Tuesday," Cian said as he marched toward his room.

"Nice work, Jack," Finnian complimented. He ruffled Jack's hair before heading out leaving Jack and I alone again.

"Come here baby boy."

Jack's face went stark red as he headed my way. He sat next to me and I instantly pulled his head down to my lap. His smile was wide as he wiggled a bit to curl his legs up on the couch. My fingers instantly found purchase in his hair. I lightly scraped my nails over his scalp as he stared at his sketchbook. He tapped the pencil a few times, his brows furrowing the longer he stared at the blank page.

"Breathe," I instructed.

Jack rushed out a breath in frustration.

"Again."

He listened and did it again and again until I noticed his body relax a bit more. He'd be better drawing sitting up but it was more about getting him to start drawing than making it perfect.

"Why not draw daddy a picture?"

Jack stopped tapping his pencil against the page instantly and turned his head to look up at me. "Like what?"

"Anything is fine."

Jack nodded and turned back to face his paper. A few minutes passed and I thought about giving him an actual place to draw but there was no need as he started to draw. I let out a sigh as I watched him. His face contoured into one of pure concentration as he etched each line. I relaxed against the couch and lost myself in the feel of Jack laying on my lap and the sound of his pencil against the paper. There was nothing better, except maybe hearing him call me daddy. I pulled up a book on my phone and hoped we'd get to stay like this forever.

I blinked a few times as Jack shifted. My attention never wavered from him for long. After forty-five minutes I was still on the same chapter.

"Is that the church?"

There was one I fell in love with when I was a child, we'd visit St. Margaret's catholic church often. We lived hours from it but mam made it her mission to visit at least once a month. We'd take multiple buses to get there in time for mass.

"Yeah, I know you said you liked it. And it had a really great structure. I heard they're going to rebuild it and make it as close as possible to the original."

It still saddened me that the church had burned down.

"Thank you."

Jack smiled and placed his book down. He cracked his fingers, stretching them out repeatedly. There were a few smudges on his hand from the pencil. I'd seen his hands like that plenty of times and still, my pulse for some reason picked up every single time.

Jack rubbed his face against my lap and my body reacted instantly. I jerked away and lifted his head.

"Why did you move?" Jack asked.

My heart was firmly lodged in my throat. For the past year I'd been stopping Jack's advances and denying my feelings for him. Giving in now didn't come easily to me.

"You were—" My face heated as I thought about what I wanted to do and how good it felt. How badly I wanted to free my cock and shove it down Jack's throat.

"Daddy Ronan, are you hard?" Jack asked. He moved his hand between my legs, and I jumped up the moment his delicate fingers grazed over my clothed cock. Shock waves attacked me from such a small touch.

"Jack."

He blinked up as if he had no idea what he was doing to me. His innocence was shattered by the smirk on his face. "Yes, daddy?"

He was using the word daddy to scramble my brain and it was working. I should have known Jack would figure out how to use it to his advantage. He wasn't manipulative per se but over the years I'd come to realize Jack wasn't like his father with an overwhelming presence that demanded respect and attention, but he still found ways to bend people to his will. I was the daddy, but I swore it felt like Jack was the one in charge.

"It's almost dinner time. What would you like to eat for a snack to hold you over?"

Jack turned around but not before I caught sight of his smile. If the others thought they'd gained the upper hand on Jack, they were in for a surprise. I knew Jack the best and still, I was easily swept by him.

"Can I have daddy?"

"No."

"Awe Daddy Ronan we can finally–."

"How about some potato cakes?"

Jack turned around, his eyes big and his mouth open. "You'll make them?"

I nodded. I knew how much Jack liked my potato cakes. It had been the first thing I'd made him to win him over. I'd been his tenth bodyguard in the span of six months. Declan had entrusted me with his son but the moment I met Jack I realized why so many before me had failed. Jack was more than the boss's son, he was his own person with dreams and ambitions.

"Fu—Fudge yes."

It was a start. My legs were moving before I'd even fully thought about what I was doing. I kissed Jack on the forehead. His lips weren't too far away; if I could taste him one time I'd be set.

"Thank you for trying."

Jack leaned into my touch, his lashes lowered resting on his cheeks. His freckles were faint on his face and a lot harder to spot normally, but when he was this close, I could count each one.

"You know we can do more," Jack said.

Heat trickled through each one of my limbs until it felt like I was outside baking in the sunlight.

"Jack—"

He pulled back before I could finish talking, his lips pressed against my cheek. Warmth fought with the desire raging through my veins.

"Sorry Daddy Ronan, I'll be good and wait." Jack moved toward his sketch pad picking it up off the couch. "Please don't take long. I—I've been waiting for a long time for you to be my daddy."

My tongue felt glued to the roof of my mouth leaving me with no choice but to nod.

CHAPTER TWELVE
FINNIAN

I COULDN'T TAKE my mind off Jack. Today belonged to me. Excitement ran through my body as I stopped jogging and fished in my pocket for the mailbox key. A smile tugged at my lips. The goal was supposed to be watching over Jack. At first he'd pissed me off, always had. I'd slowly started to realize it was because I'd always wanted this. Always wanted to drag him over my knee, spank his ass red, and put him in his place. Now that I had, I'd started to relax in ways I never expected. I'd always been uptight, but Jack was slowly changing that in some ways.

Shaking my head, I opened the mailbox. The same junk as always filled the box, but I didn't expect anything else. We weren't registered with the post office. The only reason I checked the box was to keep up appearances. We had to maintain some normalcy if we didn't want to stick out in the quiet, little suburb.

As I closed the mailbox, I froze. Something burned the back of my neck. I glanced around. No one. When I turned on my heels, my heart pounding in my chest, I sought out the source of the discomfort. Nothing greeted me but the quiet street, a few birds flying to the rock lawn across the street to look for bugs. Every hair on the back of my neck continued to stand on end as if someone was watching me. My eyes darted around, but no matter how hard I looked there was no one in sight.

"Hey Dave!"

My head snapped to the right. Our next door neighbor Mrs. Khan stood there with her little shih tzu. I tried to calm my pounding heart as it threatened to beat out of my chest.

"You scared me," I said, trying to laugh it off. "Didn't hear you walk up."

Mrs. Khan grinned. "I'm very sneaky," she chuckled. "So is Lolli." She glanced around. "You looked worried. Are you okay?"

I blinked. "Oh yeah, I'm fine. Bit of daydreamin'," I said as I reached down and pet Lolli. "I better get back home."

"To those hot guys you live with, right? Is one of them your husband or something?"

My eye wanted to twitch. Of course she was nosey, the whole neighborhood was. It wasn't all the time, but I felt eyes on us more than once. People who peeked through the blinds and stayed behind the curtain while they watched you move about your yard. They were annoying, but harmless.

"Something like that," I answered, trying to picture Ronan or Cian as my husband. *I'd take Ronan over Cian any day.* "It's my turn to make breakfast."

"Oh go on then," she laughed. "Have a good day! I'll bring over some brownies soon!" She called.

I turned, waved, and kept jogging around the block. The eerie stared-at feeling was gone at least and I'd avoided a long, drawn out conversation about gas prices and groceries being more expensive than they were in the sixties. Even at nine in the morning, it was too hot for that shit.

Stepping into the house, I threw the locks behind me. I deposited the mail into the trash before I beelined for the kitchen. As soon as I stepped inside, a plate crashed against the floor and shattered. I moved back as Jack swore under his breath. He turned his big, brown eyes on me.

"Don't tell Daddy Ronan I cursed."

I shook my head. "I'm not covering for you." I looked around the kitchen. "You're still dropping things in here I see." I tugged my shirt over my head. "I'm taking a shower. Come with me."

"Am I taking a shower with you?"

"No, you're just coming with me," I answered.

"Come on," he muttered.

I kept my chuckle to myself. Jack had been itching to get in our pants since we'd all decided to be with him. Yet none of us had crossed that line yet. Not because we didn't want to, but in mine and Ronan's case I was sure it had a lot to do with who we were and who his father was. Declan really was my friend; I didn't want to betray him. Stepping over that last line felt like a betrayal. I was desperately trying not to go there while losing that battle.

"Yes, Daddy Finn."

My heart squeezed in my chest. Three little words and I wanted to grab him, toss him into bed, and relieve the built up tension that had grown since before we left New York. As if he knew the effect he had on me, he grinned mischievously.

Oh, so he wants to play a game.

I returned to my bedroom with Jack on my heels. As I stripped out of my clothes I heard him take in a sharp breath. I glanced over my shoulder. He stood there, frozen, staring at me as I moved around my room. I gathered fresh clothes from the dresser before I pointed to a basket.

"There," I said. "I want you to load the washer and move over the drying while I get cleaned up."

Jack's bottom lip poked out. "What? More stupid chores? This isn't fair!"

I raised a brow. "I suggest you quiet that tone, wee one, before I have to show you that I am nothing like Ronan. My soft spot only exists when you're behaving. Otherwise, I'll straighten you right out."

Jack's eyes widened comically. It took everything in me not to laugh at how quickly he shut the attitude down. As I walked past him, I patted his head.

"That's a good boy. Run along and clean up. When I'm done, I'm going to make sure you know how to clean without destroying the kitchen."

"Yes, Daddy Finn."

That little lip poked right back out, but I ignored it this time. Instead, I went to take my shower. The whole time I washed the stink of sweat from my flesh I thought about Jack. It was my day. I wanted to teach him how to do things properly instead of being a mess. Declan never tried to get him to do anything, and I knew why; he was soft on Jack. Not that I could blame him in some ways. After his wife died, he just wanted to keep Jack close and safe, but he'd definitely spoiled the boy. And that helped no one.

Once I stepped out, I slipped into a pair of dark sweats and a fitted t-shirt. I picked up a hair tie from the bathroom counter and fixed my hair into a short ponytail. I wanted to be able to see clearly for what I had planned for Jack. The boy needed some order, desperately. I wanted to be the one to give it to him.

I headed toward my room, before I remembered the broken plate on the kitchen floor. *Shite. Should clean that up first.* I made a beeline for the broom and dustpan. Technically, it should have been on Jack to clean up his mess, but he'd been working hard. Besides, he had a habit of going barefoot and I didn't want him to cut his feet open. I bent over as I swept up the shards of porcelain.

"Are you cleaning for me?"

I stopped and glanced over my shoulder. Jack peered at me curiously. "Aye," I said. "It'll be quick work and then back to work."

Jack groaned. "I don't want to do the kitchen anymore," he said stubbornly, practically stamping his foot on the floor. "It's stupid."

I straightened up. "Excuse me?"

Jack chewed his bottom lip. "It's stupid," he muttered.

I opened my mouth before I clicked my tongue. "Disrespectful," I said plainly. "You're going to keep doing this room until I think you're ready to move on."

Jack crossed the space between us. He laid his hand on my chest. I stared down into sweet eyes, the kind of eyes a man might hand over his entire fortune for. He stroked his palm down my body before he danced his fingers over my cock.

"Can't I do anything to fix that?" He whispered. Jack leaned against me so closely there was no space between us. "Please, Daddy?"

It would be easy to fall for his words. Easier to indulge in the gentle caresses he unleashed upon my body. Instead, I took a step back and regained my control. The confusion in Jack's eyes felt triumphant.

"You don't get to charm your way out of things," I said calmly. "Get back to work. I have something just for you."

He huffed, crossing his arms over his chest as he glared at me. "I don't want to."

"You will," I said. "Or you'll be punished. And

remember what I said; there won't be any more fun punishments."

I left him there with his mouth gaped open as I dumped the shards of plate into the trash. Once I returned the broom and dustpan to its closet, I went back to my room. Stuffed into the closet was exactly what I needed to deal with Jack. I grabbed the items, tested them out, and once I was satisfied, I returned to Jack.

"Stand up straight," I said as I placed the spreader bar between Jack's legs. I'd had it delivered the night before and now I was glad I had. "Spread them more."

Jack let out a cute whine. "What are you doing to me?"

"Be a good wee one and do as you're told," I said calmly. "Ronan is sweet on you, he lets you do things the way you want. Me? I prefer things to be done the way *I* want them to be done. Your game doesn't work on me." I locked the bar into place. "Is that comfortable?"

Jack chewed his lip, but nodded. "Yes, Daddy Finn."

"Arms."

He stuck his arms out. I quickly maneuvered the black and purple wrist restraints into place. The buckles were fastened, and I slipped a finger underneath to make sure they wouldn't cut off Jack's circulation or hurt him. Pain wasn't the point. Teaching him to move mindfully was. I tugged at the chain between the restraints and nodded, satisfied.

"That's good," I said. "Now, turn around and get to work."

"How!" Jack scoffed. "I can barely move!"

I grabbed the back of his neck. "That's the point," I whispered against his ear. "I've watched you enough to know that you move without thinking. You're just trying to finish your task, not actually make sure it's done correctly. So, these," I said as I picked up the chain making his hands dangle, "are to help you think about every step. Now, be a good boy and get to work."

"Yes, Daddy Finn."

My lips brushed against his neck. I inhaled his scent, that delicious aroma that was distinctly his and no one else's. I wanted to take a bite. Instead, I lingered on the kiss before I moved back and allowed him to do what needed to be done. Immediately, Jack began to move, but much slower than he normally did. Every reach was calculated, every twist, turn and step was thought out. One by one he started clearing the dishes. He took his time, carefully stacking them in the dish drain.

I smiled. "See? Isn't that better?" I asked. "Since you're doing so well on this chore now, you can move on to something else tomorrow."

Jack perked up. "No more dishes?"

I shook my head. "Not for a while, no."

Jack hopped up and down on just his toes. "Yes! I'm so tired of dishes already," he sighed. "So wet. So annoying."

I chuckled. "I think you've earned a break from it. Finish the counters."

"Yes, Daddy Finn," he said happily.

Jack moved with a bit more energy. He grabbed the sponge, leaned forward and cleaned the counter carefully. Pride swelled in my chest. I really thought he'd annoy the hell out of me the entire time we were away, but there was more to Jack than what met the eye. When he had something to work hard at, he excelled. He just needed a little discipline.

Thinking about disciplining Jack made my cock hard. I reached down, adjusting myself through my sweats. He was in a pair of those short shorts he liked to sleep in. The ones that rode up when I peeked in on him at night and showed off creamy, alluring thighs. I was immediately tempted to bite him, to hold and fuck Jack until he was nothing but a quivering mess in my arms.

"What would you like for your reward?" I asked.

Jack glanced back at me. "My reward?"

I nodded as I waved around the kitchen. "You've done an excellent job. I think you deserve a reward for it. Would you like something?"

Jack's face turned pink as he gazed away from me. "I don't know," he said softly.

There was that innocence again. It made me want to laugh.

"For a man who wants to become a leader of an organization, you sure do blush easily."

Jack spun around and nearly fell. I leaped forward, wrapping my arms around him as he panted. Jack clung to me, his eyes wide. I tucked him against my chest.

"Sorry," I said seriously. "I could have gotten you hurt. That was stupid."

Jack frowned. "Are you concerned for me because of what we are now? Or because of who I am?"

I brushed dark hair from his forehead. "As much as I know your father would tear me in half if I ever hurt you, I'm worried because you almost got hurt. I'm your Daddy. It's my job to take care of you and keep you safe. Teasing you while you're restrained and upright was foolish. I shouldn't have teased you about that at all. I'm sorry wee one."

Jack pressed against me. "If you're really sorry, will you make it up to me?" He whispered.

"How should I make amends?"

"Kiss me?"

I pressed my lips to his without hesitation. All the reasons why I should; my job, my loyalties, my integrity all shattered. The moment his lips moved against mine, I moaned. My hands gripped him more tightly. I held him as close as I possibly could. As I did, he pressed forward. The hardness of his cock rubbing against my thigh broke the part of me that stayed in control and exhibited restraint. One kiss and the lad had broken my brain.

When we pulled apart, we both panted. Jack touched my face, the jingling of his chain not even drawing my attention away from those brown eyes. I swiped my thumb over his plump bottom lip.

"Do you want your reward right now?"

Jack tilted his head. "Do I have to pick?"

"Not if you don't want to. I have just the thing."

Moving quickly, I scooped Jack up and tossed him over my shoulder. He yelped, but it quickly dissolved into a laugh. That sound made the ache in my chest grow. I wanted more of Jack. *All* of Jack. He was more than I ever dared to think I could have. Someone cute, funny, cunning. Even though I'd always imagined myself with a well behaved submissive or boy, Jack scratched a part of me I didn't know I enjoyed. Taming him was just as fun as someone who obeyed my every word.

I dropped a laughing Jack onto my bed. When I crossed back to the door, I flipped the lock. I turned back to see him staring at me, curiosity in his eyes. There was something else there too. Lust. The boy exuded desire in every glance. I couldn't fucking stand it. I wanted to sate that hunger.

"Ready for your reward?"

Jack nodded eagerly. "Yes, Daddy Finn!" He smiled. "Um whatever my reward is, can you do it naked?"

My eyes widened. I hadn't expected that to come out of his pink lips.

"Cute boy," I said before I clicked my tongue. "Fine. It is your reward after all."

Jack lit up as I stripped out of my clothes. I took my

time, removing each item piece by piece before I folded them neatly. Carefully, I placed them aside. The excitement on Jack's face made it look like he was about to burst. His eyes swept from my head to my toes, then back up again. I grinned as I straddled his body.

"What? You like what you see?"

Jack swallowed hard. "I thought Cian was the cocky one, but you're just as bad."

I groaned. "Don't compare me to that asshole."

"That's a bad word, Daddy," Jack whispered.

I pinched the bridge of my nose as he dissolved into laughter. Yes, he was a real little shit, but I'd also never heard Jack laugh so much in my life. He was usually a serious boy or a whiny one depending on the day. It was rare that I heard so much joy and playfulness in his tone. I was starting to get addicted to that sound.

"What's my reward?" Jack asked.

"Right," I climbed off and carefully maneuvered Jack across my lap. Thanks to his restraints, he really couldn't move. "How about a nice, hot spanking?"

Jack squirmed on my lap. "O-okay."

"No, I'm going to need to know this is what you really want," I said. "And what do you call me?"

If it was possible, he squirmed even more. "I want it," he groaned. "Please, Daddy? Please!"

I whistled. "Who knew Jack O'Brien could use the word please?"

"Don't tease!"

"Why not? I like the way you rub your cute cock against me when I do it."

Jack rubbed against me even harder. I could feel him stiffening in those shorts. My heart raced in my chest as I slowly peeled the shorts away and dragged them down his slender thighs. There were muscles there, potential waiting to be unlocked. I ran my hand over them, mesmerized.

"You should work out with me," I blurted. "It's good for your mind, your body, and you're always telling everyone you're tough. Developing a few more muscles might help."

Jack perked up to peek back at me. "You'd help me?"

I shrugged. "Sure, why not? A wee lad like you could use some tonin' up."

Jack wiggled. "You're supposed to be spanking me, not making fun of my lack of muscles!"

"Sorry," I said. "I wasn't much bigger than you at your age, to be fair. I had to train to look the way I do now. Still do."

Jack sighed. "All I do is draw. That doesn't exactly make you stronger."

I chuckled. "No, but I think your drawings show talent. Always have."

"Really?" He whispered.

The back of my neck burned. No way in hell my face wasn't red as a tomato. I shoved him back into place. Yes, I'd admired his work for some time. And I'd agreed with his father that drawing, architecture, and a corporate future was well within his grasp. So why the feck had I just offered him a way to get stronger?

Focus.

"Daddy?" Jack called.

I brought my hand down onto his ass. He cried out. It was enough to distract us both from the conversation that bordered on too damn sweet. Too close. I was used to putting up walls and keeping people in compartments. It kept my life organized. It kept emotions out of what needed to be done. Enjoying Jack was a temporary thing. Sooner or later, we'd all return to New York and this would be over.

My stomach twisted at the thought. To chase it away, I

smacked Jack's ass again. My hand bounced against his perky, jiggly flesh. Heat licked my palm. It dispersed, radiating over his skin as he bucked and moaned. That sound was enough to drive me insane. He shoved his ass up into the air before he drew in a deep breath. I rubbed his ass instead, letting him fall into relaxation before I struck him again.

"Hey!" Jack yelped. "You can't just--."

"I can do whatever I want to your body, boy," I growled. "You gave yourself to me and you'll take every single swat I give the way I want to give it. Do you understand me?"

"Yes, Daddy," he moaned. "Harder."

That little whispered harder sent tingles up and down my spine. I raised my hand and did just that. The sound of the thwack echoed in my ears. Jack ground his cock against my thigh. His shorts had shimmied down further and I could feel his naked dick on my thigh. I could also feel the wetness his cock left behind on my skin. Jack was all worked up.

I varied my swats. Hard, soft, and then rub. Hard. Soft. Rub. By the time I was done, Jack's words had dissolved into nonsense. He shook his hips, his hard cock rubbed against my thigh. It was insane. Once I soothed away the spanking, I lifted Jack and laid him on the bed. He hissed.

"Are you okay?" I asked.

"Yes," he moaned. "It feels so good."

"I can tell," I said as I reached between his legs to fondle his hard dick. "This is all the evidence I need."

Jack groaned. "Please, please help me, Daddy."

I clicked my tongue. "Are you still trying to manipulate me today? That doesn't work on me, boy."

He shook his head hard. "It hurts," he groaned. "I haven't gone this long without cumming in ages. Please!"

Shit. I quickly remembered Cian's rule. *Although, to be*

fair, the boy has more than served out his punishment. He's been doing well. Fuck it.

I leaned down and wrapped my mouth around Jack's aching cock. The salty taste of his precum against my tongue lit up my senses. Jack bucked upward, his cock shoving further down my throat. I gagged.

"Fuck, relax." I laughed as I came up for air.

Jack shook his head. "Can't. Please."

I took one look at the desperation in his eyes and slipped his cock back into my mouth. Jack humped against my face, desperate. Eager. I allowed him to as I wrapped a hand around my length and pumped it. The tension in my shoulders built as heat swept through me. My stomach clenched.

My finger rubbed against his hole. Jack sucked in a sharp breath and I wanted to do it more. I *needed* to hear that sound as he was drowned in pleasure that only I could give him. Fuck. I wanted Jack O'Brien to be *mine*.

I spat on his hole before I sank a single digit in. Not much, just the tip. I wanted to test the waters, not hurt him. I glanced up at him.

"More, Daddy," he moaned. "I- I can take a lot!"

I pulled my mouth free of his cock again. "How do you know that?" I glared. "Do you fuck a lot of men?"

He shook his head. "A few, but Ronan runs them off mostly," he said. "Mostly I know because I have a lot of toys at home," he admitted as his cheeks blazed. "I use them on myself a lot."

The thought of Jack with a big toy stuffed up his tight ass, and I knew it was tight from the way it clenched around my finger, made me want to stuff myself inside of him. My finger slid in further. His head tilted back. His legs fell open at the knees. He practically begged me to breed his slutty little hole until he screamed for his Daddy.

131

Calm down. Not yet. I'm already crossing a line right now. I should talk to the other two first.

God, I hated that thought. My cock begged to be buried in his ass, but I ignored it. Instead, I popped him back into my mouth. The moment I did, he gasped.

"Yes, Daddy. Fuck!"

His fingers dug into my scalp as he moaned and jerked in my grasp. I took my time. I wanted to draw out every second of our time together until it was permanently seared into my brain. However, it seemed like Jack needed release. Now.

Jack's dick twitched in my mouth and I groaned the moment I was flooded with hot, wet cum. I swallowed it down as my spine tingled. Pleasure gripped my balls, tightening them. I spilled my seed over the cover and Jack's twitching legs.

Finally, I pulled free and gasped for air. Jack's eyes were distant and glossy as a huge smile covered his face. I chuckled. Reaching out, I stroked his face. Jack leaned into my touch as his eyes searched my face.

"I was pretty sure I hated you at first," Jack muttered.

I tilted my head. "I'd be offended, but I think the feeling was mutual. You're different than I thought you were."

"You too," he said. "Daddy Finn?"

"Yeah?"

"I love this. How good I feel. How you all treat me." He shook his head. "Does it really have to stop?"

As I searched his face, I knew I didn't have an answer for him. I wanted us to keep going, of course I did, but I knew that reality wasn't so kind. When we returned home, all of this would stop.

"Let's focus on what we have for now. Okay?"

Jack nodded. "Yes, Daddy." He held up his wrists. "Can you let me out? I have to go pee."

"Want me to help you do it?"

His face bloomed red. "No!" He laughed. "Well, not yet. Maybe later."

"Understandable."

I released Jack from his bondage. He tugged his shorts up his thighs before he wobbled toward my bedroom door. I watched as Jack slipped away, my heart stuck in my throat.

Letting him go is going to be a problem.

CHAPTER THIRTEEN
CIAN

JACK RAN right past me headed for the bathroom. His cheeks were flushed and there was a light sheen of sweat coating his body. I caught him right before he made it to the bathroom.

"Ugh, let me go Cian. I have to piss."

I shook my head. "Try again."

"You have got to be shitting me right now. I will piss on you."

I shoved him against the wall crowding into his space. He smelled like sex, the best scent in the world in my opinion. "Who said I wouldn't be into that?"

Jack groaned, wiggling against the door. "You're a fucking pervert."

"Says the slut." I wrapped my hand around his throat and pressed my body against his. "Did he make you cum?"

Jack squirmed, his gaze no longer meeting mine. I didn't need to ask but now I just wanted to watch Jack flounder for the answer.

"If you don't tell me, I'm going to tell Ronan that you've been swearing."

"You wouldn't," Jack hissed.

"I would."

He searched my face as if he wasn't sure if I'd tell on him or not. Normally I wouldn't. I was all for rule-breaking but when it came to Jack, I wanted to see him be punished. It was entirely too much fun.

"Crap. Yes. Happy now?"

No, I wasn't. For a man who was such a stickler about rules, Finnian was perfectly happy breaking mine. It was one thing when Jack did it and another when Finnian did. Fine, then, there was no reason why I needed to hold back.

"You fucked up twice already."

"How?" Jack's breathing was irregular, his pupils blown as he attempted to glare at me.

"What are you supposed to call me?"

His brows furrowed for a second before they shot up. "Shit. Daddy Cian."

"That's right."

I shoved Jack into the bathroom and followed right behind him. I flipped the lock on the door and crowded into Jack's space.

"Wait, I really do have to pee," Jack said. His hand on my chest felt hot burning through the shirt I was wearing. I couldn't imagine what it would feel like without the barrier of clothing between us.

"Then I'll help."

Jack's brows nearly kissed his hairline. "No thank you."

"Wasn't asking."

I shoved him near the toilet and yanked his shorts off his hips. I slapped his inner thigh earning me a yelp from him as he lifted his leg like I wanted. I pulled his shorts free and tossed them to the side.

"What are you doing?" Jack asked.

"Stop questioning Daddy and go pee."

Jack glanced over his shoulder, a nervous look overtaking his face. "I can't, you're making me anxious."

"You know just what to say to make me hard, huh?"

Jack shook his head. "No, you're just crazy."

Maybe.

I snapped my fingers and pointed toward the wall and Jack huffed as he turned around. He held his soft cock in his hand and aimed at the toilet. I grabbed his hips and before Jack could turn back around, I parted his cheeks and dove in. I dragged my tongue over his hole.

"Wait—" Jack's words were broken off as he moaned.

His hole clenched around my tongue begging for more. *What a greedy body.* My cock twitched in need. I wanted to slam Jack down and bury all eight inches of my cock in his tight ass. I bet he'd milk me dry. I moaned against his puckered flesh.

His fingers tangled in my hair. If he planned to push me away, he quickly changed his tune as I lapped and teased his hole.

"Oh fuck."

I pulled back, smacking my lips as I tried not to laugh at him. "You're supposed to be peeing, remember?"

Jack's entire body was trembling. "I can't."

I reached around him and pressed against his abdomen. Another groan left him as he bent forward.

"Daddy Cian I—"

The first trickle of piss cut off Jack's words. I spread his cheeks and devoured his hole like a man starving. No person or catastrophe could get me to stop. Jack's moans grew louder and louder bouncing off the walls.

A knock at the door gave me pause. "Wee one, are you alright?"

Jack went stiff. "Shit." He whispered.

He glanced over his shoulder at me. His big brown eyes

pleaded with me to come up with a magical solution for the predicament we were in. I smirked up at him before I bit the firm globe of his ass.

Jack slapped his hand over his mouth, keeping the scream at bay.

Damn. I moved back a little to admire the mark. My stomach was on fire at the sight before me. I wanted to mark every single inch of Jack and hear his screams as I did.

"Jack?"

Fuck Finnian. I wanted him to open the door and see just how slutty and hungry I made Jack. But then the fun would be over, and I wasn't quite ready for that.

"Daddy," Jack whispered, snapping my attention right back to him.

It was pure insanity how easily I was being dragged along by a simple title. How many times had men and women called me daddy in the bedroom? But none of them ever created the strange sensation bubbling in my stomach. It felt as if I'd eaten a hive of bees and they were buzzing around inside of me. It was impossible to ignore or even comprehend.

I winked at Jack. *Show Daddy how bad you can be.*

"Why did you lock the door?" Finnian asked as he wiggled the knob around.

Jack looked as if he was about to have a panic attack. He chewed on his bottom lip nervously looking at me and then the door and back again.

"Answer him," I whispered.

I moved back and flipped the shower on to give us a little more time. I grabbed Jack's ass once more and spread his cheeks. His hole was still glistening from my spit and I mentally groaned as I dove back in. My tongue swiped over his entrance poking at it as Jack attempted to talk.

"I uh—" His words were broken off as he tried not to let his moans out.

There was no stopping now. I wanted to hear him lose his mind. He needed to feel chaos at my hands. I wanted to break Jack until he was nothing but a cumming mess who could only live for my cock. His fingers tightened in my hair, nails scraping over my scalp adding to the pleasure that already raged through me.

"I'm fine. Need—shower," Jack finally forced out.

I nipped at his hole and teased him more, loving the way he pushed back against me. He bent over more, giving me better access.

"Are you sure? It sounded like you were screaming," Finnian said.

"Is Jack okay?" Ronan's voice broke through the thick wood door.

Jack tightened around my tongue, he attempted to stand back up straight. I forced him right back down; they weren't going to stop me from enjoying my meal.

"Daddy," Jack hissed.

That's right call for me, baby.

"I'm Fi—Fuck!"

I shoved two fingers in at once, heat wrapped around my digits, and sucked them in deeper. Jack's body was perfection. He took my fingers in without any issues and pushed back as if begging for more. He balanced on the balls of his feet as his head fell forward. His fingers moved through my hair as he lost the grip he'd had.

"Jack, open the door right now," Ronan said.

"We're going to get caught," I teased Jack.

Curling my fingers, I sought out the bundle of nerves I knew would drive my slutty boy insane. The moment my fingertips brushed against it Jack lost it. He moaned, barely able to cover his mouth.

"Pl-ple-please," Jack whimpered.

"Cum for Daddy."

The moment I said the command, Jack lost it. His hole tightened around my fingers to the point I couldn't move them anymore. His hips shook as he painted the walls with his cum.

I stroked him through it, not wanting him to stop for a second. Jack batted at my hand and attempted to push me back, but I wasn't going anywhere. The second I could move my fingers I did. I played with his prostate until his legs caved and I was forced to catch him. He shook his head, mumbling something I couldn't hear over the shower. I dragged him close, shifting my fingers inside of him so I could continue to fuck his hole.

"I can't...cum..again so soon." Jack's whimpers were like music to my ears. His words meant nothing to me.

"We just need to train your body. Don't worry, I'll help you."

Jack shook his head, but his ass sucked on my fingers as if it never wanted to let me go. I stood him up, pulled a dead Jack closer to me and kissed him. I sucked on his tongue and watched as he lost it even more. He clutched onto my shirt and ground his soft cock against me. I reached between us and wrapped my hand around his length. Jack tried to pull back from the kiss but I deepened it, not letting him escape me for even a second. I stroked his cock, loving the way he beat at my chest wanting to be let free. His cries were muffled by my lips.

A hot splash of cum hit my torso and soaked into my clothes as Jack was forced to cum again. It was a small one and not nearly enough to sate my hunger, but it was fun regardless. A single tear slipped free, and it was better than gutting a bastard. I pulled back to watch it fall down the side of his face. I wanted more just like that. I had a new fixation.

"Daddy Cian, please." Jack leaned against me, his entire body trembling.

If I wasn't careful, I'd lock Jack up and keep him as my toy. Declan, life, my job be damned.

"Go hop in the shower. Quickly."

I released his cock but not before I gave him another firm stroke. I slowly pulled my fingers free from his ass.

"Fuck," Jack groaned.

"Such a bad little slut," I whispered in his ear.

"You're killing me."

I hummed. "I can show you how it feels to die at my hands. I promise you it will be something you will never be able to forget." The idea of killing Jack brought on two emotions, one I knew and understood, the other was one I'd need to analyze later.

"Jack, you're still okay?" Finnian asked.

The man was a worry wart. I expected it out of Ronan, not Finnian. I rolled my eyes and turned toward the linen closet in the bathroom.

"Yes, Daddy." Jack opened the shower curtain and stared at me. *What should I say?* he mouthed.

Instead of answering him I pointed at his cock and opened my mouth wide. I formed a circle with my finger and thumb indicating I wanted to suck my boy's cock. Jack's face went bright red, and he quickly jerked the curtain back in place. I held back my laughter as I turned and finished setting everything up, I was careful to make as little noise as possible. Checking my phone, I found Finnian and Ronan standing outside the bathroom.

Jack's hair was plastered to his face as water droplets ran down his body. Fuck I wanted to continue to play with him. I wanted to make him cum again and watch him lose his mind. Jack said he couldn't cum so soon, but I bet I could get him to cum multiple times in a row.

I climbed the shelves and squeezed myself up on the top. It was a tight as fuck fit, nearly as tight as Jack's ass had been around my fingers.

"How?" Jack whispered.

I winked at him as he closed the door. Contrary to the muscles on my body, I was flexible. I had to be for my work. Hiding wasn't my favorite part of it, but I needed to be able to disappear at a moment's notice.

The sound of the door opening reached my ears, and I slowed my breathing down. Jack ran the water washing his hands as the other two stepped into the bathroom.

"Daddy Finn. Daddy Ronan," Jack said sweetly.

A chuckle sat at the back of my throat. He was anything but innocent; he could play it all he wanted but Jack was a filthy boy, and I was here for it.

"What were you doing in here?" Finnian asked.

"Using the bathroom."

"What was all the noise?" Ronan asked.

"Me."

It wasn't a lie, but it wasn't exactly the entire truth either. Oh, my boy was being naughty. The rings holding the shower curtain rattled as someone shoved it open. Who the fuck would hide in the shower? It would be the first place anyone with a single brain cell would check. Fucking amateurs.

"Jack, what aren't you telling us?"

I held my breath waiting to see what my boy would do.

"I made a mess," Jack said.

"You did what now?" Ronan asked.

I bit down on the inside of my cheek so hard I tasted blood. It coated my tongue, erasing the taste of Jack all too soon. Shite. I nearly laughed. I could imagine Ronan's face, he'd probably be ready to wrap Jack up in a blanket and Finnian he was either angry or confused. Both, I'd pay to see.

Should have put a camera in the bathroom. I made a mental note to place some in there just in case there was another incident like today.

"I knew you had to go but I didn't know you had to pee that badly," Finnian said.

"No, it's not your fault, sorry daddies."

"It's okay. Next time I guess I'll make sure to help you," Finnian said.

"I'll make a note of it too," Ronan added.

"We don't have to talk about it," Jack rushed out. "I, um, need to clean it up."

The room was blanketed in silence that was twisted with awkwardness. I wished I could be down there. A part of me wanted to kick the linen closet door open and jump out. The other liked hearing Jack struggle to explain himself.

"Do you need help?" Ronan asked.

Of course, he did. The man was soft with Jack it was hard to believe he was the same Ronan I knew from a few years back. Before he'd become Jack's bodyguard, Ronan had been training to become a reaper for the Irish mob just like me. We had the same mentor, and he'd been just as good at killing. He might not have loved it as much as me but very few did.

"No, I got it." Jack cleared his throat. "Uh, are you two going to watch me?"

"Hurry it up boyo. I have a few more things planned with you."

"Yes, Daddy Finn."

The bathroom door closed and a few seconds later Jack

opened the closet door. He glared up at me and I couldn't help but smile.

"You're a very naughty boy."

If looks could kill, I'd be dead twice over.

"It's all your fault."

"Didn't you get to cum?" I asked.

Jack looked away from me searching the far wall of the bathroom as if it had something interesting on it. "Are you coming down?"

"No."

"Aren't you uncomfortable?"

I was hard as fuck stuffed and twisted up like a damn pretzel; uncomfortable wasn't a strong enough word to describe the state I was in.

"Want me to come down and play with you some more?"

Jack slammed the door in my face. I laughed, unable to stop myself. *I can't believe I thought it was going to be a boring assignment all because I wasn't killing someone. I was very wrong.*

CHAPTER FOURTEEN
JACK

I DROPPED onto the ground as Cian laughed. He stood over me and grinned. I both hated and loved that look. It was batshit crazy, but it made him even hotter when he did it.

"Are you done, princess?" he asked. "Come on, get up."

"You almost punched me in the face!" I growled. "And I'm too hot."

"How? I made sure to dress you in something light."

I glared at Cian. He'd helped me into a short blue and white mini-skirt, blue panties, and a matching lacy bra. The look was completed with a pair of fishnet stockings. When I asked where he kept getting these outfits, exactly in my size, Cian just smiled and told me to get ready for training. I still had no answers. And I still wasn't sure I wanted any.

"Water," I groaned.

Cian picked up the water bottle and squeezed it. Water hit me in the face and cascaded down my body while I blubbered and gasped. I swiped a hand down my face as he laughed. I hopped to my feet.

"What the hell is your problem? You know Daddy's are supposed to be nice, right?"

He shrugged. "I'm not nice. Never said I was." He

squirted more water at me and dodged my fist. "Besides, you'd be bored if I were another Ronan. You need someone who's not going to treat you like breakable glass. No, you need someone who's willing to break you and smile while doing it."

A shiver racked down my spine. *This goddamn guy.* No matter how much I wanted to deny Cian, my cock throbbed and my hole clenched. So maybe I liked that he was rough around the edges. I wouldn't want more than one Ronan, there was no one like him. And I wouldn't want another Finnian; I would never be done cleaning. Cian gave me a break from the hovering and I could breathe a bit more except for when he looked at me like he wanted to devour me whole.

Like now.

"Don't look at me like that," I muttered as I snatched away the water bottle.

"Like what?"

"With that dirty look on your face."

Cian stepped closer to me. "You love it."

I nervously tried to drink some water. Instead, it splashed out, dribbled down my mouth, and tried to choke me as I squeezed too hard. I choked as I tried to regain my composure.

Great. I look like a total dork in front of him!

Cian grabbed the bottle and tilted my chin up. He placed the bottle between my lips and squeezed. I expected another joke or for him to splash me in the face. Instead, he held the bottle for me while I gazed up at him in awe. Right when I thought I had him figured out, Cian did something that I couldn't explain. He was a mystery.

When I pulled back, I burped. Cian chuckled.

"Nice one," he said.

My cheeks heated. "I can do much better than that." I

glanced around quickly. "But I shouldn't. If Ronan hears, he'll lecture me about manners."

Cian shook his head. "I will never understand that man and you two together."

"What do you mean?" I frowned.

"The Ronan I knew was way different," he said. "That man can take someone out before they even know they're being watched. He was almost as good as me when he trained to be a reaper. Almost," he pointed out. "No one can beat me."

I rolled my eyes. "Sure Daddy, whatever you say." I paused. "Did Ronan really train to be a reaper?"

Cian shrugged. "Your father took him and said he needed a bodyguard. It came out of the blue. Just like that he was gone and became your personal maid and ass wiper."

"Ronan has never wiped my a-butt!"

"Sure, yeah. Whatever you say, princess."

I ignored him, but I couldn't stop trying to picture Ronan as a reaper. He was the one that averted his eyes if I walked into a room half-dressed. The person that insisted I ate my vegetables and took a shower every night so I wouldn't have to do it in the morning when I was half asleep and cranky. He cut up my food, tidied my room, followed me around endlessly. *Is Cian sure it's my Ronan?* No matter how hard I tried to picture it I came up blank.

I shook my head. That was too confusing to think about.

"Daddy Cian?"

"Hmm?" He asked as he sucked down a sports drink.

"Did I do good at training today?"

He removed the bottle and wiped his mouth. "Meh."

I narrowed my eyes at him. "Why can't you be nice for even a minute?"

Cian stepped so close to me I moved back on instinct. "Is that what you want? For me to be different?" he asked. "You've said that before. I ain't changin' who I am for no one, so get that outta your thick head now."

I blinked. "Wow," I muttered. "That accent really leaps out when you're mad."

Cian flipped me off. "Shut up."

I grabbed his middle finger and lowered it. "I don't want you to change," I said slowly. "I mean, I know I said it before, but you were driving me crazy!" My teeth sank into my bottom lip as I tried to conjure up the right words. "I like you the way you are, Daddy."

"Yeah?" He asked.

I nodded. "I mean, you're mean, crazy, impulsive, perverted, a butthead, blackmailing—."

"Blackmailing!"

"Controlling, mean, bullying—."

"Alright," he growled. "You've said mean more than enough times."

"—Jerk." I smiled. "But I'm into it."

Cian moved closer. "That's it, I'm putting my cock in your tight little ass," he said as he undid his pants.

I blinked at him. "Is that a punishment or a reward?"

Cian stopped in his tracks before he advanced on me. I turned and ran to the other side of the yard. He barrelled after me, but nearly tripped as his pants wrapped around his thighs. I ducked his advance and doubled back.

"Oh you better get your little ass back here right now," Cian growled. "I should have shoved more than a few fingers in you yesterday!"

"What?"

I stopped and nearly ate fake grass as I whipped my head in Finnian's direction. He stood by the back door, arms crossed over his chest. The look on his face said he could kill. *Oh shit, he heard that!*

Finnian walked over to me. Every step felt like I was about to get my ass handed to me. I swallowed thickly, my instincts told me to run but I was rooted to the spot. My fingers danced along the skirt I wore before I gripped it, trying to hold on and dive for cover. As soon as Finnian saw my muscles flex, he grabbed my arm and yanked me close.

"When did that animal touch you?" he asked. When I didn't answer he spoke rapid fire Irish so quickly I couldn't even understand. "Is that what you were screaming about last night?"

I opened my mouth before I snapped it shut. "I don't know how to answer that, Daddy Finn."

"Do not lie to me again, boy," he growled. "That will earn you more of the punishment I have in store for you. I can assure you that you won't enjoy it."

My mouth went dry. "But Daddy Cian said..."

"You knew it was wrong, right?"

I shuffled back and forth. "Yes, Daddy."

"Then you'll still be punished." He turned his gaze on Cian. "Don't worry, you won't be the only one."

I still didn't want to tell on Cian. One look from Finnian though and I wanted to fold. The man had a way of looking right into my soul that knocked the air from my lungs.

"We were playing around in the bathroom," I muttered as I glanced over at Cian. He looked impassive, like he gave no care one way or the other. "Daddy Cian hid in the closet when you two came in."

"Where?"

"At the top."

Finnian laid a hand on my head. "I know I said we wouldn't put you in the middle, but I want to know something; what exactly did Cian do to you?"

"I shoved my tongue so far up his tight little ass I tasted heaven," Cian laughed. "And then I fingered him until he came. Twice. You broke my rule, I broke yours. I think that's fair. Right, Finn?"

I stepped back as the two of them faced off with each other. *Oh crap.* I'd never seen two people who looked like they wanted to murder each other more.

"Where's Daddy Ronan?" I asked. If anyone could calm them it was him.

"Out on errands," Finnian said shortly. "And there's nothing stopping me from finally putting you in your place, Cian."

"Bring it fire crotch."

I groaned as I buried my face in my hands. Fire crotch? Really? Why did he even know that?

My eyes darted from one to the other. As my heart squeezed in my chest I knew I should say something, anything. But my tongue stuck to the roof of my mouth like it had been glued into place.

Why not let them hash it out? After all, they seem like they need it.

The tension in the air was almost too much to take. Even with the sun setting, heat poured into my body making it even worse. To top it all off, I had never been so horny in my entire life. The thought of two jaw-dropping men coming to blows made me want to lift my skirt, wrap a hand around my cock, and stroke off until I was raw.

Cian moved first. It was a mistake. Finnian dodged his attack and slammed him onto the ground. A gasp fell from Cian's lips before he tried to drag in a breath of air, but couldn't. I winced. I'd only had the wind knocked out of me once during a horseback riding lesson. Needless to say, I never attended another one and the instructor came up missing.

Finnian grunted as Cian wrapped his legs around his waist and slammed him into the grass. I winced. They both dragged themselves to their feet before they came to blows all over again. I watched that scary look come over Finn's face, the same one I'd witnessed when he grabbed me up in the car.

He's not joking around.

Cian went after him, but I winced before he even dropped. Finnian put his foot on Cian's chest before he tilted his head.

"If you want to keep going, be my guest. I can guarantee you that you'll be sorry though. Want to try?"

Glaring, Cian tried to shove Finn's foot off. "How the fuck—."

"You're not the only one that trained with your mentor. And I was doing it when I was twelve." He ground his foot against Cian's chest. "I told you there were rules. Yes, I screwed up but let's be honest; you messed up as soon as you dressed Jack in one of your perverted little outfits. And then you made him lie for you." Finnian shook his head. "Terrible."

"What do you want me to do about that?" Cian snapped. "That's all in the past."

"I want you to take your punishment," Finnian said. "Don't set a bad example for our boy."

Ice dripped down my spine at his tone. It was equal parts terrifying and fucking hot all at once. My cock practically begged to be touched by now, but I kept quiet. Clearly, it wasn't the time to ask for that.

Cian tried to sit up. Finnian shoved him right back down again. The unhinged look in Cian's eyes made me want to retreat all the way back into the house, into my room, and underneath my bed. Instead, I shook my head.

"Okay, no more fighting," I said. "That's enough."

They both glanced at me.

"Is this bothering you?" Finnian asked.

I shrugged. "It's making my stomach feel weird," I muttered as I gripped it. "Can we stop now?"

Finnian glanced down at Cian. "Can we?"

Cian blew out a sharp breath. "Fine. I'll take the punishment."

Finnian glared down at Cian for a minute more before he took his foot off of Cian's chest. He held out a hand. Reluctantly, Cian took it and was hauled to his feet.

"You go to my room," Finn told Cian. "And you," he turned to me, "you're writing me lines. I want one sheet front and back completely filled out and neat."

I groaned. "What? Daddy come on..."

"I will not lie to Daddy Finn."

"That's such bullshit!"

Finnian stopped and turned on me, making me swallow. "Since you want to complain and the sentence is so short you can double it up."

My jaw dropped. Finnian stared as if he was just waiting for me to screw up and make another complaint. Instead, I forced myself to shut my mouth like I should have done from the beginning and marched after them both.

Should have known I can't get out of anything with Finn. What a hard ass.

MY HAND CRAMPED as I glared at the page before me. Finnian and Cian had been gone for way too long. I'd already showered, changed into my comfortable shorts and t-shirt, and got to work on lines in Finn's room. They'd both disappeared into Cian's room a long time ago. *What are they doing in there?*

I conjured up images of them both covered in blood from beating the shit out of each other. My back tensed. There was no way in hell they'd keep hurting each other, right? I didn't even have a phone anymore. Contacting Ronan and letting him know the situation was out of the question. All I could do was wait.

The door swung open just as I dotted the I over Daddy Finn on the last line. My brain felt like it wanted to explode. Every slow, mind-numbing moment that dripped past as I did such a boring task made me want to never lie to Finnian again.

Shit, that's why he gave it to me. Well, it worked. From now on, I'm telling him the truth.

My eyes snapped up to the doorway. "Daddy Finn, am I done now or—."

The words were knocked right out of my mouth by the image in front of me. I tried to speak, but failed. Finnian's hand was wrapped around Cian's arm as he led him further into the room. Cian grumbled the whole time, a fierce glare on his face that I never wanted to be on the receiving end of.

"This is a load of bollix!" Cian snapped.

I slapped a hand on my mouth to keep my emotions reeled in. If I wasn't a hundred percent sure I was still alive, I would have thought I'd died. Or was experiencing some kind of intense hallucination. Just in case I pinched my arm. Sharp pain radiated up my flesh. Nope, I was wide awake.

"The fuck are you grinning at?" Cian asked.

I stifled the noise that tried to wrestle itself free from my mouth. I was in a state of both shock, admiration, and completely turned on. Cian was dressed in one of the slutty outfits that he loved to see me in. A tiny, solid red mini skirt barely fit him correctly and it hid *nothing*. Underneath I saw his cock and balls pressed into the same matching red fabric. Even the bra he liked to make me wear was the same. His hard, pierced nipples poked through.

I could see why he liked me in the outfits now.

"Doesn't quite fit," Finnian said nonchalantly. "But I think it'll do for now."

I barely registered what he said to me. I was entirely hyper-focused on the fact that the skirt, panties and bra looked good on his huge frame even if they didn't fit. His tattoos that spread all over his chest, up his neck, down his arms and to his hands looked better somehow when wrapped in lace and a soft skirt. I reached down and grabbed my hard cock.

"Holy shit," I muttered.

"Language," Finn said before he frowned. "What the hell? Ronan is rubbing off on me."

"Shoot, sorry," I said quickly before I stood up and walked over to my tattooed, bad attitude Daddy. "You look like a slut."

The words fell from my lips before I could stop them. One minute I thought about how hot he looked and the next I remembered his endless torture. As they both stared at me I gave them a sheepish grin.

"It's true though," I said.

Cian made a move toward me. "You little brat. Come here!"

Finnian grabbed him by his hair and dragged him backward. Cian growled, but Finn calmly shoved him to his bed. I watched him topple into it, my heart lodged in my throat.

"Bring me the lube, boyo. It's in the nightstand."

I jogged over to the table more than a little excited to see Daddy Finn sink his hot, hard cock into Daddy Cian. Just the thought of it made my nipples and dick so hard that if the wind blew too hard I'd cum in seconds. My fingers grazed the bottle of lube. I happily tugged it out and passed it to Finn as he kept his knee in the center of Cian's back.

"What the fuck are you doing?" Cian growled.

"Putting you right back in your place." Finn squeezed lube onto his fingers before he pushed them into Cian's panties. "Stop squirming. You said you'd take your punishment, remember?"

"I didn't think *this* was what you meant! You have-- Ah, fuck!" Cian hissed. "Oh fuck," the words turned into a moan as he shoved his ass up.

Fire erupted in my veins and threatened to consume me. *That's so hot. It's too hot! Fuck I'm so horny!*

Cian groaned as Finnian's fingers twisted in his hole. Instead of fighting like I thought he would, it seemed like Cian loved it. *Why am I so surprised? He's such a pervert, of course he loves it all.* I grinned to myself as I walked up to the bed. I dragged my fingers up Cian's barely clothed skin before I climbed in front of him. He glanced up at me.

"Does it feel good?"

He tried to growl and shake Finnian off, but it was only a half-assed attempt. Instead, I watched as his cheeks tinted the most intoxicating shade of crimson. My fingers brushed over his lips.

"Are you embarrassed that you like it?"

"Fuck no," he muttered.

I clicked my tongue. "You shouldn't lie, Daddy."

Cian gazed away from me. It was impossible to miss the look of embarrassment on his face. Not that he had anything to be embarrassed by. I thought it was exciting that he was so wild and free. No one could stop Cian from being himself and he didn't give a fuck what anyone thought. That was the kind of man I wanted to be.

"You're doing great, Daddy," I whispered as I turned his head back to me. "Can you let him up a little?"

Finn raised a brow. "What are you doing?"

"Giving Daddy Cian a treat."

Finn let Cian up. I quickly pushed my shorts down enough to release my cock. Cian stared at it. The hungry look in his eyes warred with a different emotion. I reached out, cradling his cheek before I shuffled closer.

"What the hell's with that look on your face?" Cian asked.

"You're so hot," I moaned as I rubbed my cock against his lips. "There's nothing better than seeing a big, wild, tattooed man moan in pleasure. I've always thought that was so interesting. I've watched lots of porn with guys like you on the bottom." I tilted my head. "Do you want Daddy Finn's cock in your ass?"

Cian growled. "I don't—."

"Don't lie," I said, making my voice as stern as possible before I grinned. "Come on, you can admit it. We're the only ones here." His lips parted as I slipped my cock inside. "Admit it and I'll let you do whatever you want with me."

Cian's tongue darted across his bottom lip. I searched his face as he seemed to think about what I'd just said. I wasn't going to back down. Nothing could stop me from wanting to see the two hottest men in my life touch and fuck each other.

"Tell me," I whispered. "I want to hear it. Please, Daddy? Admit it, and you can shove your dick in me while he fucks you."

Cian groaned. "Fine!" He grunted. A cut off moan slipped from his lips. "I want it."

I shook my head. "You have to be more specific."

Finn snickered. I glanced up at him and pressed a finger to my lips. If he started messing with Cian, then he wouldn't want to do it. And I *craved* it now. I wanted to watch Cian fall apart on Finn's cock while he was stuffed inside of me.

"I want Finnian's cock in my ass," he ground out.

I shivered. "Say it one more time?"

"You're fucking pushing it, boy!"

"One more time," I groaned.

His eyes flashed, that defiance in them that I had started to love. "I want Finnian's cock in my ass. I want that shit to destroy me. Come on, already," he growled over his shoulder. "Stop playing and put it in!"

Finnian shrugged, but the lust on his face was clear as day. "Since you beg for it so nicely, I'll give it to you."

My mouth watered as Finnian slipped out of his clothes. Every time he stripped he had a habit of doing it slowly as if he wanted to drag it out and make everyone that watched him lose their minds. Mostly me. Finn's fingers came free from Cian's hole and made Cian moan hard. His hands gripped my thighs.

"Get all the way naked," Cian said.

I hopped off the bed. Unlike Daddy Finn, I had no patience. I stripped out of every piece until I was stark naked. When I glanced up, both of them had paused. They stared at me like I was the most tantalizing thing they'd ever laid eyes on. The back of my neck heated as I shifted from one foot to the other.

"Stop staring at me," I muttered.

"How could we?" Finnian asked. "Goddamn you look delicious." He shook his head. "I don't agree with this Cian taking you first shit."

"Oh fuck off!" Cian snapped. "He's the one that wants it!"

That was true. I did want it.

"I don't care," Finn cut in as he snagged a condom. He

tugged it over his cock as I stared the whole time. "You can try to fight me, but we both know you'll lose. Besides, none of us has talked about who gets Jack first."

God I loved when they talked about me like I was some amazing prize. The fact that they all wanted me made me love it even more. I climbed back onto the bed. Cian's eyes stayed on me. He looked ravenous, like he'd starve if he wasn't able to take a bite of me soon. I wriggled further down the bed until my cock was in reach of his mouth.

"Want a taste?" I asked.

Cian didn't hold back. He opened his mouth, shoved my dick inside and sucked. My heart flipped in my chest as his head bobbed up and down. The whole time he stared up at me. I reached up and toyed with my nipples. Cool metal greeted my fingertips as I tugged and rubbed them in time to Cian's quick, sure sucking. Groaning, I rested my hands on the bed. My head fell back as I gave myself over to how good it felt to have Cian between my thighs.

"Oh God that's good," I groaned. My fingers faltered as I tried to find his hair in the dark. When his silken locks greeted my fingers, I shoved him down. "More, Daddy." I panted. "I need more!"

"Greedy slut," Finnian muttered.

I opened my eyes and lifted my head to smile at him. He continued to stare as if he was transfixed, but I was too far gone to care about how I looked or came across. Cian was right; I was a slut. And I planned to enjoy every second of it while I was locked away with my Daddies.

"I'm your greedy slut," I moaned. "Both of yours." I grabbed the bottle of lube and drenched my fingers. As they watched, frozen, I shoved two fingers in my hungry hole. I pressed deeper, my heart in my throat as I rocked into Cian's mouth. "Please, fuck him," I groaned as I gazed at Finn. "I don't want to cum until I see that."

"Demanding too," Finnian said as he clicked his tongue at me, but grinned. "I have to admit, I don't want to resist." He slapped Cian's ass roughly making him moan around my cock before he mumbled what I could only guess were curse words. "I know you love it, don't complain."

Finnian climbed onto the bed. He tugged Cian to his knees making his mouth disconnect from me. I groaned in frustration.

"Behave," Finnian said shortly. "Or I'll make you sit in the corner and watch."

An embarrassed whimper slipped from my lips. "No, no, I'll be good Daddy!"

"Good boy. You'll get his mouth back shortly."

Finnian plunged his cock into Cian's ass. No stretching, no slow taking his time, nothing. I watched Cian's eyes widen before he groaned and fell forward. Finnian didn't wait, he slammed into Cian's ass, pulled out, and did it all over again. I watched as Cian gripped the bed, fighting for his life as he was fucked uncontrollably. He bit into his forearm.

"Can you do that to me, Daddy?" I asked. "Please?"

Finn grinned at me. "Soon enough, wee one."

I could barely sit still. The excitement threatened to bubble out of my chest as I watched the two of them. Their fighting had turned to fucking. It was really the best outcome, better than I could have hoped for. I watched, transfixed, until Cian brought his head up. He looked flushed, that same uncertain look in his eyes as he stared at me.

"Does it feel good?" I whispered. "Looks like it does."

Cian groaned. "Yeah. It feels... fuck me! It feels good."

I gripped my neglected cock. "Don't leave me out of the fun!"

Cian's hands gripped my hips as he dragged me closer.

As soon as my dick disappeared between his plump lips I was in heaven. I rocked back and forth as I continued to finger fuck my ass. As much as I wished it was one of them inside of me, I knew they had to be on the same page when one of them finally, blissfully fucked me. Even if I wanted to say screw the rules, it wouldn't work. I didn't want the three of them to fight. I wanted them to love me.

My mind nearly imploded with that thought. One swipe from Cian's tongue and I forgot about everything. The three of us moved in unison, the sound of our moans enough to make me want to cum on the spot. Instead, I held off so I wouldn't miss a single second of the show in front of me. Cian's nails dug into my skin, hard. I cried out and he loosened up.

"No," I shook my head. "Do it again Daddy Cian. Please!"

His nails returned to my flesh. My balls tightened as electricity danced up my spine. It didn't help that the two of them moaned and grunted while I tried to have some form of control. All of that was destroyed as Cian pulled free and stroked my cock hard and fast. He panted as he gazed into my eyes.

"Cum for me."

Fuck!

Three words and I was shoved from a cliff over the edge. I cried out, my hole clenched around my fingers. Spurts of cum splattered all over Cian's face as he threw his ass back against Finnian. I stared as the two of them dissolved into pure, animalistic fucking. Cian grabbed my cock and shoved me back inside, ignoring how sensitive I was. I shoved at his face, but as the pain mixed with pleasure, I didn't try all that hard.

"What the hell is going on?"

All three of us froze. Our eyes all snapped to Ronan as

he stood in the doorway to Finnian's room. His eyes darted over all of us. I watched as redness creeped up his neck and colored his cheeks.

Oh shit. He's pissed.

It was rare I ever saw Ronan angry. Normally he kept the same calm look on his face as if nothing bothered him. Now? It looked like he could and would kill every last one of us. I swallowed thickly as I squirmed. Cian's mouth made an audible pop as he pulled free of my dick.

"Want to join?" Cian asked.

As Ronan's eyes landed on me, I forgot how to speak. Yes, I wanted him to join more than anything. How long had I fantasized about feeling him inside of me? Instead, a lump formed in my throat that refused to go down. What if he viewed me differently now? My chest burned in the worst way.

Oh shit.

CHAPTER FIFTEEN
RONAN

ANGER TWISTED with desire swarmed me all at once making it impossible to think, let alone move. Jack still had his fingers stuffed into his hole, his cock glistened with Cian's saliva.

"Would you hurry the fuck up," Cian growled.

"Daddy Ron—"

I held up my hand stopping Jack from calling out to me. My mind was a mess, and it was impossible to think straight. *What should I do?* I wanted Jack, there was no questioning that but having him with the other two all at once? Was I ready for that? I took in the scene again: Finnian buried in Cian and Jack kneeling in front of Cian.

No one spoke as the seconds ticked by. My mind raced to an answer. Did I take Jack out and demand they didn't touch him? Call this whole thing off? But if I did, I wouldn't have Jack but more importantly, Jack would be upset. The thought of seeing Jack hurt by my words or actions made me physically uncomfortable. I rotated my shoulders trying to ease the tension out of them.

Then there is only one right way to go about it.

I grabbed the front of my shirt and started to unbutton it.

"Jack, rip open his shirt. If we go any slower I'm going to lose my mind," Cian said.

Finnian slapped his ass but all it did was make the crazy bastard moan and smile. Jack's big brown eyes trained on me. He was still frozen as if he wasn't sure what to do. I'd felt the same the moment I stepped through Finnian's door. I hadn't known what to expect but to see them all fucking hadn't been it.

"Baby boy, you heard your daddy," I said.

Jack snapped his mouth shut and withdrew his fingers from his ass. He wiped the lubed-slicked digits off on his thigh and crawled over to me. My cock was hard instantly. It didn't take much. All I needed was Jack to get turned on. His smiling lately did it to me. I'd taken more cold showers than hot ones lately. Being secluded in a house with the one man that had been my temptation for well over a year now was like telling a drug addict not to do the drugs that sat right in front of them. It was damn near impossible and took every ounce of my willpower. That willpower vanished, pissed in the wind as Jack worked on unbuttoning my shirt.

It was going too slowly, and for the first time, I had to agree with Cian. I wanted to move at my own pace. I was liable to hurt my boy if I wasn't careful, but they'd already touched him and played with him. He made it to the last button, and I caved to the dire pressure in the pit of my stomach and shoved off the shirt. The pants and underwear were quick to go as I grabbed Jack up.

Our mouths clashed together in a heated kiss that took my breath away. Once I started, there was no stopping. I mapped out every inch of his mouth, tracing his tongue with my own, making sure I got every taste of him down to memory. Jack whimpered. I wasn't sure if it was from feeling so good or lack of air. Either way, I ate it up like a starving man. My hands were just as greedy. It was as if the dam on my desires had been broken and I was flooded with an immeasurable amount of want.

"This is why you don't deny yourself," Cian teased.

"Shut the fuck up," Finnian groaned. He pulled back until only the tip of his rock-hard cock rested inside of Cian. He slammed forward rocking the bed and the psycho on his knees.

"Fuck."

I let Jack go for only a second, I hadn't expected it but watching the two of them was hotter than I could have imagined. They fucked as if they were trying to tear each other apart.

"Holy fu—"

"Watch your mouth," I said automatically.

Jack slapped his hand over his mouth, his eyes wide and focused on my cock. I wasn't exactly lacking in the dick department.

Cian laughed but it was short-lived as Finnian didn't let up. Finnian whistled.

"Daddy, your cock is—"

"Monstrous," Cian supplied.

Jack nodded as if he couldn't have thought of a better word. I wrapped my hand around my cock stroking it lightly as I stared at my boy. "But you can take it. Right baby boy?"

Jack bit his lip, his eyes glued to my cock with hunger shimmering in the brown depths.

"You can do it, wee one. Take Daddy Ronan's cock while we watch."

My heart was going to break free of my ribcage any second now. I wasn't going to be alive much longer with how hot the situation was turning. I knew one day if I'd ever had Jack, I'd make it sweet for him, at least for the first time, but having the other two there made that impossible. All I wanted to do was ravish Jack until he was blubbering broken mess.

A pearl of precum dripped from my head and rolled down my cock before I caught it and used it as a little lube to keep stroking my cock.

"Go ahead and taste him slut," Cian coached. The other two had stopped moving. Everyone's eyes were on Jack; it was impossible not to stop and stare.

Jack licked his lips leaving a sheen on them as he leaned forward. His lips parted and his tongue slipped out as he took the head of my cock into his mouth. The moan that left him sent vibrations straight to my balls as he attempted to take more of my length into his mouth. His lips were stretched and slightly paled as he took what he could.

"A little more, baby boy," I groaned.

My hand rested on the back of his head, coaxing him to take more of me. There was no way he was going to be able to take me fully down his throat, not this time at least. We could work on that another day. A shiver raced down my spine just imagining my cock deep in Jack's throat.

Tears dripped from Jack's eyes as he took more of me in. He looked up through his thick wet lashes driving me more insane. Cian appeared next to him and he lapped up the tear that ran down Jack's cheek with a moan.

"Fuck you even cry pretty," Cian said.

I nodded, catching the tears from his other eye and bringing it to my mouth. Jack's pupils were blown as he sucked and lapped at my cock. Finnian moved behind Jack, his green eyes locked with mine.

"We weren't going to fuck him yet."

My stomach dropped at the news. Oh, I'd had every intention of sinking into Jack and claiming a piece of him.

"But now that we're all here, how about it? You want to take Daddy Ronan's cock first?" He asked Jack.

Cian snickered. "I want to say that I'm good with not going first if I get to watch Jack get split in half."

I moved my hand away and Jack pulled off my cock with an audible pop. He sucked in air greedily wiping at the saliva coating his bottom lip and chin. He blinked away the tears that clung to his eyelashes.

"We don't move unless you say something boy," Finnian said.

I waited on bated breath for Jack's answer. He looked to Cian and then to Finnian before he turned to me.

"Daddy Ronan will you fu—" his head tilted, and I groaned.

"This one time, it's okay."

Jack smiled. *I just want to attack him.* The restraints that held me back for so long were useless.

"Will you fuck me first, Daddy Ronan?"

"You two good with that?" I forced out. I didn't want to ask but luckily my brain hadn't shut off completely.

"Like I said, I want to see Jack cry." Cian grabbed Jack's face and kissed him, not giving a damn that Jack's mouth had been wrapped around my cock moments ago.

Finnian shrugged, his gaze drawn to Cian and Jack making out. Then there was no objection to me taking our boy. Finnian tossed something at me and I caught it on instinct. I held the condom in my hand, staring at it as if it was some foreign object. I'd been so lost to the desire coursing through my veins that I'd forgotten about it.

Cian released Jack and the moment he did, Jack had all of five seconds to suck in air before Finnian was grabbing him next. If Cian tried to devour Jack, Finnian dominated Jack while kissing him.

"Fuck this thing is getting in the way," Cian groaned.

For the first time since I'd walked in, I noticed Cian was wearing the skimpy outfit that he'd put Jack in. The skirt was way too small and the bra was painted onto his flesh. He snatched it all off and tossed them to the side.

"I don't think I gave you permission to take those off," Finn said.

Cian flipped him off. "Take it out on my ass. It was biting into my skin."

"I will."

What the heck had happened in the short time I was gone? I looked between the two and then at Jack. I had a feeling it was Jack's fault that they'd all ended up in bed. I blew out a breath and guessed it was better than them seconds away from killing each other.

Finnian turned Jack around and his lips were up for the taking. I moved in, grabbed his face and pressed our mouths back together. Our tongues twisted together and it was like coming home after being gone for way too long. The knots in the pit of my stomach loosened up the longer I kissed Jack.

Jack wrenched free, his face flushed as his mouth was left open. He moaned, his eyes rolled to the back of his head. I glanced over his shoulder and smirked at the three fingers Finnian had in our boy. Cian played with Jack's pierced nipples toying with them roughly.

Our boy. It was new and yet it felt oddly right.

Finnian withdrew his lubed covered fingers.

"Wait, don't stop," Jack whimpered.

"Don't you want something more than my fingers?" Finn asked. He turned Jack's head back my way.

Jack groaned, licking his lips as if I was a steak and he hadn't eaten all day. That was it, something in my brain snapped and I was on the bed before I knew what I was doing. I grabbed Jack and brought him closer to me. His back was pressed firmly against my chest, my cock nestled between the firm globes of his cheeks.

"It's like an animal when it loses its shit," Cian said.

Jack and Cian faced each other. I ripped the condom open and rolled the latex over my length in record time.

"Move him closer," Cian said.

We moved as one until Cian could get ahold of Jack's cock. My cock was nestled against Jack's hole, just a little push forward and I'd get to finally take him. My pulse raced as I tried to reign in my excitement. I slowly moved forward, pushing past the first ring of muscle. Heat seeped in past the condom and wrapped tightly around my cock in a vice-like grip. I got nearly three-quarters of my dick in Jack before he started pulling away.

"I don't know if I can take all of you," Jack confessed.

"I believe in you, Jack," Finn said.

He shook his head back and forth but I could feel his body fit around me like a glove. There was no room and yet I wanted to push on. I shallowly rocked forward.

"Daddy, wait I—" Jack's words were broken up as his head turned right and left against my shoulder. His hole tightened around my cock dragging me in deeper and promising to never let me go.

"Fuck," Finnian groaned as he slammed into Cian like a man possessed. His eyes were glued on Jack as our boy lost his mind.

It wasn't enough. I needed Jack to know just how much he meant to me and how badly I'd wanted him. Cian's fingers brushed against my thighs as he gripped Jack's ass cheeks. He pulled them apart and I sank the remaining two inches inside.

Jack screamed and it was more beautiful than anything I could have ever imagined. The three of us groaned and I knew I wasn't the only one affected by the sounds coming out of Jack. I pulled back slowly, loving the way Jack's body gripped my cock. He shook his head, but it was too late, there was no stopping us. I slammed forward forcing Jack's cock down Cian's throat and the full length of my dick inside of him.

Another guttural cry came from Jack as I matched Finnian's crazed pace. Every time he slowed down on Cian, I did the same to Jack. It was driving us all insane. Even Finnian looked as if he was barely hanging on. Sweat beaded my brow as I fucked Jack. There was no tenderness like I'd planned. I was owning my boy and making sure his body knew who it belonged to.

I moved my hands around Jack and twisted his nipples between my fingers.

"Daddies wait—I—" Jack shook in my hold as I slammed forward.

Cian popped off Jack's cock, drool and precum decorated the lower half of his face. He looked as if he was in euphoria with Finn's cock plowing his ass and Jack's cock stuffed down his throat. "Go ahead slut. Cum for your daddies."

He took Jack's length back into his mouth and Jack started losing it. The words that came out of his mouth were no longer English. It was a bunch of half-finished words and moans.

Jack's channel tightened around me stopping any of my movements as he came. He wasn't going alone because the climax hit me out of nowhere. I wanted to drag it out, but my body wasn't having any of it. Pleasure crashed into me and robbed me of any thought.

I came filling the condom, although all I wanted to do was fill Jack.

"Fuck," Cian growled as he crashed on the bed.

Finn wasn't that far behind grunting as he came. He

discarded the condom in the trash bin before staring at the bed. His breathing was erratic and face flushed. I picked Jack up with the help of Cian and we scooted closer together. Finn laid down. The bed was too small for four grown-ass men who were all well over six feet. Cian alone took up most of the space. And yet none of us rushed to get up. Jack was draped over our bodies, his brown eyes glazed over as his lids lowered with every passing second. He was going to be out like a light soon.

"You have got to be bleedin me," Cian groaned.

I glanced over at him, but he was already moving. He picked Jack up off us and kissed the boy before depositing him between me and Finnian.

"Where are you going?" Just as Finn asked, the sound of the doorbell rang throughout the house.

"To deal with that nosey as fuck neighbor. If I scoop her eyes out and burn her ears off, maybe she'd stay her geezer ass in the house."

"Cian."

He was gone before Finnian could utter a single word. Finnian was up in seconds snatching up his trousers to chase after Cian. "He didn't even put on clothes. Fucking gobshite."

I should probably go help. Finnian plus a pissed-off naked Cian was a recipe for disaster. Then again, after finding Finnian fucking Cian maybe it would come out differently.

"This bed is too small," Jack said. He moved closer, pressing his face into the crook of my neck. dragging all of my attention to him.

I still couldn't believe I'd held Jack. My cock had been buried inside of him. It twitched as if the memory was enough to make me want to go again.

"Daddy, I'm tired."

My heart pounded wildly against my ribcage. "How tired?"

Jack pulled his head back and his pupils were blown but it was impossible not to take in the fatigue showing on his face. His lids kept drooping close.

"We need to get you cleaned up."

"Later...Please."

I sat up and pulled Jack up with me. "Not happening. You need a good washin."

Jack groaned. "Fuck the bath."

"Language." My tone was flat and left no room for the softness that I held normally for Jack. I'd heard him curse and I knew he was doing so around the others. Finnian would correct him, but I wouldn't be surprised if Cian wasn't encouraging Jack's bad habits.

Jack's eyes widened and he sat up alone. "Sorry, Daddy Ronan."

"I have to punish you."

Jack whimpered and his lower lip trembled as he looked up at me through his thick lashes. An arrow shot right through my heart, and I wanted to crumble that very second. One curse word wasn't that bad. And the boy was trying. That was all I'd asked for. I could let him get away with it.

"Daddy," Jack called out in a sultry voice that had my cock ready for another round and my body craving to be plastered against him once more.

I shook my head and slipped out of Finn's bed. "You can either follow me or your punishment will be twice as long."

Jack pouted as he threw a small fit on the bed. I patiently waited for him to be finished. When he saw I wasn't going anywhere, he placed his hand in mine.

"My legs won't work, can you carry me?"

My stomach tightened into knots. "Of course, baby boy." I scooped him up and cradled him close to my chest.

"Daddy Ronan, do I really have to do a punishment right now?"

I nodded. "Are you going to be my good boy and take it?"

The commotion at the front door got louder but if anyone could handle it was Finnian. He'd figure out how not to let Cian murder the neighbors. I needed to focus on my boy. I walked into the joining bathroom and sat Jack on the counter. He hissed at the cold coming into contact with his ass. I opened the closet and fished out a fresh bar of soap and unwrapped it.

"Open your mouth."

Jack looked to the bar and then I saw the pout coming a mile away.

"Don't try it. Open up for daddy."

"That's not fair," Jack whined but he opened his mouth. He squeezed his eyes shut as I put the bar of soap in his mouth.

"Now close." I placed both of my hands on his thighs and ran them up and down. "You're going to hold that bar in your mouth for five minutes."

Jack grunted around the bar. He kept his eyes screwed shut however, the rest of his body had relaxed against my touch. He probably didn't notice how he leaned closer to me every few seconds.

"You're doing so good for Daddy." I kissed his nose, avoiding the bar of soap. "I got you a present if you keep being good, I'll give it to you."

Jack sat up straighter at my words of encouragement. Time passed by quickly and not once had Jack tried to wiggle out of the punishment.

I took the soap bar out of Jack's mouth, and he hopped

off the counter. He twisted around and went right for the sink and rinsed it out. He spat a few times, wiping his mouth with the back of his hand. I stood behind him and stared at our reflections. There was nothing in my life that could have prepared me to become Jack's daddy. I was floored that he'd pick someone like me. I kissed his cheek.

"You did so well. Daddy is proud of you." I watched his reflection as a shy smile came over his face.

"I really am sorry, Daddy. I'll do better." He turned around and draped his arms over my shoulders. Both of us were still stark naked but there was something far more intimate going on between us.

"Thank you."

Jack smiled up at me and warmth enveloped my chest. I couldn't stop staring at him. I forced myself to move.

"Let me go get your present."

I ran out of the bathroom and grabbed my pants. I glanced at the bed still in shock that we'd all had sex in the small queen size bed. I fished out the bracelet I'd made and brought it back to the bathroom to present to my boy.

"Hold out your wrist."

Jack obeyed and I hooked the tracking bracelet around his arm. It was platinum that wasn't too heavy but didn't draw the eye either. Jack stared intently and I brought it to my mouth kissing the cool metal.

"The night you went out scared the living shit out of me. This is so Daddy always knows where you are. Can you promise me you will never take it off?"

Jack chewed on his lip as he stared at the bracelet. "What if I want to go out with friends?"

"Then you tell me, Finnian, or Cian. As long as we know where you are. I don't ever want to feel like I might lose you," I said. Jack had no idea the amount of fear that had sliced through my veins. The copious amounts of possibilities that had flashed in my mind.

"Okay, Daddy I won't take it off."

The tension in my body eased at his words. "Come here, baby boy." I scooped Jack up in my arms and kissed him gently. I took my time devouring him.

Jack broke free on a moan; his lips were red from all the abuse they'd taken today. It only made me want to kiss him more.

"Can you take a bath with me?"

"I would love to." I wouldn't want to be anywhere else.

"Oh, wait, it's Daddy Cian's day." Jack glanced at the door and as if summoned, Cian barged in.

"What are you doing with my slutty boy?"

"He needs to get cleaned up."

"I like him dirty," Cian said.

Of course, he did.

"Daddy Cian, would it be okay if I took a bath with Daddy Ronan? Unless you want to take a bath with me?" Jack asked.

"Eh." Cian hopped up on the counter still naked. "I'll just watch." He propped his elbows on his crossed legs and rested his head on his hands.

"Jack's right. You are a perv."

Cian smiled. It was the kind of smile you'd see on a hyena, unnatural and terrifying. "Thank you. Now next time, we need to go over the use of condoms."

My back stiffened. I'd preached to Jack over and over again about the safety of sex and now Cian wanted to go condomless.

"Why?"

"Our boy needs to be stuffed with our cum till he can't hold it anymore." Cian's blue eyes focused on Jack. "You want that slut, don't you?"

Jack whimpered and the air in the bathroom heated. Cian's idea was sounding less crazy and more plausible.

"Yes, I want my daddies to breed me."

I don't know what good I did in my life to deserve this, but crap was I happy. I glanced up at Cian and I could tell he felt the same. "We will talk about it later."

For now, I needed to wash my boy and take proper care of him.

"Daddy Ronan, were you training to be a reaper?"

I froze at Jack's question. Sweat collected at the base of my spine slipping into my trousers as I attempted to get my heart rate under control. My blood rushed making it nearly impossible to hear anything besides my pulse.

"What?"

Jack put down his sketch pad and turned off the cartoon playing in the background. He turned to face me. His big brown eyes bore into me waiting for my answer. "You know, before you became my bodyguard were you going to be a reaper?"

Finnian and Cian knew but out of the two, my money was on Cian telling my sweet baby boy that I'd nearly become a hired killer for the mob.

"That was a long time ago."

"Holy sh—sugar muffins."

My left eye twitched. It was hard not to laugh when Jack was trying hard not to curse. The boy came up with some of the weirdest phrases I'd heard. But more importantly, I needed to know if he was afraid of me now.

"Can I ask you more questions?"

I audibly swallowed. I wasn't ashamed of my past and I wasn't one to shy away from it either. I knew the day I met my maker I'd pay for the souls I'd taken part in robbing from this world. It was a fate I openly welcomed. My mam always said there was never any good without bad. The world couldn't function on peace because it didn't exist outside of war.

I opened my arms and Jack scrambled over to my lap. This was going to be the only way I'd be able to answer him. "Ask your questions and I will answer all of them as truthfully as possible."

Jack leaned back and it made it slightly easier that he wasn't facing me as he asked his questions. "Okay, have you killed anyone?"

"Yes."

"Was it for the family?"

"Yes and no."

Jack went stiff but he didn't turn around. He stared down at his fingers fiddling with them. "Was it personal?"

"Some."

"Is it okay if I ask how many?"

"Fourteen." I knew the exact dates, places, and how I'd killed them. Each face was etched into my memory and no matter what, there would be nothing that would erase them.

"Do you regret coming to watch me?" Jack's body went rigid in my lap. His shoulder bunched up as he leaned slightly forward.

My arm went around Jack as I pulled him back against me. My lips burned to kiss and because I could, I gave in to the need, peppering kisses up and down the column of his neck. I didn't stop until his shoulders dropped and he tilted his head to give me better access.

"There is no regret. I had no idea this is what would

come out of it but even back then when Declan asked me to watch over you it'd been a blessing."

"You didn't like killing?"

This was the question I'd been afraid of. I hesitated as I tried to come up with my answer.

"He loved it," Cian said. He plopped down on the single chair in the living room with a beer in his hand. Our eyes met and all I saw was the insanity.

Jack turned around in my lap and met my gaze blocking Cian. "Daddy?" He was too adorable to resist.

"Yes, I liked it."

"Then why did you give it up?" Jack's brows dropped and scrunched together. I reached up and smoothed them out.

"Because I didn't want to like it."

Jack turned all the way around and straddled my lap. "You didn't want to become like Daddy Cian?"

"Hey! What the fuck's wrong with me?"

"You're crazy," I said.

"You're an eejit," Finnian added.

"I'm just fucking creative and fun unlike you two. Isn't that right, princess?" Cian winked at Jack and instantly the boy's face was flushed.

"I like that he's crazy," Jack whispered.

"Your taste in men has always been questionable." I shook my head at Jack. Remembering all the guys I'd chased away left a sour taste in my mouth. None of them had been worthy of my boy.

"Yeah, he's always gone after those pussy boys with fake power. No way in hell they'd be able to make you cum."

I went still at Cian's words.

"Cian, you make it sound like you've been watching Jack," Finnian said.

"Yeah, Daddy Cian." We all stared at the psycho of the group.

He draped one leg over the other and leaned back on the chair. A devilish smile on his face. "We were talking about Ronan."

"Now we're talking about you," Finnian said.

I wouldn't be surprised if Cian had watched Jack but I was impressed the nut job hadn't acted until now if that was the case. Cian was compulsive; he went after what he wanted and it was either handed to him or he took it.

"You waited?" I asked.

Cian's blue eyes flicked up to mine and then back down to Jack. They softened slightly. "It's time for me to go surveil the area.

"Don't start anything with the neighbors again."

"They keep their nosey asses to themselves, and I won't have to shoot them," Cian said.

Finnian pinched the bridge of his nose. "We are here secretly. Don't draw unnecessary attention to us."

The garage door slammed shut before the sound of the garage opening reached our ears. Cian was good at his job but he was a loose cannon.

Jack watched Cian go. "Is it me or did he just run?"

"He did." Finnian said.

"Do you have any other questions for Daddy?"

Jack's head tilted as he closed his eyes and his brows furrowed. "Would you kill again?"

"Yes."

"What the heck are you two talking about?" Finnian asked.

"I was asking Daddy Ronan about his past. He was going to be a reaper before becoming my guard."

Finnian nodded. "He was good at it."

Praise from Finnian felt good as it settled in the middle

of my chest. The man wasn't easy to impress. He'd trained under Cian and I's mentor long before we did. He was the star pupil we'd heard about the entire time. The fact he acknowledged me filled me with a sense of pride.

"What do you two want for dinner?" Finn asked.

"Can we have nachos?" Jack asked.

"I think I have everything. I'll make a cheese sauce. Spicy or a little spicy?

Jack and I answered in unison. "Spicy."

He laughed and it filled the house with warmth. I always wanted to hear Jack this happy. *I love you*, circled around in my head. I knew I loved Jack.

"Oh, one more question," Jack said.

I nodded for him to go ahead and ask it.

"All those times I tried to seduce you, did you almost fold?"

I smiled, unable to stop myself. "A few times."

Jack whooped and went to get off my lap. I stopped him before he could make it off. I wrapped my arms around him. This might bite me later, but if doing any of this taught me anything, it was I had to take a chance.

"I love you." I cupped Jack's face and kissed him softly. "You don't have—"

"I love you too," Jack interrupted and kissed me back.

"Thank you."

Jack shook his head. "Don't thank me, just never stop loving me Daddy."

How could I? Jack glanced over to the kitchen, and I knew he was looking at Finnian cook. His journey with the others was for him to figure out. I'd loved Jack for a long time. It was only now that I'd been able to act on it. I just hoped the other two came to the same conclusion I did. Jack was the one for me and he deserved every ounce of love.

CHAPTER SEVENTEEN
FINNIAN

Jack ran beside me. He panted, but he didn't stop moving as we turned the corner and continued our jog. I smiled. *He's trying so hard.* My chest swelled with pride as I admired him. A week later and he was showing so much improvement. I'd always thought Jack was just a spoiled, lazy, soft shit, but he'd started to show me a different side of himself.

"Wait," Jack stopped, his hands propped on his knees. "I need water."

I handed over my bottle. Jack had brought his own, but he'd finished it less than halfway into our jog. He took the bottle from me, pressed it to his lips, and ended up spilling more than a little bit of it down the front of his shirt. He gasped as the icy cold water splashed on his flesh.

"Oh, sugar honey iced tea," he growled.

I quieted a snort. As I gazed at him I was hit with just how much I'd changed. I'd always been a stickler or as Cian said, I had a stick shoved up my ass. Now? Whenever Jack did something that should have irritated the fuck out of me, I found amusement in it. When he made a mistake, I moved on quickly. Did I still want him to do things right? Of course. But I took it slow, showed him how to do it, talked to him until he got it right. I didn't lose my shit over it or write him off. Jack was a smart, strong, capable young man, more than I ever thought I'd see.

Or maybe I'm not so hard on him anymore because I care about him.

My chest tightened as I watched him brush water from his shirt. It was more than that. Maybe it was because we were locked in a small house together, but... I felt more for him. And it grew every single day. What should have been a simple assignment had turned into so much more.

"Why are you staring at me, Daddy?"

My heart flip-flopped. "No reason," I said. "Come on. We're almost back home. I'll make you breakfast."

Jack perked up. "Anything?"

I nodded. "Anything. You've been doing so well lately. You deserve a reward."

He grinned. "Then I want pancakes, bacon, eggs, sausage..." He ticked food items off on his fingers.

I shook my head as I started to move again. "Where are you going to put all this food?" I poked his stomach as he caught up with me.

Jack laughed before he slapped my hand away. I stared, mesmerized. He always frowned back home. Maybe the Arizona heat was doing his brain some good. Something had changed, that was for sure.

"I'll race you back!" Jack called.

He took off and left me in the dust. "How were you dying five minutes ago and you're fine now!" I called after him. "Get back here!"

I picked up speed, but allowed him to stay ahead. The view of his ass was better from where I was.

I was distracted by the sound of a car. Reluctantly, I was forced to draw my eyes away from Jack's form and look around. A black car drove by, headed to the corner and disappeared around it. Once it was gone, I relaxed. *I'm turning into a paranoid person.* My gaze turned back to Jack.

Until the car resurfaced again.

My stomach knotted. *It's no big deal. They might have forgotten their keys and need to head back home. There could be a million scenarios that explains why that car is here.* I tried to stay calm.

"Jack!" I called. "Come back here. Now!"

He stopped and turned to look at me.

"What's wrong?"

"Come here," I growled.

Without another question, Jack turned and jogged back in my direction. As soon as he was in reach, I tucked him against my left side. I tried to look into the car and figure out who was behind the wheel, but the windows were tinted. Back home, it would have raised red flags. Out here, tinted windows were normal, a way to keep the blazing sun out. Even knowing that, my stomach stayed in knots. Something didn't feel right.

"Finnian?" Jack frowned. "What's the matter?"

"Just stay close," I said as I turned on my heels and doubled back. "We'll go around the other way and jump the back wall."

"What?"

I grabbed Jack's hand. He didn't fight, didn't argue with me. Instead, he ran with me. We rounded a corner as we dipped through an alley and came out the other side. I led him in another direction and then another before we were right behind our house.

"Quick," I lowered myself and offered my locked hands. "I'll give you a boost J—."

185

I glanced up in shock as Jack vaulted over the back wall. There was a thump as he dropped to the other side.

"Are you okay?"

"I'm fine," he called. "I'll get Cian."

"Have him check the cameras."

"Okay!"

Gotta hand it to him, the wee brat knows how to pull it together when he needs to.

I glanced around before I moved a huge stone out of my way. After I dug down, I yanked out the bag and dumped one of my guns into my lap. After I checked it and the clip, I clicked off the safety. Jack was safe. That meant I could hunt in peace.

I made my way back out of the network of alleys before I was deposited onto the street. The black car rolled down the block as if they were looking for something. *Or someone.* Fire raced through my veins. Jack. What if they wanted my boy?

Then I'll send them back to New York in pieces.

It had to be one of the factions back home. The Triads or the Italians. Whichever side Declan had chosen, the other was on our asses. My spine prickled with anxiety. I turned and glanced behind me. The car slowed before it sped off. My finger twitched on the trigger. Shooting through the window wasn't an option. One gunshot and every neighbor on the block would be on the phone to the cops. I couldn't protect Jack if I was hauled off to jail.

I loosened my grip as the car drove away. Carefully, I tucked my gun into my shorts as I glanced around. The neighborhood settled back into that eerie, too quiet calmness that I should have gotten used to by now, but hated. It was worth being crammed into a bed with three other men on nights when the silence became too loud.

"Finn!"

Jack threw himself at me as soon as I stepped inside. He wrapped his arms around my neck and held on so tight I thought I'd get choked out and end up passing out. I wrapped my arms around him as well and held him tight.

"I'm okay," I muttered. "I'm fine."

"You scared the crap out of me!"

"What happened?" Ronan asked.

They'd both walked up on us without me even realizing it. We'd gotten closer, all of us. I was always aware of my surroundings, but around them I was relaxed. Even their footsteps were familiar now.

"Nothing," I said matter-of-factly. "Jack, why don't you run into my room and get me a shower ready. I need clothes too."

He gazed up at me. "I can handle it," he pleaded. "Don't push me out."

"I'm not." I pushed my fingers through his soft, dark hair. "I really need that shower though. Want to join me?"

Jack looked apprehensive, but he lit up a bit too. Finally, he nodded. I smiled as I ruffled his hair.

"Go on, wee one. I'll be in shortly."

He sighed. "Okay, Daddy."

The moment he was gone we all stood still, like statues. Finally, the shower turned on. Collectively, we all heaved a sigh of relief.

"So, what really happened?" Cian asked.

"Possibly nothing." I rolled my shoulders as I tried to disperse the tension I still felt in my muscles. "Or maybe something. A car, it followed us. They seemed to slow down when I was with Jack, but I can't be sure. It could have just been a neighbor minding their own business."

Cian frowned. "Was it?"

"I don't know. They drove away. Didn't run, didn't get

out. Like I said, it could be all in my head. Someone looking for an address or setting up the GPS on their phone."

"But?" Ronan interjected.

"Something didn't feel right about it."

Cian crossed his arms over his chest. "Trust your instincts," he said, quoting our old mentor. "If you think shit might be going down, then we fall into high alert status."

"No more leaving the house," Ronan added. "Jack will have to stay inside for the time being."

I shook my head. "I agree. He's going to hate that." We all stayed silent until I broke it. "I'll break it to him. After I call Declan."

The phone that I'd stashed away weeks ago was still taped underneath the kitchen sink, buried under a mountain of cleaning products, sponges, and plastic bags. I crouched down, removed the duct tape and turned it on only the second time since I'd purchased it.

I dialed Declan.

"Is Jack okay?" Declan asked.

As if he could see me, I nodded. "Yes, he's fine. Taking a shower in the other room."

"Then what's wrong?" He growled. "It has to be something or you wouldn't be calling me."

"It's nothing major sir, but I had an incident this morning." I related it to him as I paced. "Is there any news from your end?"

"Yes," Declan said. "I've taken my side with the Vitale family. You need to be on the lookout for the Triads. Qiang isn't happy with me. However, it made more sense to trust in the Vitale's. For now."

"Understandable sir," I said. "We'll keep Jack safe," I assured him as I glanced up at Cian and Ronan.

"I don't have to explain what will happen if anyone hurts my son, right?"

"No, sir."

"Good. Ditch this phone."

I hung up and smashed the phone against the counter. Pieces of it flew in different directions before I plucked out the SIM card. I tossed the whole, useless mess into the trash.

"He sided with the Vitales," I told them. "We need to keep a very close eye on Jack. The Triads could be anywhere."

Ronan frowned. "How would they know he was here?"

I shrugged. "You never know what contacts they might have."

"What about those guys he was with?" Cian growled. "Where are they? I'll rip their faces off!"

I pinched the bridge of my nose. "I doubt Elio would have anything to do with the Triads. All we need to do is protect Jack." When they both nodded, I grabbed a bottle of water from the counter. "I need a shower. Cian, keep monitoring. Ronan, do a few neighborhood sweeps today. Casually. Be careful coming back home."

They both nodded once they knew their assignments and started to head off.

"Cian?" I called.

"Yeah?"

"Be careful. If you see anything out there, tell me. Don't go rushing into shit."

He looked me up and down. "You almost sound like you give a fuck about me."

I shrugged. "And what if I do?"

Cian's eyes widened for a split second before he turned around and shrugged on his way out. "Then you're crazy."

"As crazy as you are," I added. I shook my head as he ran away once more. There was definitely more to Cian than what met the eye. He was a hell of a lot more sensitive than I ever would have guessed.

I walked into the bathroom and stripped out of my clothes, tossing them into the hamper as I went. The curtain rattled as Jack poked his head out. Water rolled down his face as he looked at me, worry etched on every inch of him.

"Everything okay?" He asked.

"Yes, it's fine for now," I said as I climbed in with him. I carefully thought about my next words before I decided Jack should know. "He sided with the Italians. We have to be on the lookout for any Triad blowback."

Jack frowned. "Is my father going to be okay?"

"Of course." I pulled him against my chest. "Declan knows how to handle himself."

"Unlike me," he muttered.

I shook my head and grabbed him by the chin. I tilted his head up. "No, I think you're more capable than we all realized. I used to view you as some soft, stuck-up brat, but that's far from the truth. There's a hell of a lot of good in you. And you know how to move when things get dicey. Those are good qualities for a man to have."

"I'm still not great," Jack said, as he tried to suppress the smile that attempted to break through.

"Cian said you've improved every time you two train. I've watched you. Even when it's not Cian's day, you two are fighting. Even your sparring with me has gotten better. You'll get there."

"And then I can protect my family," Jack said, resolved as he nodded. "It's what my mom asked of me, you know? Before she died, she told me to look after my father. I have to take over eventually so he can finally rest."

My chest tightened. "I think that's a noble goal."

"Really?"

"I do," I said. "Crazy, given the chance you have for a way out. But still, noble."

Jack smiled. "I get it from Cian," he laughed before his face fell. "I'm still worried about him."

"Me too," I admitted.

He tilted his head at me. "You really like my father, don't you?"

"No one else gave me a chance the way he did. I owe him my life." I laughed shortly. "And now I'm fucking his son."

That old twisted ache returned to my chest. As much as I enjoyed being Jack's Daddy and screwing him every which way to Sunday, in the end, I'd betrayed Declan. I was supposed to watch over his son, not drag him into bed. Even if I protected Jack with my life, eventually everything we'd started would have to come to an end.

How the hell am I supposed to deal with that?

Something wet and hot wrapped around my cock. I thrust forward on instinct as I dragged in a ragged breath. I gazed down. Jack looked back at me, his cheeks flushed as he ignored the water that dripped into his face and bobbed his head back and forth. My toes curled against the tub. I pushed my hand into Jack's hair, grabbed his silken locks and yanked him closer.

"Fuck, that's good," I moaned. "Are you trying to distract me? Or make me feel better?"

"--hy -ot -oth?"

I laughed as he tried to talk with my dick in his mouth. Why not both. Of course that's what Jack would say. I appreciated it. My mind was completely consumed with pleasure. Every thought disappeared as I rocked into Jack's sweet mouth.

"Come on, boyo. Give me more than that. Work that pretty tongue."

Jack did just that. He pulled free as his tongue ran up and down my length. He slipped the tip of his tongue into the head of my cock and made me shiver. When he pulled free he traced over my balls. One after the other he sucked them into his mouth, toyed with them, and scraped me with his nails. Jack made me crazy. I wanted to fuck his face until he came without me even touching him. I wanted to bite every inch of him until he was clearly marked as mine.

As ours.

I should tell the guys that. Maybe we'll mark him before we return him.

Every good thought that had been in my head disappeared in the wake of Jack's eager mouth. Logic, restraint; it all flew right out the window and all I could think about was him. I pulled Jack free of my cock and bent over. My lips pressed against his. The salty precum that lingered on his lips belonged to me. Me. I shoved my tongue inside, desperate to keep tasting until I had inhaled all of him. When he pulled away he panted, his chest rising and falling as he stared up at me with stars in his eyes.

My thumb drifted over his bottom lip. "Jack?"

"Yes, Daddy?" He whispered.

I swallowed thickly, my heart in my throat. The words I wanted to say tingled the tip of my tongue like I'd just bitten into hot peppers and held them there. I opened my mouth, but the words refused to leave. When I said nothing, Jack took me back into his mouth.

"Fuck... That's good," I groaned as I rocked forward. I gripped his hair harder as I shifted. "You're doing so good, boy. Just like that. Keep your mouth working."

Jack moaned.

"Are you my good boy?" I asked. "You want to taste my cum?"

He nodded his head up and down. The moans that

vibrated up my cock only made me want to cum faster. I tugged him forward completely until his nose was pressed against my pelvis.

My muscles tensed as Jack choked and gagged, but he worked harder to please me. "Such a good boy. You're doing a good job taking my cock like this. Fuck!"

Nirvana hit me hard as I pulled back enough to make sure Jack tasted more of me. I watched as I spurted into his mouth as his pupils dilated, and he touched his cock between his thighs. He pulled back and stuck his tongue out, showing me how much he'd caught for me. I almost grabbed him and fucked his mouth all over again.

Jack's tongue dipped down and dripped my cum all over the side of the tub as he came too. He fucked his palm hard and fast, his eyes on me the whole time. I crouched down and matched his strokes. As soon as he came, I caught it in my palm and lapped up every drop while he moaned.

"You're so hot, Daddy Finn."

"You make me this way," I muttered.

"What do you—mmm."

I dragged Jack into a long kiss. I didn't want him to know that no one had ever made me this way. That I lost my sense of control when I was with him.. That was too much to give anyone right now.

When we pulled apart, I helped Jack to his feet. I wrapped my arms around him, content to stand in the heat of the shower for a little while longer before I had to get out and deal with the real world. A world that might want to take away someone I'd started to love.

CHAPTER EIGHTEEN
CIAN

I moved in the dark shadows of the room. Light snores came from the bed. My hand wrapped around Jack's ankle, and I snatched him down Finnian's bed. All three woke with a start.

Jack's big brown eyes focused on me and the moment he realized it was me, he flopped back down.

"Cian," Finnian growled. His gun was aimed right at my heart.

Hot.

I shook my head. I wasn't there for Finnian, although I wasn't opposed to a repeat. There was something about the way we fucked that had my body hungry for more. Finnian fucked me as if he wanted me to submit to his cock. I did and I'd happily fight him and do it again.

"Daddy?" Jack whimpered. His eyes were half closed as he rubbed at them.

"It's my turn," I said.

Finnian still held his gun up and glared at me as if I was some lunatic. Maybe I was. Who the fuck knew? All I understood was I wanted my slutty boy now.

"It's three in the morning," Ronan groaned. He wiped a hand down his face pulling the sheet back over Jack.

I snatched it away and tossed it to the floor.

"Perfect time for what I have planned."

Finn sighed as he looked at Ronan.

"Jack is tired," Ronan said, yawning.

He slipped down the bed stretching his arms over his head. There wasn't a single tattoo or piercing on his body but it didn't diminish just how dangerous he could be.

"Princess, it's okay if Daddy touches you, right?"

Jack whimpered, but he nodded his eyes closing again.

"He'd agree to eating nothing but vegetables right now." Ronan shook his head.

I shrugged. It didn't matter to me. I was going to have Jack, and it was happening regardless of how the other two felt.

Finnian sighed. "There is something wrong in that head of yours."

I winked at him as I flipped Jack back over. The tight sleep shorts slid off his slender hips with ease. My breath caught at the mint green see-through panties he wore. Fuck he was such a perfect slutty boy.

"Shite," Finn groaned.

"You didn't," Ronan said as he peered down at Jack along with me.

I twisted our boy around just to get a view of the front. His cock was nestled in the tight fabric begging to be played with. The moonlight seeping through the blinds glinted off his cock piercing.

"I did."

"Where the hell are you getting this stuff?" Finnian asked.

"Are you complaining?" I asked.

Finnian shook his head. Even Ronan couldn't say

anything against it, my choice of attire for Jack was spot on. I stroked his cock through his panties. I groaned at the feel of warmth that seeped past the fabric. I played with his piercing knowing just how much Jack liked when we did. Our boy squirmed on the bed, his right leg hiking up as he shamelessly thrust against my palm. Jack shook his head and batted at my hands on his cock.

"Daddy! It's too early." His slaps were weak and they tickled me more than anything.

"Quit yer gurning. You're already hard."

Jack moaned as I pulled the panties back and stroked his cock.

Whore.

Finnian cleared his throat, reminding me that we weren't alone yet. "Did you make sure there was no one out there?"

It had only been a few days since Finnian's run-in with the strange car. We were still on high alert. I didn't doubt Finn. On my runs around the neighborhood, I'd felt eyes on me as well. I couldn't tell if it was the nosy-as fuck neighbors or a potential enemy. Either way, no one was going to touch our boy.

"Ya."

I leaned forward and grabbed Jack's panties between my teeth and yanked back. The fabric tore with ease as I ripped it from his body. Jack grunted, sleep leaving his eyes a little more. *Can't have that just yet.*

"Lube," I held out my hand.

One of them knew where it was. I didn't have the mental capacity to go searching for it. If they took much longer, I was bound to fish out the knife strapped to my ankle, slice into my hand and use my blood as lube. That was how desperate I was for Jack.

"Here," Finn said, handing me the lube.

Blood play for another day. I wonder if my princess will let me cut him open as he bounces on my dick. The thought alone had my cock rock hard and ready to sink into Jack.

I turned Jack back over and his arms curled around the pillow as he sighed in relief. If he thought for a single second I was giving up, he had another thing coming. His puckered hole greeted me as I parted his firm cheeks. My lubed fingers circled Jack's entrance before I pushed two fingers in.

"Ah!" Jack's hips went up and my fingers sank deeper, wrapped up in soft heat.

I didn't wait for him to adjust as I pumped my fingers in and out of his ass. He took each one. His hole sucked me in every time I pulled back. The heat alone surrounding my fingers was enough to drive a man insane. Add in the tight feel of Jack's ass and there was no wonder I was a mess for him. Ronan groaned at the sound of Jack's whimpers. We both gazed at him. He was still half asleep as I worked my fingers into his hole.

"I want to fuck him without a condom," I said.

Ronan and Finnian sat up. "Cian, we didn't agree yet," Finn said.

I grunted and pulled my fingers out of Jack's hot hole. I spread his cheeks and pulled our boy's lower half up. Showing the other two Jack's hole. "You're telling me this hole isn't meant for breeding?"

"We didn't say that," Finn said.

His voice was rough, and I didn't think it had anything to do with him just waking up. It had everything to do with his desire for the slutty boy in my hands.

"Daddies," Jack moaned.

He glanced over his shoulder at us. His lashes fluttered and I stuffed my fingers back in his hole.

"Shh it's okay, princess. Daddy just wants to play with your hole a little bit."

"You want to ruin him," Ronan said.

And you don't? I glanced at him smirking at the hungry glint in his brown eyes. Yeah, he wanted to wreck Jack just as badly as I did.

"When was the last time you were tested?" Finnian asked.

"The results are on the screen in my room along with Ronan, Jack's and yours. You got tested eight months ago. Jack and Ronan went together five months ago and I went right before we headed out for this trip."

"I'm not going to ask how you know that or even why it feels like you prepared for this to happen," Finn said. He blew out a breath. "Our test results are good. I haven't been with anyone since that test."

Ronan shook his head. "Me either."

I wouldn't be surprised if Ronan hadn't been with anyone since he started babysitting Jack.

"Princess, I need you to wake up a bit." I pressed against his prostate and Jack let out a loud moan.

"I haven't." He shook his head. "Heard you." His breathing was erratic to the point he couldn't get his words out.

Guess he's not asleep anymore.

"No one for a year," Jack finally said.

"See now we are all in agreement." My patience was getting thinner by the second. *How much longer must I be tortured?*

I curled my fingers inside of Jack massaging his prostate relentlessly. I found a thrill in the way his body spasmed around my fingers.

"Da-daddy ple—"

"Fine," Finn said. He leaned forward and kissed the top of Jack's head. "I'll go out and check the neighborhood."

Ronan did the same. "I'll go watch the cameras."

I smirked. "Switch the left monitor on."

A confused look came over Ronan's face before his brown eyes settled on Jack. Clarity came over him quickly.

"How long has there been a camera in my room?" Finn asked.

"Since we got here."

Finn groaned. "We are going to talk about that."

I waved him away. "Yeah, take it out on my ass later."

The moment we were alone my entire focus went to Jack. I sucked in a breath and all I could smell was him.

"I can't wait anymore."

I stripped out my clothes in record time letting them hit the floor wherever. Finn would lecture my ear off about being clean in his room, but it was going to be well worth it.

"You want my cock don't you, princess?"

Jack parted his lips and I almost wished one of the other guys were there to shove their cock between his pillowy lips. Jack had the perfect mouth for sucking cock.

"Yes," he moaned.

Need trickled down my spine and wrapped around my balls. I was either going to cum from Jack's voice alone or go completely insane. I squirted lube on my cock and lined up with his hole panting at the notion of sinking into him bare. I was going to be the first one to fill our boy up with cum.

"Fuck, I want you bad."

"Daddy Cian, please."

His pleading always got to me. Jack could plead for me to lay on a bed of needles, and I'd do it just to hear him whimper for me.

I'm the one who's fucked.

I pushed forward sinking into the tight heat of Jack's ass.

Every inch of my cock that sank in was another piece of me that belonged to Jack. I bottomed out and forced myself to go still. *So, fucking tight.* I couldn't get my tongue to work as it stuck to the roof of my mouth.

"So full, Daddy," Jack said as he rocked back against me.

I came a little unable to stop myself. Jack clenched around my cock, and I swore.

"Are you trying to drive me crazy?"

The little minx chuckled. I was going to show him just how funny it was to make fun of his daddy. I pulled out until the tip of my cock rested in his entrance. I slammed forward, cutting off his snicker. I did it again until I set a punishing pace. Pleasure ripped through me like a heated blade. There was no stopping it and all that was left for me to do was bask in the fire that enveloped me.

I changed angles seeking out Jack's prostate. The moment I found it, my boy went insane.

Who's crazy now?

His moans were no more than growls, and any time he attempted to talk it slurred as if he was drunk off our sex. Jack clawed at the bed. The pillow flew across the room as our bodies crashed tougher. The base of my spine tingled; it was the only warning I got as my orgasm rocked through me. Spots danced in my vision, but I fought against them even wrapped up in my pleasure. I wanted to watch Jack fall apart as I filled him with my cum.

"Da—" Jack's voice cracked as his words turned into a scream. His hole tightened around my cock, milking me of every single drop of cum I had.

We collapsed to the bed and even then, I was reluctant to leave his hot body. I rocked my softening cock inside of him as long as possible, shoving my leaking cum back in where it belonged. Breathing, let alone speaking, was the last thing on my mind as my lungs burned.

That's it, I'm addicted.

My soft cock slipped out and I whimpered at the loss. I'd have to get back in soon. Jack chuckled as I dropped onto the bed next to him.

"You want to fuck me again already."

"I'd stay in you 24/7 if that were possible." Jack shook his head, his eyes dropping closed again.

I did what I'd come accustomed to when it came to having someone like Jack. I dragged him closer to me. Jack turned in my arms, a light sheen of sweat clung to his freckled flesh. The early morning rays bounced off of him, giving him a golden glow.

"Daddy."

"Hmm?"

"Why do you call me princess?"

"You don't like it?"

Jack shrugged. "At first I thought you were doing it to piss me off. Now, I don't know, it sounds sweet."

I balked at the thought of me being sweet. Brutal, ruthless, and crazy had all been used to describe me. No one had ever said I was sweet.

"I did do it to piss you off. Still do. You're delicate like a princess."

Jack's elbow connected with my side dragging out a grunt of pain as I tried to keep from laughing.

"I didn't say it was a bad thing." I gathered his fist in one hand and rolled over on top of him. "Keep being bad and I'll get Finn in here to strap you down."

Jack batted his thick lashes like the tease he was. "I thought you liked me being bad, Daddy."

"Keep it up and I will fuck you again until you cry."

Jack visibly shivered. He made me want to tear into him all over again. I never thought having a taste of him would make me so addicted. I'd been perfectly fine watching him from afar, but now that I had Jack, there was no going back. He was mine. Ours.

I glanced at the door. The others had a claim on Jack just as much as I did. I wasn't stupid. I saw what they gave Jack. Finn gave Jack order and someone to lean on. Ronan was his safety net. He could be his childish self with Ronan and know he'd be taken care of. But what did I give him besides a good time?

Jack tapped my forehead dragging me out of my head.

"What are you thinking so hard about?" He smirked at me as he moved closer. "Smoke is leaking out of your ears."

I thought about it for five seconds. There was no use dwelling on it. "What do I give you?"

Jack's brows lifted as he stared at me. "What do you mean?"

I relayed what I thought about his relationship with Finn and Ronan, and how they worked for him. But when it came to me, I was stuck. Why keep someone around who bullied him and pushed him around for the fun of it? All I could come up with was sex, which I was fine with, but there was a strange part of me that wanted to be something less... replaceable.

"Oh, easy." Jack kissed me. "Freedom, duh."

"Duh?"

Jack didn't have any hang-ups on his answer like I did. *How was he so sure?*

"Yeah, with you I get to be myself. I mean I get to be myself with Finn and Ronan but it's different. I get to fuck up knowing you will laugh at me but will fuck up right next to me. Oh, and you don't hound me to be anything but myself. Ugh I feel like I'm all over the place with this." Jack wiped his hand down his face hiding away his cute pouty lips as he scrambled to explain it to me.

"That's where I'm stuck too. There is something in the

pit of my soul that says you're mine, but I can't understand it sometimes. It's kind of like when you go for a kill and you're not sure how you want to go about it. You know it's going to be a great one and that it will excite you and give you a rush like no other, but you're stuck with this sensation in the middle of it that you can't possibly describe because it's just always there and then you wonder if you're going to mess up the kill and the feeling will be gone."

Jack scooted back, his brows furrowed and mouth dipped in a frown. "I.. I don't—umm." He glanced behind him at the door before looking back at me. His brown eyes were wide and searching my face. "Do you want to kill me Cian?" he whispered.

"I've thought about it often."

I smiled. I couldn't help it. Jack's death had been in many of my dreams, and it was always a good one when it was done at my hands. He'd be a gorgeous corpse. I probably wouldn't ever part from it. I couldn't keep a plant alive but I sure as shit knew how to preserve a body.

"Are you thinking about killing me right now?"

I blinked a few times at the worry in Jack's big brown eyes. "Maybe."

"The fudge?" Jack sat up.

He groaned as he looked between his thighs. I smirked at the sticky mess covering him.

"I would keep you."

Jack's head snapped up, his eyes bore into me as if I'd lost my mind, but I felt more sane than I ever had before. There was no unbearable itch to go out and kill. I wasn't craving the thrill of taking someone's life, at least not like before. Having Jack in my arms curbed some of my twisted desires.

"I don't know if that's worse or better. What would you even do with my corpse? Wait I don't want—"

"I'd fuck you all the time. Hold you at night as long as I could. Dress you up and keep you clean. We'd spend every single second together. You would never escape me."

Jack's mouth hung open as he stared at me.

"Is that not normal?" I asked.

Didn't other people feel this way? When they professed that they couldn't live without someone, wasn't this it? If it wasn't then, weren't they all lying?

"Nope." Jack shook his head and shut his mouth. Silence weighed down on us as he continued to stare me down. "You're serious."

"We would never part."

"That's—" Jack's head tilted as he nibbled on his lip. "Sweet?" He dragged out the word as if he wasn't sure what to say.

"Then you will—"

He lifted his hand, stopping me from asking anything.

"First let's unpack some—" He wildly gestured at me, "of this."

"I thought you liked me the way I am?"

My stomach tightened in knots preparing for what Jack wanted to change about me. *What am I lacking?* He'd leave me behind and I'd never have Jack in my arms again. Panic was an unfamiliar feeling. Even when Jack had snuck out, I hadn't panicked. I knew he'd done it and I spun the situation to my benefit, but there was no other way to describe the ants crawling up my skin feeling happening all over my body.

"Stop whatever has you looking at me like you're going to cut off my legs and arms so I'll never be able to run from you."

"That's a good idea."

"Daddy Cian!"

I shrugged. It was. I settled down and forced my body to

relax. I wanted Jack alive or dead but since he was alive, I needed to know what I had to do to stay with him.

"First, let's be clear, I like your crazy even if it's terrifying." Jack ticked off each thing on his fingers. "Second I'm not going anywhere and even if I tried, you'd hunt me down, right?"

I sat up instantly and reached for Jack. "There is nowhere that I wouldn't be able to find you."

Jack's shoulders relaxed. "See, and lastly the whole killing me thing is not allowed but—" Jack cleared his throat and sat up straighter. His gaze darkened and I swore I was holding the boss and not the sweet slutty brat I'd claimed. "If I choose to go out it can only be at your hands. You never let anyone kill me, am I clear?"

"Yes." It was the only response I could give him. It was a demand and nothing else.

"Good till then, no killing me. I think it's selfish of you to keep my corpse to yourself. What about my other daddies?"

"I'd let Finn and Ronan visit."

Jack tapped his pouty lips. "Okay I think that's fair."

"What's fair?" Finn asked. He pushed back his shoulder-length auburn hair. His green eyes flickered between the two of us in his bed.

"You get to visit Jack's corpse, but he stays in my possession."

Finn opened his mouth and then shut it.

"Daddy Finn, nod your head."

"There's less in that head of yours than I thought," Finn said. He headed for the shower but before he disappeared, he glared our way. "Change the sheets and then get in the shower."

Jack groaned. "I didn't get to go back to sleep."

"Time to train, wee one."

"Outside?" Jack asked.

I shook my head as Finn shouted no.

"How much longer do I have to be stuck in here?" Jack groaned.

I kissed him. "Let's mess up the sheets even more."

Jack's frown flipped to a smile as he chuckled. "Daddy Cian you're going to get in trouble."

"Come on, be daddy's slutty boy and ride my dick."

I never wanted to let this go, whatever this feeling was that twisted and knotted in the middle of my chest. I wanted to hold on to it forever and in order to do so I knew I needed to keep Jack. He was the source of this magnificent feeling.

CHAPTER NINETEEN
JACK

I TUGGED my sweater over my head and lifted it to my nose. We'd been away from home for weeks, but Ronan had even packed the laundry sheets I loved. It still held that soft, fluffy, warm smell I loved. When I pulled the sweater down smiling, I felt eyes on me.

"What?" I asked.

"You know that thing is falling apart, right?" Finnian asked. "You should toss it and get a new one. I can have one delivered."

"No!" I wrapped my arms around myself tightly.

"It's just a sweater," Cian said.

I shook my head harder. People could talk shit about my sweater, but it was the one thing I'd never give up. No one could take it away from me. If they tried, they'd be pulling back a stump after I gnawed off their hand.

Ronan walked into the kitchen and patted my head. I leaned into his touch. It was almost as comforting as the sweater I now had to protect from Finnian and Cian.

"Leave him alone," Ronan said. "If either of you touches that sweater I'll be forced to do something... drastic."

A shiver coursed up my spine. The way he said it; his

tone cold, his eyes dead, and his fist clenched, I felt as if he'd make good on that threat. Why did I find that equal parts hot and terrifying? A better question was why did I like it?

Cian pushed his chair back. "I kind of want to see that." He grinned. "How crazy do you think Ronan would get?" He cracked his neck back and forth as he reached for my sweater.

Ronan stepped in front of me.

"Will you two knock it off?" Finn growled. "Couple of morons."

I moved around Ronan. "It's okay, he just knows how crazy I am about this." I rubbed the fabric between my fingers. "It was my mother's," I blurted out trying to get the words to slip free before I got choked up. "She died when I was really young. Cancer," I muttered. "We were close. All of us. Most people complain about their parents, but mine were great. I didn't even know what our family did back then, I didn't care. The only thing that mattered was how happy I was."

"I'm sorry," Finn said. "I know how much it affected your father."

I nodded hard. "Yeah. It really fucked him up." I blinked. "Sorry, Ronan..."

He shook his head. "Fuck Cancer."

My heart squeezed. "Yeah. Fuck cancer." I sucked in a deep breath as my eyes watered. I rapidly blinked away the tears. "Anyway," I cleared my throat. "This sweater was one my dad wore a lot in college. He gave it to my mom once and she never gave it back." I grinned. "He used to tell her all the time to give it back, but she'd just tease him. It still smells like her because of Ronan. He never lets the dryer sheets she used run out."

Ronan pulled me into him so quickly I nearly fell. I leaned against him and let him hold me. It felt good to be in his arms. He stepped back just enough to tilt my head up. Ronan gazed into my eyes and I almost teared up all over again. Shit. He always broke down the parts of me that I wanted to stay intact. I meant what I said; I wanted to take over someday. How could I do that when Ronan turned me into a giant baby?

He kissed my cheek. "It's okay to be vulnerable," Ronan whispered.

My heart skipped a beat as I leaned into his palm. "Thank you."

Finnian grabbed me the moment Ronan let me go. "Sorry we made fun of your sweater. That was an asshole move."

I chuckled. "No, it's okay," I said. "You didn't know." I hugged him tightly as he kissed the top of my head. "Besides, it's okay. She's the reason I want to take over. I promised her I would look out for my father. As much as he pisses me off and drives me insane, I love him. It's my job to keep the family business going. And I'm going to do it. No matter what I have to do to make it happen."

Finn hugged me harder until I felt like I couldn't breathe. "I'll help you, boyo. Don't you worry about that."

"I'll always be by your side," Ronan said.

I smiled at the two of them. It felt good to know they had my back. Eventually, we'd go back home. Knowing they stood with me made me stand up a little taller.

For the first time, I realized that Cian was quiet. I glanced over at him. He looked like he wanted to say something, but he shifted from one foot to the other. He opened his mouth before he snapped it shut again.

I felt as lost as Cian. He clearly was uncomfortable, but I didn't have the right words to comfort him. I just smiled at him before I walked over and hugged him too. Cian squeezed me tight, the air between us thick with tension. I wasn't surprised he didn't know what to say; I'd spilled a lot of my life in his lap, and Cian was closed off on a good day if it wasn't him being a bully or saying he wanted to kill me.

When I stepped back, I stared at him. Cian nodded briefly and I stuck beside him as the panicked look I'd seen before started to calm.

"Ronan and I need to run into town," Finn said as he picked up his keys from the bowl on the counter. "Are you two going to be okay here?"

I nodded. "I'll be alright."

Finn glanced at Cian. "You good?"

"Yes."

I stared at Cian. One word? The man had been talking nonstop since we'd gotten here. My stomach tightened.

"We'll be right back." Ronan kissed me deeply before he stepped back.

Finn left me with a kiss as well before they both walked away. As soon as the front door closed I sighed and turned back to Cian.

"You don't have to say anything," I said. "Emotions kind of make you uncomfortable, huh?"

Cian shrugged. "Maybe."

"Maybe?" I pushed.

Cian rubbed the back of his neck. "I didn't grow up in a touchy, feely household. I don't even remember having an attachment to my parents before they died." He shrugged. "So I don't know what it was like for your family."

"And that makes you feel weird."

"What is this? A goddamn therapy session?" He scoffed as he moved around me to the coffee maker. "Keep your stupid sweater. No one's gonna take it from you," he growled.

I smiled at his muscular back. Cian was sweet in a weird as heck way. Just the way he said it felt as if he would shoot anybody who even tried to take my sweater away from me. *He'll be a good guard dog when we get back home. No one will ever be able to lay a finger on me.*

Cian glanced over his shoulder. "Quit starin' at me!" He snapped, that thick Irish accent coming through. "Stop it already or I'll fuck you up, princess."

I grinned harder. "Do you promise, Daddy?" I leaned forward more. "Will you force your cock in me and make me cry for you?"

A shudder passed over Cian. I laughed as I grabbed a mug and poured coffee into my cup. He was so predictable sometimes. I loved it.

Once I doctored my coffee, I moved to the couch and sat down. I had the whole day ahead of me and nothing to do. All of my chores were completed, I was sick of TV, and I was still banned from a phone. I wanted to call Sayge and the guys over, but my daddies had strictly forbidden it.

I'm so tired of lockdown.

Dealing with thoughts of my mom had made that old sadness come back. It creeped in, clenched me tightly, and refused to let go. I groaned as I laid on the couch face first.

Maybe I should just go to sleep. I can't be bored if I'm asleep.

"Hey."

I turned my head to look at Cian. "Yes, Daddy?"

"Want to go to the park?"

I jumped up and landed on my still sore ass from me and Finnian's last spanking session. "Ow!" I hissed and rubbed at my butt as I shifted my weight off of it. "We can leave the house?"

Cian shrugged. "I don't see why not? Nothing's been going on and the park is nearby. Besides, I'll shoot anyone if they start shit."

I rolled my eyes. "If you shoot someone then we're all going to jail."

"Fine. I'll strangle them."

I contemplated it for all of five seconds before I hopped up. "Okay!"

"We have to be back before those two though," Cian grunted. "I don't want to hear Finn's mouth."

"You love it when he lectures you," I pointed out. "It makes you go crazy because you know he'll bend you over and—."

"Enough," Cian growled. "Are you coming or not?"

I smiled at him. He was rough around the edges, but I could tell he wanted to make it up to me. I didn't have a problem with the fact that he couldn't express himself all the time. But I wasn't about to turn down a get out of jail free card either. I needed to stretch my legs, explore, do something other than stare at four walls or I would finally go insane.

"I'm coming!" I tugged my sweater over my head carefully and folded it up on the couch. "Okay, now I'm ready."

Cian wrapped an arm around my back as he escorted me to the door. When our eyes met, he smiled. That one gesture was enough to make my heart pound in my chest. Even the psycho of the group made me feel like I would melt.

"We should head back soon," Cian said as he sat on his swing, a cigarette dangling from his lips. "Seriously, I don't want to hear Finn's mouth today."

"Don't be cranky," I said. "I told you it's okay. Just because Finn and Ronan are softer—."

Cian groaned. "Will you shut up?"

I snickered under my breath. For once I had something to tease him about and I would milk it for all it was worth. Especially when it was the one time I saw his cheeks turn pink. I needed more of that.

"Stop it," he growled.

I laughed. I pushed off the ground and swung back and forth carefully to avoid my feet running into the wood chips so I didn't go flying.

"You really want to run shit back home?" Cian asked.

I nodded. "Yeah, of course. Are you going to help me?"

Cian tilted his head. "Would I have to stop being a reaper?"

I shrugged. "Only when I really needed you. Otherwise, I wouldn't mind if you kept doing your job."

Cian blew out a breath. "Then, of course," he said. "Although I still don't think you're ready. Someone's gonna kick your ass."

"You don't trust your training?"

He shoved a thumb into his chest. "I'm the best trainer there is. You're a delicate little princess though."

"I will throw wood chips in your face."

Cian clicked his tongue. "You do that and I'll fuck you in them."

I winced. "That sounds painful," I muttered.

Cian smirked. "That's the fun part."

I rolled my eyes as he laughed. There was no doubt in my mind he'd think that was hot. All I could picture were splinters in my knees. No thanks.

"We should head back."

I yawned. "Yeah, I guess so." I stood up and stretched. "Do I have to put your hoodie back on?"

"Yes."

I groaned as I tugged the black hoodie over my head. I

was going to bake in the sun, but at least we weren't far from home. Already I'd dreamed up visions of ice cream. Cian took my hand. As we walked, he squeezed it. I loved when he held me. It was such a small thing, but I wanted to stay close to him all day just like this.

"Jack."

"Yeah?" I glanced up from our hands to a van as it skidded to a stop.

Four men hopped out. As they ran toward us, I froze. Cian reached for his gun, but before he could even get the safety off I watched them jump him. I stared in shock, the world around me eerily quiet before it came back all at once.

"Get off of him!" I screamed.

I ran toward Cian as arms circled around my waist. My feet lifted off the ground. I kicked and swung my arms, but whoever had grabbed me was strong. He tossed me over his shoulder as he spoke Chinese to his partners.

Shit. Triads!

I elbowed him in the back of the head. The man faltered, swore, and punched me in the side. I grunted as I prepared to hit him again, but we'd already reached the car.

"Get him in!"

They shoved me inside. I kicked out and caught the man who'd been holding me in the chest. He choked, holding his sternum as I glared at him. My brief moment of triumph vanished as a fist crashed into my face. Blood rushed from my nose as they all jumped back into the van.

"Let's go!"

I turned to the window and my heart dropped as I saw Cian lying on the ground, face down. He didn't move. Was he even breathing? I lunged forward only to be shoved to the cold, hard floor. Something was yanked over my head. All the light disappeared as I was plunged into darkness.

"Cian!"

I screamed until my throat burned. The more I tried to fight, the harder I was held down. I heard the familiar sound of zip ties as I was restrained and left on the floor.

"Fucking pain in the ass," a man growled.

"It'll be worth it."

I panted before I forced myself to calm down. If I kept panicking, I would never get back to them. I would never go home again. And I had to. There were people I loved now, people that I swore I would protect the same way they protected me.

"Stop squirming!" A foot kicked into my side.

"I'm going to kill you," I said calmly. "All of you."

Their laughter didn't phase me. I'd been laughed at my whole life. I kept my body relaxed as I imagined them covered in blood. One way or another I'd make sure everything I imagined came true.

CHAPTER TWENTY
RONAN

SOMETHING WAS WRONG. We stepped through the front door into utter silence.

"Finn."

"Clear the house first."

He dropped the grocery bags to the ground and pulled out his gun. I followed suit as we made our way down the front hall. We split in the kitchen as we crept through the place. The only sound reaching my ears was the hum of the air conditioner and Cian's computer setup. But no Jack or Cian.

"No one's here," Finn said. His mouth was in a flat line as we looked at each other.

"No sign of anyone breaking in either," I said.

All the locks were intact, no windows were broken and no blood. Knowing Cian there was liable to be a dead body around if something happened.

Panic crept up my spine leaving a chill that felt bone deep. We both looked at each other before rushing outside. *Which way should we go?* My heart felt as if it was permanently lodged in my throat.

"You go that way. I'll head this way," Finn ordered.

Before Finn could get a step away, I stopped him. "We don't have phones, how in the hell are we going to—" My words died instantly as a figure headed our way.

I blinked a few times as Cian came into focus. He was covered in dirt and blood. One of his eyes was bloodshot as if he'd been hit there one too many times. The closer he got, the easier it was to see a blood vessel had popped. His lip was swollen and he was favoring his right leg. But what stuck out to me most was who was missing. There was no Jack.

"Where is he?" Finn asked before I could even get my mouth to work.

Cian bared his teeth at us like a rabid animal. "They —fuck."

Finnian stepped closer to Cian. "Where the fuck is Jack?"

"They took him."

Took Jack? My world came down faster than it ever had. Everything went dark and it wasn't until Finn snapped his fingers in front of my face that I realized I'd completely tuned out. I blinked a few times as they came into focus. Finnian and Cian were arguing back and forth. I knew Finn was trying to get all the information he could from Cian, and I should be listening, but my head felt too heavy. I needed Jack here, but he was gone. Remembering that fact only made the pressure worse. How could we have lost him?

Everything suddenly went quiet and the fog plaguing my head lifted. "The tracker," I shouted.

Both of them stopped talking and stared at me.

"What?" Finn asked.

"I picked up a tracker for Jack a while ago. He has it on."

Cian's eyes widened and he turned on his heels and ran to the house. "Hurry up! What's the fucking code to it?"

I jogged in after him and relayed the information to

access Jack's tracker. I could picture it clearly, he had it on when we left. The likely chances of them knowing it was a tracker and not some bracelet were slim. I held my breath as Cian's fingers flew over the keyboard. What felt like an eternity was more than likely a few minutes before a blinking dot appeared on the map.

"Found him," Cian said.

I squinted at the map and my heartbeat pounded in my ears as I stared at where Jack was.

"Let's go, it's going to take us at least thirty minutes," Finn said.

I snapped out of my trance as Cian got up and pulled a huge case from under the bed.

"When did you get all of this stuff?"

Cian glanced after opening the case. He passed over a few unmarked guns and loaded magazines.

"I'm the one who restocks the hideaways of weapons." Cian slapped the clip in his before standing back up. "I'm going to kill every single one of them."

Finn nodded. "I'll reach out to Elio. We will owe him a favor, but at least we won't have to worry about clean up."

My stomach was knotted as I peeked at the dot again. It was still in the same place. "They haven't moved."

"Not yet," Cian said.

He grabbed the laptop off the makeshift desk. His movements were jerky. Cian didn't say it but I could tell he was beyond pissed that someone had not only gotten the drop on him, but they'd taken Jack right from under him.

"How many were there?"

Cian cracked his neck as we raced toward the car. I slipped in the backseat as Finn got behind the wheel and Cian took the passenger seat.

"I told you already. Four jumped me, but I'm pretty sure

there was more than that. Someone snatched Jack up so five plus the driver six."

"But there could be more," Finn said.

Anger rushed over me like little hot pokers stabbing into my flesh. It was better than the panic that made me move slowly.

"Who?" I asked.

Cian didn't need me to explain what I was asking. Our eyes met in the rearview mirror.

"Triad."

"You're certain?" Finn asked.

He nodded. "They were speaking Chinese. Something about getting the Irish to switch sides."

How dare they drag my sweet boy into this mess? Jack wasn't even a part of the mob yet and they decided to involve him all because Declan chose a side. They weren't going to win him over now. If there was one thing Declan didn't play about, it was his son.

"Calm down Cian. You're going to bounce a damn hole in the car floor," Finn groaned. As we slowed at the stop light he looked at me in the backseat. "Both of you get your heads on straight. We will find him and bring him home. No losing your shit till he's safe."

I bit the inside of my cheek filling my mouth with the coppery tang of blood. The pain did little for me but it was enough to push everything back.

"Okay."

"Cian," Finn growled.

"They took him from me."

Normally Cian was confident, boisterous, and annoying but what he sounded like now was defeated.

Finn punched him. "That means you need to get him back. Are we clear?"

Cian nodded. "Ya."

I didn't blame Cian. It could have been any of us and it'd been quiet for the past two weeks. Nothing had stood out to us, but that apparently had been the chance they'd been waiting on. I swore the moment Jack was back in my arms, I was never going to let him go.

WE SLIPPED OUT of the car and traveled by foot to the secluded area on the horse ranch. There wasn't a single animal in sight. Gravel and sand crunched under our feet. Finn gestured for each of us to take a side. Cian went to the right, Finnian taking the left that meant the back was on me.

I skirted around the house slowing down as the light of the porch became more visible. A man paced the back porch with a cigarette in his hand. A phone was pressed to his ear. I couldn't hear him clearly, but a few words hit my ears and I knew he was part of the Triads. The moment his back turned, I rushed at him. My hand wrapped around his mouth and the other cupped his chin. It all happened in less than ten seconds. I jerked to the left with all my strength. The first crack was okay, but it was the second one that I was looking for. The resounding pop hit my ears and I let the body drop to the ground. I didn't bother moving him as I opened the back door.

The farmhouse layout was open and I made quick work of seeing if Jack was around. A bullet zipped past me and landed in the sheetrock behind me. I dropped down and rolled back into the kitchen. The gun was in my hand, my muscle memory coming to the rescue. I fired off a few shots and dodged the ones coming my way. There was even more noise outside. Looked like I wasn't the only one caught in a fight, hopefully one of the guys found Jack.

A bullet landed in the cabinet near my head. I fired back and moved the moment I heard the grunt followed by a body hitting the ground. I ran over to the man scrambling for his dropped gun as he pathetically put pressure on his lower abdomen. I kicked the gun away and went to shoot him when something shiny caught the corner of my eye.

Cian crashed in with two guys. I spared him a glance, but he'd already killed one of them and was fighting the other. Blood splattered him from head to toe.

I picked the bracelet up off the floor in the living room. *Jack.* My heart felt as if it was ripping in two. My vision blurred for a second before I forced down my emotions. My stomach tightened as I pocketed the bracelet. There were no signs that indicated Jack was dead. For now, I'd go off the notion he was alive and waiting for us.

We're coming for you, baby boy.

The man on the ground scrambled away on his hands and knees. If he thought he was going to escape me, he thought wrong. I snatched his ankle and yanked him toward me. His hands slipped from under him; his face slammed into the floor. His feeble groan did nothing for me. I held his leg up and slammed the heel of my booted foot down on his calf.

The wet cracking noise filled my ears and pulled at a piece of my soul I thought was buried deep inside of me. The bone in his leg cut through the soft fabric of his pants. It was easy to make out the bloody muscles still clinging to the broken bone. The bellowing, aching screech that I wrenched from the man's throat was just as satisfying, but it did nothing to ease the pain that continued to radiate in the middle of my chest.

I flipped him around and shot one hand. I grabbed the

other. I brought my knee up and his arm down, snapping it like a twig.

Finn stepped into the room and took one look at the man on the floor and then Cian behind me sitting on a corpse. "Where is Jack?" Finn asked. His eyes were wild as if he was barely containing himself.

Cian was a lost cause. He was stabbing at a body on the floor sitting on top of it. The blood wasn't even splattering every single time he drove the knife into the body. It was a corpse. Most of its blood was a pool under its body. Cian's blue eyes were dull as if no one was home.

"I know nothing." The man spat.

Finn didn't need to say anything as I dropped the man's hand and held his head. I pushed my thumb into his eye. His screams were nothing more than white noise. The pop of his eye echoed up my fingers and traveled the length of my arm. Hot blood gushed out as I scooped the rest of what was his eye out. Stringy pieces clung to the thin flesh as I ripped it away and flung it to the side. More blood splattered on the ground as I made my way to his other eye. No man who'd seen my boy should be allowed to see again.

I paused as a thought occurred to my muddled brain. "Did you touch him?"

The man was too busy screaming that he didn't hear my question. I glanced over at Cian. He glared daggers at the man. I knew he wanted to be the one torturing him. The fact he let me do the honors spoke wonders of our growing bond. I don't think I could sit patiently by as we waited for this piece of shit to answer us.

The man trembled as blood coated the entire right side of his face. "I—" His mouth opened and closed as he shook in front of us.

"He's going into shock," Cian said.

I crouched down and slammed my knuckles against his

sternum. His eye widened. The empty socket gushed more blood. He sucked in a breath choking on it instantly. The distant look in his eye vanished.

"You're wasting our time," Finn said.

The unmistakable fear that showed on his face would have made me laugh if I didn't imagine the same look on Jack's face when he was snatched away from Cian. My body was moving before I could think about what was happening. My fist cut through the air and crashed into his face. His teeth cut into my knuckles, but it wasn't enough to stop me. I pulled back to do it again and again.

"Ronan, enough." Finn stopped me, his hand in the middle of my chest.

His green eyes held me captive. He didn't have to say it. If I kept going, I risked us never seeing our boy again. I pulled a tooth free from my flesh and tossed it to the side.

The man shook his head and blood poured from his mouth. "Please." He repeated the word as if it meant anything.

"Tell us what we want to know," Finn said. He stepped closer. "Next time, I won't stop him."

There wasn't going to be a next time. He was dead if he didn't tell us soon where to find Jack. I was going to make sure he begged for death.

"They went to the private airport, pl-please... Just stop."

"You shouldn't have touched what's ours."

I felt my lips move and my vocal cord vibrated with the words, but everything felt as if I wasn't there. I was a spectator to my body's actions. I turned away and headed to the car. I didn't give a damn what happened to him, my only focus was getting to Jack.

"I'd make you suffer but we don't have the time," Cian said.

I glanced over my shoulder as he dragged his blade shallowly over the man's throat. Blood bubbled to the surface and soaked into his clothing.

"Let's go get our boy," Finn said.

Cian jogged over to the car to join us. My mouth wouldn't move. Maybe that was a good thing. I didn't trust what might come out. Cian slapped his hand on my back. Our eyes met and I could tell he was barely holding it together. The nut job loved Jack just as much as I did. It seemed the same could be said for Finn. He wasn't chasing after Jack because he was Declan's son no, he was doing it because Jack for all intents and purposes was ours.

"We'll murder every single person who touches him," Cian promised.

I nodded. There was nothing in this world that would keep me from Jack. Never again.

CHAPTER TWENTY ONE
JACK

My CHIN RESTED on my chest as my arms burned. They'd tied me to a hard chair that made my ass sore. I shifted trying to relieve the pressure, but nothing could. My arms were too tight. I carefully ran my fingers over the rope. If I stayed where I was my hands would go numb. Then I really wouldn't stand a chance.

"What are we waiting for?"

"A phone call, Jun," the man snapped. "Once Declan tells us he wants his son back then we'll know he's ready to play ball. This is what the boss wants. Got a problem with it? Tell him."

"No problem," he growled. "I'm just tired of us sitting on our asses."

The next words he spoke were in Chinese. I had no idea what he said, but as long as he kept talking, I could keep trying to work on the knot in the ropes. My bracelet had fallen off when they stripped me at the last location. They'd checked every inch of me for trackers and never realized there was one on the floor. My hope had dwindled when I was redressed in baggy, scratchy jogging pants and a t-shirt and shoved into a van. They were being careful, making sure my guards couldn't follow us.

I swallowed thickly. The thought of being left in their hands, never seeing Finn, Cian, or Ronan again made me feel sick to my stomach. My fingers faltered. I had to get back to them. I couldn't trust that they'd hand me over to my father once he changed sides. Everyone in my father's part of the world was a snake. If anything, they'd keep me for however long they saw fit, dragging my father along until they couldn't get anything from him anymore.

A shiver worked up my spine. I'd told my father I would lean into architecture, but that was a distant dream. He needed me home and by his side. If I'd been with him, they wouldn't be able to use me like a puppet for their fucked up little scheme. My flesh grew hot as I picked at the rope harder, my fingers raw as I worked.

Footsteps halted my progress. I let my hands drop. A light clicked on overhead. I blinked, trying to adjust quickly.

"Ah!"

I held my tongue as I was jerked up by my hair. The man that peered into my face looked like he wanted to kill me.

I licked my lips. "Can I have some water?"

He scoffed. "Why the fuck should I?"

"Jun, give him water," someone called.

He clicked his tongue before he shoved my face to the side. I slowly lifted it once more and glared. Jun disappeared, but returned with a bottle of water. I watched as he cracked it open, relief flooding me when I heard that familiar sound that meant it hadn't been opened. They'd talked about drugging me, but I wasn't stupid. After we drove away from Cian, I calmed down. It was better to be alert and kidnapped than out of it and vulnerable in the hands of these men.

Jun shoved the bottle into my mouth and let the water fall. It poured so quickly that I tried to gulp it down. Most of it splashed down my chin, some up my nose. I coughed as he took the bottle away while laughing at me. My heart clenched. It felt nothing like when Cian teased me. *I'm going to kill you first.*

"They were right when they said you were pathetic," Jun said, shaking his head at me. "Who knew Declan O'Brien's son was such a little pussy?"

"Jun!"

"What?" The man laughed. "What is he going to do? All he does is draw little pictures and fuck men. Nothing special at all."

I spit in his face. The resounding crack of his fist against my face temporarily made my ears ring. I shook my head, shaking it off as I turned to face him again.

"Wipe that look off your face, bitch," he growled. "Daddy's not coming to save you. We might be together for a really long time." He reached out, this time caressing my cheek. "I'm sure I could fill that sassy mouth with something big and hard."

"Enough, Jun." The man stepped into the doorway, his eyes narrowed. "One more time and I'm calling Qiang."

"Calm down, Bo." He straightened up. "I'm just toying with the little pussy."

As they walked away, the door was closed and the light was turned off. I was cast back into the darkness of the supply closet. I listened for the sound of the lock, but it never engaged. They didn't think I was strong enough to get out. Just like everyone else, they underestimated me. I had underestimated myself too. Then I fell in love with three crazy as fuck men who I called Daddy. Nothing would stop me from getting back to them.

I tugged harder at the ropes while they talked outside. I yanked and pulled. The rope bit into my arm, burning my flesh. I pulled harder ignoring the pain while I concentrated on what was ahead of me; the men I loved. The ones that had all given me their hearts in some way. Men who would love and protect me until the end of time.

The first wrist ripped free and I quieted the yell that echoed in my throat. I frantically worked at the next knot, then the next one around my ankle. As the ropes fell away my heart started to race. I rubbed at my wrists, trying to get my circulation going as I forced my legs to move. My hands frantically moved along the shelves until I found what I was looking for. I'd spotted it the first time they left me in the room, a pipe that leaned against the shelving unit. I closed my eyes, took in a deep breath, and released it the way Ronan had taught me when I was worked up. Carefully I shifted to the left and felt something cool. I picked it up carefully.

I cringed at the slight clinking sound of the pipe as it dragged across the ground. When the sound of rushing foot-steps didn't greet my ears I sighed. I weighed the pipe in my hand. Not too heavy, not too light. I'd be able to knock down a few of them and keep going. Carefully, I made my way to the door and gripped the knob. I positioned myself the way Cian taught me.

The moment I threw the door open, I stepped out. Shocked faces turned to stare at me. I took that moment of surprise and swung my pipe at the first person in sight. Bo, Jun's little friend. Or boss. Or whatever the hell he was. The pipe cracked against the side of his face. Blood splattered in my direction. I grinned.

"He got out!"

The chaos that ensued fueled me forward. I took another shot at Bo's head. it caved beneath the weight of the pipe as I lifted it and kept hitting until he stopped moving. Someone grabbed my waist. I fought and squirmed in his arms until he dropped me to the ground. As soon as I rolled away a foot landed where I'd just been. I grabbed the man's ankle, tugged and he slammed onto the ground.

"Fuck you," I growled.

I ducked as a bullet ripped through the air. A sharp, piercing pain sliced across my cheek. I felt the blood roll and drip down my flesh as I stared at Jun. The gun in his hand shook. I smiled at how pathetic he looked now that he was on the other end of fear.

"Who's the pussy now?" I asked.

"Take him down!"

I ran. Gunshots rang out after me, but I turned a corner and kept going. We were in some building. Through sets of doors I could make out what looked like a hanger. Two planes were inside, but it was dark. We were on the other side where a string of offices were. I glanced around.

What's the best way out of here?

"He's back here!"

I ducked into one of the offices and moved behind the door. I forced my breathing to calm as I stared straight ahead, waiting. The sound of footsteps rushing past would have made me relieved, if I didn't hear another set walking up to me. They took their time, pushing open the door as far as it could go until I was squished against it. I waited, my heart pounding in my ears until I jumped out and struck.

The pipe connected with a man's face. He crumbled before he even had the chance to scream. I kept hitting him until pieces of his brain showed through fragments of his skull. Panting, I flicked the pipe to disperse the viscera. I wiped a hand over my head to get rid of the sweat. My hand wrapped around the cool steel of his discarded gun. I picked it up and kept going.

Two down. A bunch of fuckers left to go.

I crouched as I exited the office. Cian's training and Finn's lecturing about being careful had helped apparently. That and the crazy ass blood that pumped through my veins. My father had passed on his genes in earnest. And my mother? She was no saint. It had taken work to be everything my father wanted me to be; upright, studious, calm. Now I could be myself and I had weeks of my Daddies training to back it up.

Hands wrapped around me. I grunted as I was slammed into the wall. The pipe fell from my hands, clattering to the floor.

"If you move I'll blow your brains out."

The hot, moist breath that snaked across my ear made me shudder. It was enough to make me want to vomit. I carefully sucked in a breath, but I stayed still.

"Not so tough without the pipe, huh?" He laughed against my ear. "Now we're going to beat the shit out of you while we wait for your father's call. Should have stayed where you were."

He yanked me away from the wall. I turned, a smile on my face as I squeezed the trigger of the gun. Now, that was the one thing I didn't need any help with. Maybe my father always knew I couldn't escape my fate. He'd taught me to use a gun since I was young.

I leveled the gun and shot the man in the head to add to the bleeding wound in his stomach. He dropped and I kept moving.

Keep moving.

Those words played in my head on a loop. I focused on them, making my way through the building as I fought to get outside. Once I was there I had no idea what I'd do, but it would be better than being in here. There was only one thing I had to do for sure before I got out; I wanted Jun. I kept the pipe by my side just so it would taste his skull and cave it in the way I'd done his friend.

I doubled back the way I came. There were too many of them prowling around near the hangar now. I had to find another way out before I ended up surrounded. The gun I had only held a few bullets now. I popped the magazine and counted them. *Less than I thought.* I would be fucked if they got the upper hand.

Besides, Cian would be pissed if I died here. It would be like his training was for nothing. I imagined his smug face as he talked about how delicate I was. No way in hell could I die here. I'd never live it down.

Footsteps grew closer quickly drawing me back to the present. I raised the gun only to have it knocked out of my hands as a body plowed into me. I grunted and lashed out, kicking until my foot connected with someone's flesh. Jun glared at me.

"Come here you little bitch!"

I kicked at his face this time. My foot connected with it, but pain flared. I quickly grabbed my foot as Jun held his mouth.

"Shit," I muttered. "Just my luck that I'd kick you in the tooth and get hurt."

He spat out blood. "You're going to pay for that."

I rolled out of his way as he launched himself at me. As soon as I stood up, I ignored the searing pain in my foot and met him head on. My fist connected with his face. I took the punch to my stomach, tightening it to absorb the blow as much as possible. It still hurt like hell, but at least I was on my feet. As soon as Jun tried to step back, I elbowed him in the face. He took that time to spin and kick me in mine.

I laughed as blood dripped down my face. My fingers

swiped through it before I rubbed them together. I glanced at Jun.

"You really think you can win?" He asked. "I've been at this longer than you've been alive. Trust me, the only thing that's going to happen is me pinning you to that floor and fucking you to within an inch of your life with my cock."

I rolled my eyes. "Trust me, I've had great dick. Yours couldn't even compare. I think I'll just cut it off instead."

"Try it."

The challenging glint in his eyes made me want to do it even more. I wanted to do unspeakable things to this asshole until he was nothing but a pool of blood, broken bones, and cut up flesh on the ground. I would devour him until there was nothing left. Not even my Daddies would be able to have a piece of him. When I told them all the vile things he'd said to me, I'd have to offer them myself instead. I was sure that was a better prize than getting to kill Jun. They should like that.

Jun raced for me. I let him. As soon as he was close, I ducked and drove my fist into his crotch. Screw fighting fair. I wanted to get out of there alive.

A door flew open and both Jun and I's head whipped in that direction.

My heart raced as Cian rushed through the door. He looked at me, smiling and covered in blood as soon as our eyes met. I sighed with relief.

He's okay. Thank you!

I didn't know who I was grateful to, but I was. Seeing Cian lying on the ground like that had conjured up all of my worst fears. But he was alive. Alive and as insane as ever.

The fist to my left cheek jogged my memory about where I was. I heard Cian shout my name. The room was flooding with the men who'd run out. We didn't have time to stop and stare, now was the time to fight so we could get home.

"Focus on you!" I shouted.

I launched myself at Jun. My fist crashed into his face as we both fell to the ground. I didn't stop.

Now that my daddies were here, I was more determined than ever to go home with the men I loved.

CHAPTER TWENTY TWO

CIAN

THE PAIN WAS WELCOMED. I took every blow that came my way. I didn't bother to block; I didn't even focus on the man before me. My eyes were glued to Jack. *Holy shit he's doing it.* I whooped as Jack head-butted the big fuck trying to take him down. My boy didn't let up either. Jack followed through with a swing of the pipe that was covered in blood. *Just how many fuckers has he taken on?*

"Hell yeah, princess! Hit him again."

My head whipped to the side as my vision blurred. I turned back to watch Jack but found some other ugly bitch in my face. I sneered at him. I was fine with him hitting me as long as he didn't get in my fucking way. I wanted to watch Jack. The man blocking my view cocked his fist back and I dropped low. He saw it coming as he lifted his knee. I let him ram it into my abdomen as I hooked my arms around his leg and twisted. We crashed to the ground together.

I was up and on top of him in seconds. I didn't have time to waste on him; every second I spent looking down at him I wasn't watching Jack beat the living shit out of this guy. Fuck that. I wanted to watch my princess get messy.

I jabbed the guy in the throat and he instantly went into

a wheezing, coughing fit. He attempted to throw me off but I wasn't budging as I grabbed the knife from my back pocket. At some point, I'd run out of bullets or maybe I lost my gun. I wasn't sure and I didn't care. No matter what I'd find a way to kill.

The knife carved out a hole in his neck. Blood splattered all over my face and I was forced to wipe it away as I sought out Jack again. They'd moved but he was still going toe to toe with the man. I got up the moment another figure ran at Jack.

I snatched the knife out of the man below me and threw it halfway across the room. It struck the man running in his left calf and brought him to his knees.

"Don't get in the way," I growled as I marched over to him. I didn't hesitate as I broke his neck.

My gaze met Jack's briefly. "You got this baby."

I could make out the slight smile on Jack's face as he doubled his efforts. The pipe scattered to the floor but Jack wasn't letting up. My heart pounded away. Everything in me said go rescue him but the tiny voice in the back of my head knew Jack needed to do this. He needed to show himself that he could be at the top.

The sound of footsteps headed our way and I groaned. What the hell were Ronan and Finn doing? There were more guys than the few that had come and snatched Jack from my arms. My blood boiled at the fucking memory. I took down two more men blinded by rage.

"I'm sick and tired of you bastards interrupting. I'm trying to watch my princess kick ass."

I came toe to toe with another bastard. He swung a crowbar, aiming for my head. Fucking bitch was trying to take me out. I knocked his feet from under him and slammed my body down on top of his. His foul-smelling breath hit me in the face. I punched him in retaliation.

Once I started, I didn't stop even as his nose broke under my assault and his teeth cracked in half. He went still under me. I couldn't let up, not until he was dead.

"Son of a bitch." Jack's voice hit my ears and I whirled around just in time to see him take up a stance and shoot the man in the back of the head.

Now that's sexy.

I scrambled onto my feet. I moved instantly, unable to hold back any longer. I ran toward Jack. My body warmed as we crashed together. My arms wrapped around his waist melding our bodies together. I never wanted to be apart from him again. His brown eyes searched my face, his blood-covered fingers tentatively touched my cheek and around my eye. The pain was nothing more than an ache but under Jack's warm touch, it almost felt better.

"I was so scared."

"You could have fooled me, you were kicking ass," I said.

I was so fucking proud of him. Jack was soft and dainty with us but from what I just witnessed he wasn't like that with anyone else. My cheeks burned from smiling so much.

Jack shook his head. "Not for me, idiot."

My head tilted as I tried to figure it out. "Ronan and Finn are here." I turned my head to look for them but Jack stopped me, both his hands pressed against my cheek.

"I was scared you were dead." His brown eyes shimmered with unshed tears.

Has anyone ever cried for me? My stomach knotted and the need to drop him and take a few steps back crawled up my skin. A shiver worked its way free and Jack wiped at his face.

"Sorry, you're not good with emotions."

No, but I wanted to be for him. I'd never be Ronan, or even Finn, but Jack had made it clear he wanted me. I shut my brain off. It wasn't going to help me. Instead, I took

Jack's lips into a slow kiss. I tried conveying everything through touch. It was the easiest way to explain that I was okay. I was happy that he was okay. That I never wanted to be without him. That I—.

I pulled back resting our foreheads together. "I love you, Jack." My heart pounded in my chest as his eyes widened. "It might not be the traditional way of love but I'd live for you and only you."

Killing for Jack was easy. I'd taken more lives than I could remember some days. There was no question if it came down to it and I needed to die for Jack I would without hesitation, but I'd dedicate the rest of my existence to Jack. There would be nothing outside of the man I'd given my heart to.

"Daddy." The tears broke free, carving a way through the dried blood on Jack's face.

I hated when people cried and yet all I could think was how enamored I was by Jack.

"I love you too," Jack said.

A weight lifted off my shoulders I hadn't noticed was there. I would have been fine if Jack hadn't said it back.

"Jack!" Ronan shouted.

I let our boy go as he turned and ran into Ronan's arms.

"Are you hurt anywhere?" Ronan asked. He had gone quiet after Jack had been taken. It was a strange relief to hear his worried tone. "You're covered in blood."

"I'm fine, Daddy Ronan." Jack groaned. "And you're one to talk, you're soaked."

"Everyone good?" Finn jogged our way. The moment his green eyes landed on our boy his shoulders dropped and the tension in his face fell away.

Jack turned around and Finn was right behind him pulling him into a hug.

"Not hurt anywhere?"

Jack groaned. "Daddy Cian didn't worry this much."

"He's an idiot," Finn said.

"Hey I can hear you."

"Good," Finn said.

His tone was a lot lighter. We were all glad to have found Jack alive. We headed toward the car with no one saying anything. Instead of getting in the passenger seat, I sat in the back next to Jack. He laced our fingers as he rested his head on Ronan's shoulder.

"Thank you daddies."

Finn started the car as I turned to look at Jack.

"For what?" Ronan asked.

Jack yawned, his eyes barely opened. "For coming for me. I—love you guys." His head fell forward and Ronan caught him. Jack was still holding my hand even as he passed out.

"We never let this happen again," Finn said, breaking the silence.

There was no argument. I nodded as Ronan did the same. We'd protect Jack no matter what.

CHAPTER TWENTY THREE

JACK

As soon as I stepped out of the tub, Daddy Ronan wrapped a towel around my body. He'd cleaned me up the night before, but I was entirely too exhausted to do anything but sleep. I leaned against him as he held me tightly. Over his shoulder I watched as Finn and Cian climbed out of the shower as well. It had been a tight fit with all four of us, but I needed all of them right now. I wanted their touch, their attention, their love.

My eyes moved to Finn as he carefully inspected a wound he'd sewn up on Cian's cheek. His fingers moved over it as he lectured Cian to be more careful before he started bleeding again. I smiled at Cian's annoyed look. He might say he hated it, but he didn't move away from Finn. My stomach tightened.

They definitely have a thing for each other. Good for them.

Finn glanced at me and I tilted my head at him. He was the only one that hadn't said the words. I could guess that he cared about me, but I wanted to hear it. I wanted to say it back to him. He went back to picking at Cian and I frowned.

"Jack? You okay?" Ronan asked.

I smiled at him. "Yeah."

"Are you sure you're not hurt anywhere?"

"You've looked me over three times. So have Cian and Finn." I shrugged. "I told you Daddy, I'm fine. A little sore, but fine."

"Do you want more pain medicine?"

I nodded. "Sure, why not?"

Ronan disappeared to the kitchen to grab the medicine while I carefully secured the towel around my waist. Once it was in place, a hand ripped it away. I glanced up at Cian. He invaded my space as he leaned toward me.

"Who said you could cover that body up?"

I swallowed thickly. "Daddy Ronan."

"Yeah? Well I didn't. You could have been killed yesterday. I fully plan to breed you until your belly is full."

I touched my stomach on instinct. "I don't think you have that much cum," I whispered.

"Believe it, princess. Besides, I've got these other two. They'll help me."

Ronan frowned. "Help you do what?" he asked as he handed me the medicine and a glass of water.

"Just Cian being a pervert," Finn said. "And a moron."

"You two can lie all you want. I'm fucking our boy." He tipped the glass up more as I drank from it. "Hurry up. Down the fucking hatch. Get in the bedroom."

I tried not to choke. "You're demanding," I grinned. "Who says I want to?"

Cian's eyes flashed. That dark look that came over him made every inch of my skin feel as if it were on fire. I pushed forward, all for tempting that withering gaze.

"Bedroom. Now," Finn said. "Unless you're injured."

All three of them stared at me like I was a high priced steak and they'd just starved for three days in a row. I drew my tongue across my lips and chuckled as they tracked the movement. My men. My daddies. I held them in the palm of my hand and I loved it.

"Who's going to stuff my hole full of cum first?" I asked. "I need to be fucked until all of yesterday's bullshit is erased. All I want to think about are my daddies and their hard cocks."

"Fuck," Ronan groaned.

I chuckled. "Language, daddy."

Ronan grinned at me. "Of course. What was I thinking?" He held out his hand and I held it. "Let's stop that rule at the bedroom door. I don't think I'll be able to be well-behaved in there."

"I sure hope not." I stopped and glanced over my shoulder. "Are you coming Daddy Finn?"

"Of course."

I waited until he moved before I turned and headed for the bedroom. As soon as we were inside Cian grabbed me and tossed me into the bed. I yelped as I bounced before I laughed. Ronan gave him a dirty look.

"Be gentle with him."

"Why? It's not like he can't handle it." Cian grabbed the lube from the bedside table. "I saw the way he took down the enemy. The boy is built a hell of a lot tougher than you pretend, Ronan."

Ronan gave Cian a disapproving glare. I beamed with pride. They'd gotten to see me in action. I'd gotten to see them too. Cian had told me when we woke up how feral Ronan had been. Apparently I was right when I called him a dolphin; he looked the most innocuous, but he was the deadliest of them all. I was proud of my daddies. All of them. They'd saved my life.

"Daddy Finn?" I called.

"Yeah, boyo?"

"Why are you avoiding me?" I asked as I climbed onto the bed and shifted to the middle. I tilted my head at him. "What's wrong?"

He frowned. "I'm not avoiding you."

"Yeah you are," Cian said. "We can all see it."

Even Ronan nodded. Once I saw they all agreed with me I turned back to Finnian. He frowned. I wanted to rub the lines that creased his face and ease his worries. But I couldn't do that if I had no idea what was wrong with him.

"Why are you hiding?"

Finnian crossed the room and growled. "I'm not."

"Is it because you love me? And you were worried last night?"

Finn stopped dead in his tracks. I knew I'd figured it out as he backed away a little. I scrambled to grab his hand. Pulling him back toward me I shifted to my knees so I could be closer to him.

"Do you love me?" I asked.

Finnian glanced away. "We're going home tomorrow. I talked to your father this morning and after everything that happened he thinks it's better for you to come home. Said he made a mistake sending you away." He shrugged. "Play-time's over."

My heart squeezed in my chest. No. I wasn't about to let them pull away. They'd given themselves to me. I owned every inch of them the same way that they owned me. My daddies were *mine*.

"No," I said firmly. "I'm not giving any of you up."

"You have to," Finn muttered as he gently removed my hands. "There's no way this can work when we return. Your father will kill us."

"I don't give a fuck," I snapped. I glanced back at Ronan. "Sorry, but it's true. I don't." I glanced at each of them. "I survived because I had all three of you. No way am I going back to being on my own."

"No one can tear me away from you," Cian growled. "I'll kill anyone who tries. And yeah that includes your dad," he said as he crossed his arms over his chest.

"Don't kill my father," I sighed before I looked at Ronan. "How do you feel, Daddy Ronan?"

He stood up a little straighter. "As much as I respect your father and know how protective he is over you, I would like to continue what we have. The thought of not having you makes my skin crawl," he growled before he seemed to collect himself. "I plan to speak to him when we return. I'm not going anywhere."

I smiled at him before I turned to Finn. "Are you really willing to give me up?"

"No," he spat before he sighed. "Of course I don't want to lose you."

"Then say you'll fight like hell to keep me." I held his cheeks in my palms. "Don't abandon me, Daddy," I whispered. "Please."

Finn's arms wrapped around me. "I would never do that to you."

"Then tell me you love me," I whispered as I brushed my lips over his. "Tell me how much you need me."

"I need you more than I could ever put into words," he groaned. "You're mine. I love you, Jack."

I melted against him. "I love you too."

Our lips pressed together and Finnian tried to devour me. We fell into bed as he continued to slide his tongue against mine. His teeth buried in my bottom lip as he tugged it out and rolled his hips against me. The hard caress of his cock against my body sent me into a tailspin. I needed them now.

My legs spread on their own as Finnian attacked my

neck. He kissed and sucked on my throat before he bit. I cried out. The pain radiated through me before turning into pleasure. As he soothed the spot, Finn moved down my body and left a string of kisses as he went. Cian appeared on my left side and attacked my throat next. He moved around, kissing and sucking until he too bit me. My back arched up from the bed as my cock stiffened.

"Daddy Ronan," I begged.

"I'm right here baby boy," he whispered. His lips kissed my ear before he sucked the lobe between his teeth. "I don't plan on letting these two mark you without me."

I sucked in a breath and whimpered on the exhale. The burning pain of teeth buried in my flesh magnified as they all bit me at once. My cock was so hard I felt like I would burst if someone didn't stick something in me soon.

"Please," I moaned. "Breed me. Fuck my slutty hole. Please, please."

Cian chuckled. "Told you he was a slut," he said. "Who gets him first?"

"We should be fair," Finn said.

"Fair?" Cian growled. "I'm the one that got knocked the hell out for him yesterday. I'm going first."

"No," Ronan said. "I'll go first. I want him."

"Once your big cock goes in him it'll take two of us to fill him up again," Cian muttered. "Monster dick."

"That's not nice," Finn said.

I groaned. "Daddies please! I'm so horny," I said as I squirmed. "Will one of you fucking take me already? Come on!"

Finn clicked his tongue. "Impatience. We'll have to punish you for that."

Ronan nodded. "I have to agree with Finn. You need to learn your manners again."

"Fuck that!" Cian called. "I'm going first-- Hey! Let me go!"

Finnian dragged Cian even closer, his hand tightly wrapped around Cian's ankle. I watched as Finnian spat on Cian's hole and stuffed his fingers inside his ass. Cian groaned, shoved back, and glanced up at me with lust in his eyes. Fire ignited in my belly and spread as I watched my Daddies go at each other.

"Daddy Ronan?" I called. When he glanced at me I smiled. "Can you fuck me while I suck Daddy Cian's cock?"

"Whatever you want baby boy," he said as he tilted my head up. He kissed me. "Get on your knees and arch that pretty back for me."

I scrambled to get into position as he picked up the bottle of lube. Finnian moved both himself and Cian closer until they were in my reach. I wrapped my lips around Cian's cock and sucked. The groan that left his lips was music to my ears. I took him in deeper until Cian's cock was in my throat. He gripped my hair and humped my face as he panted.

"Fuck yes," he groaned. "That sweet little mouth of yours should be illegal, princess. Fuck me."

"Lube?" Finn called.

Ronan's fingers sank into my hole. He worked them in and out, stretching me as Cian's cock shoved roughly down my throat. I came up coughing and drooling as Cian groaned. The sound of Finn fucking Cian, that sharp smack of skin against skin only turned me on more.

"Sorry wee one," Finn said. "Got a little excited. You okay?"

I coughed and swallowed thickly. "Do it again."

"Slut," Cian said affectionately. "Fuck, I ove that about you. Get those lips back around my dick."

"Yes, Daddy."

I did as I was told while Finn fucked Cian. My mouth stretched, my throat burned, but it was all worth it. I just needed more, something to scratch the itch that had consumed me. Ronan, as if he'd read my mind, shoved his cock up my ass. I saw stars as my back bowed and I shoved back toward him on instinct. My breathing stuttered as Ronan gripped my hips and fucked me wildly.

I pulled my mouth free. "Daddy Ronan don't hold back," I moaned. "Harder. I need to feel your cum!"

"Anything for you, baby boy."

Before I could say another word he slammed into me harder. My hole stretched, a delicious tingle running through me as it settled and turned into pure pleasure. I gripped Cian's body, my nails sinking into his flesh as I took him into my mouth again. The moaning, groaning sounds that filled the air around me turned me on even more. All three of my daddies were so close. I could die just like this and I'd be happy.

I cried out as hot, wet cum filled my hole. As I pulled free from Cian's cock I panted. Saliva rolled down my chin, but Cian didn't care. He kissed me hard, a growl on his lips like he wanted to eat me whole. When he pulled back, Cian slapped at Finn.

"Our turn," Cian groaned. "We're taking him together."

I lit up. "Together? Both of you?" My heart raced. "Really?"

"Think you can handle it, princess?" Cian asked.

I nodded so hard I felt like my head would pop off. Ronan kissed me before he took Cian's spot. I let myself be moved around like a doll, a toy for them to pose and shift until they were happy with where they put me. Finnian laid beneath me while Cian took up a spot behind me. I made a mental note to make Cian be the one to face me next time. He could hide for now, but I wouldn't let that stand forever.

"Ready?" Finn asked as Cian lubed up their cocks and my hole even more.

"Ruin me, Daddy."

I didn't have to urge them on. Both Cian and Finn stuffed their cocks inside of me as my mouth opened and closed without a sound. My hands gripped the sheets tightly as I let out a guttural moan. I panted, my eyes rolling up before Ronan grabbed a fistful of my hair. He pushed my head down.

"Lick baby," he commanded. "Don't stop."

My brain became fuzzy as I bounced on their cocks. They stretched me, fueling me toward my own orgasm as I tried to keep up with what was happening. My skin tingled, heat washed over me and my eyes rolled back as I came hard on my daddies cocks. My nails dug into Finn's skin. He groaned, shoved his cock in deeper, and then they both flooded me. Ronan added onto it as he decorated my face with a few shots of cum.

I panted as I swiped Ronan's seed into my mouth. He tilted my head up before he kissed me so hard I nearly lost my breath and suffocated altogether. When he pulled back I sucked in air until my lungs burned.

"Love you," I muttered as I flopped onto Finn. My eyes started to close despite how badly I wanted to keep them open. "Sleep."

"You sleep, I'm going again," Cian said as he smacked my ass hard and made me jump. When I groaned, but didn't move he laughed. "I'll take that as you're cool with it."

"Never said that," I muttered, a smile on my lips.

Cian could do anything to me and I'd be happy as hell. No matter if he wanted to hold me, love me, or completely ruin me I was into it all. A sharp bite mark sank into my ass cheek and I yelped.

"Love you," Cian muttered against my skin.

"And I love you," Finn added as he caressed my chin and kissed me again. "Rest."

"Love you too," Ronan left a kiss on my forehead. "I'll make sure Cian doesn't go overboard."

The smile on my face stayed in place as my eyelids fluttered. As happy as I was that I would soon be home, I would miss this. Out here, it was just the three of us. No one could come between me and my daddies and I loved it that way.

I could only hope that when we returned home they all stuck to their words because I couldn't live without them. My heart would shatter into a million pieces if I ever tried.

EPILOGUE

JACK

I FIDGETED with my clothes as I sat in my father's office. Finnian stood behind me along with Cian while Ronan sat at my side. We'd been directed to the office by my father's secretary, but he hadn't arrived yet. Ronan reached over and adjusted my shirt, flicking off an invisible speck of dust. As his fingers grazed my wrist, I breathed a little deeper and told myself to calm down. I met his concerned eyes and gave his hand a squeeze.

"It's going to be okay baby boy."

My heart squeezed as I nearly melted at his words. I sat up a little straighter. "You're right. I've got this."

"You better," Cian growled against my ear, the heat of his breath sending a shiver down my spine. "If you get taken away from me I'm going to find a way to sneak into your window at night and pound your ass while you're half asleep."

I grinned. "You already do that. Well the second part."

"Yes, but the breaking in is the real concern princess. I won't be gentle."

I yelped as my jaw dropped. Cian had nipped my earlobe! I rubbed it as I turned back to glare daggers at him.

I knew the man was insane, but every once in a while he really proved it. *I should probably think about running from him.*

The thought of that made me laugh. Yeah, right. There was no way in hell I could get away from Cian. If I tried he would just hunt me down and probably kill me. Thank God he was on my side or he would be truly terrifying.

Cian smiled at me. I turned back around in my seat and shook my head. Finnian's hand landed on my shoulder. He squeezed it and I relaxed even more.

"We're all right here for you, boyo."

I touched his hand gingerly. "I know, Daddy. Thank you."

We pulled apart as the door opened. My father walked in, flanked by two men. I recognized them briefly as members of the Vitale family. I hadn't seen them in years, but they still looked the same. One glanced at me and I forced myself not to wither beneath his cool gaze.

I stood up and held out a hand. "Jack," I said briefly.

"Benito." He shook my hand before he glanced at the rest of my men. "And this is my brother, Enzo."

Enzo didn't offer a hand. Instead, he nodded. I noticed that he kept his distance though, choosing to stay alongside the wall rather than interact with us. I'd heard things about Enzo, that he was odd. He seemed like every other mafia man to me; cool and aloof on the outside. He was probably batshit insane on the inside.

My father cut through the bullshit and hugged me right away. The heavy hand that slapped my back was familiar. Comforting. When we pulled apart, I nodded at him.

"You seem... different," he said.

I gave him a small smile. "Maybe I grew up a little."

"A lot." He touched my cheek. "And you're okay, son?"

"Better than ever," I confirmed. I waved a hand to the

available seats in my father's office. "Mr. Vitale, feel free to have a seat. Ronan, we'll move over here."

I felt my father's eyes on me the entire time. He looked at me as if I'd grown a second head. A tight knot formed in my chest at the impressed expression on his face. *Finnian taught me well. So did Ronan.* They both made me better than I was before. I appreciated them for that.

Once they sat down I moved beside my father's desk. He glanced at me once more before he straightened up and focused on the Vitale brothers.

"We were sorry to hear about the unfortunate incident that took place out in Arizona," Benito started. "Although we're glad that you're okay. We sent some efforts out to help the Laureati with cleanup."

"Appreciated," my father said. "Jack handled himself just fine."

"No problem," I said calmly. I tried not to jump in the air and punch my fist at the sky. Did he see me as a real contender? Someone who could do this job? I swallowed my emotions. "So, what's the next step now that we're on your side?"

"We're working things out," Enzo said evenly. "The Triads are moving, but we have some idea of what they're doing."

"Which is?" I asked.

Benito's gaze flickered from me to my father and back again. "It's a lot to go over. Sufficed to say we're keeping an eye on things for now. All I need your family to do is keep their eyes open, watch out for the Triads, and keep your head down if they come gunning for it. We'll have your back, but we can't be everywhere at once."

My father grunted. "Qiang wouldn't even have gone that far. He doesn't give a damn who lives or dies during this war and he's certainly not trying to protect anyone. All he sees is blood."

"Well, he's going to get it," Benito said.

The look on his face spoke volumes. A shiver worked up my spine as he gazed off into the distance, as if he could already imagine ripping Qiang's head off and handing it to him. Cian cleared his throat. I glanced up at him as he glared at me.

He mouthed the words. "Watch it."

I gave him a sheepish look before I cleared my throat and focused again. *He's going to kill me for that later. It's not my fault this man is a living legend!* I wanted our family name to be as strong as the Vitale's. I wanted to go toe to toe with them and come out better. My hand tightened into a fist. I was that much more determined now to prove myself.

"Well thank you for coming to update me on all of this," my father said as he stood up again. "I know this could have been handled with a phone call, but I appreciate you coming to meet face to face."

Benito shook his hand and held it tightly. "No, I want you to know that I appreciate this alliance that we've formed. I know peace between us has always been tentative, but perhaps going forward we can establish a much closer business relationship."

"I don't see why not," my father said. "We'll talk soon."

Benito shook my hand once more. "Good to meet you, Jack. I assume you'll be in on future meetings?"

I glanced at my father. The unsure look on his face was all too familiar, but at least he hadn't outright said no. I turned back to Benito.

"I hope so."

Benito nodded before he released my hand. Enzo did the same. They filed out as quickly as they had come in. I heaved a sigh.

"Jack."

I turned to my father. "Yes, Dad?"

He looked me up and down. "You did well," he said. "I'm proud of you."

Seriously, had I died back in Arizona and gone to heaven? There was no way in hell my father had just said that he was proud of me when it came to the family business. He'd said it to me before of course; when I got good grades, when I graduated college, when he took a look at my architectural sketches. In this capacity though? Never. I felt like my heart would leap right out of my chest at any moment.

"Thank you," I said, forcing myself to stand up taller and act mature in this situation. "Will I be in on the next meeting?"

"Perhaps," my father said. "You really want to be, don't you?"

I nodded. "I always have."

Sighing, he pushed his fingers through his salt and pepper hair. "You know I don't want you in this life."

"I know."

"And you still want it?"

I nodded. "I'm not leaving your side. There's no more shipping me off to get me away from it." I swallowed hard as I stood my ground. "Mom wanted us to be together. That's what I'm going to do, stay with you."

My father shook his head. "You're as stubborn as she is."

I grinned. "Yeah I am. So you know, it's not worth it to even fight."

He laughed as he slapped a hand onto my back. "Fine, fine," he finally grumbled. "You're never going to let it go, are ya?"

I shook my head. "Nope. You taught me too well."

My father dragged me into his arms and hugged me so

tightly I thought I'd break. When he stepped back, he cleared his throat, and glanced around the room. I watched as my men all stood a little taller. They hadn't moved since the Vitale's left.

"Well, business as usual," my father said as he took his seat again.

I shook my head. "No," I said slowly. "I need to tell you something." I sat back in my seat and glanced at him.

"Go on," my father said, his brow raised as his eyes roamed over all of us.

I swallowed thickly. "These three are my..."

What are they? What do I call them? I can't say these are my daddies? Inappropriate. Boyfriends? Lovers? Definitely not that.

My mind raced as I considered the possibilities. No matter how many times I'd rehearsed this conversation in my head, I never got this far. I knew how my father was. He was the type of man that drew a gun first and asked questions later. Most of my imagination revolved around me trying to get him not to shoot. Now I was stuck.

"Sir," Finnian said. "We all care a great deal about Jack. I think—."

My father held up a hand. "Jack can tell it to me," he said as he turned back to gaze at me. "What do you want to say?"

A lump caught in my throat. "I wanted to say that they're... mine." Yeah, that felt right. "I want all three of them to start working with me. And I want to be trained to take over the business. You can't do this forever and I don't want it passed to someone who won't appreciate all your hard work."

My father laced his fingers together. "You want them to work for you? That's it?"

I shifted uncomfortably in my chair. "Sure."

He leaned forward. "And this has nothing to do with the fact that you're all... together?" He asked.

I stared at my father. One of my men fell into a coughing fit, but I couldn't even turn around to try to place who it was. My mouth opened, snapped shut and then opened again as I tried to force my brain to restart.

"How... How did you?"

"I'm not an idiot," my father said. "The things that have been said. What I've heard?" He shrugged. "It wasn't that hard to put the pieces together. Am I right?"

I bounced my leg up and down. "You're right." I glanced back at them. "They're my boyfriends. And I need them."

My father sat back a bit. "Boyfriends." He glanced at them. "I don't think I sent you to Arizona to seduce my boy."

"That was not our intention, boss," Finnian started.

"Never," Ronan added. "I've watched over Jack for years and I just want to keep watching over him."

Cian leaned on my chair and put his chin on top of my head. "We'd all kill for him. Especially me. And I won't be leaving him alone."

"Cian," I hissed.

He moved back. "I mean it."

My father dragged his gaze from them to me. "And this is what you want? Three men?"

"I don't care what anyone thinks," I said. "All of them are mine. I need them to take over, to support me. So no, you can't kill any of them."

My father raised a brow, but there was a grin on his lips. "Who said I would?"

"I know how overprotective you are."

"True." He stood and walked over to us. "And all three of you will look out for him?"

My father's eyes narrowed. "I don't need to tell you all what I'll do if Jack gets hurt, right? Physically or otherwise?"

"No, sir," Finnian said.

"I would rather die than let anything happen to him," Ronan added.

Cian leaned on me again. "I'll fight anyone over him, so yeah, I'm good."

My father shook his head. "You always were unconventional." He sighed as he raised a shoulder and dropped it. "You're a grown man now. Your decisions are your own." He looked me over. "I really am proud of you." His phone rang and he fished it out of his pocket. "I better take this. Go home and rest. I guess I need to find a new reaper and second."

"No way in fuck!" Cian called. "I'm always up for a hit."

"And I'll still be by your side until you retire, Declan," Finnian added.

I nodded. "I wouldn't want them to give up what they are or what they do. I'm fine with them keeping their jobs."

My father grinned. "Look at you, sounding like a boss." he nodded. "Alright. Then things will continue as usual." He answered the phone. "What the fuck have you done wrong now?" He growled as he stormed out of the office.

I breathed a sigh of relief. My stomach was still in knots. My father was really going to let me be with them? I stood up and turned. As soon as I did, all three of my daddies practically rushed me. I laughed as I was covered in a deluge of kisses. I couldn't tell whose mouth was whose as I kissed each of them back.

"You did so good," Ronan moaned against my ear.

"I have to agree. I'm proud of you too," Finnian added as he placed a kiss on my neck.

"Can we take him home already and fuck him?" Cian

asked, clearly over it all. "Or I'm going to fuck him on that desk!"

I quickly gathered my stuff. "We'd better go before Cian gets everyone killed. Let's go, Daddies."

As I approached the door they pulled away from me. They flanked me as we exited the office. I'd never felt more protected or more loved in my life.

Thank you so much for supporting us. Writing Jack, Cian, Ronan, and Finnian's story was such a blast. Three daddies and one boy has been an idea in my head for a long time and I'm so glad Skyler Snow and I had a chance to write it. By far Cian is my favorite but then again it's not a surprise that I love the crazy characters.

We both hope you enjoyed the fun smutty ride that was Problems. We have more coming your way. Tony's book will be next, Trouble!

We would greatly appreciate if you would take the time out of your day and leave a review informing other readers on your thoughts about Problems.

Want more Brea and Skyler or to even get access to bonus scenes join their patreon Twisted Tales.

Keep updated on what Skyler Snow is working on, Subscribe to her **Newsletter.**

Skyler Snow is the author of kinky, steamy MM books. Whether contemporary or paranormal you'll always find angst, kink and a love that conquers all.

Skyler started off writing from a young age. When faced with the choice chef or author, author won hands down. They're big into musicals, true crime shows, reality TV madness and good books whether light and fluffy or dark and twisted. When they're not writing you can find them playing roleplaying games and hanging out with their kids.

Come join my Facebook reader group. My angels get exclusive teasers and first peeks at covers. Both my dark Pen name Wren and my light name Skyler share the space. It can range from light and fluffy that Skyler just loves to the dark and depraved that Wren is known for. So come for the books and stay for the great community.

MORE BREA ALEPOÚ

Keep updated on what Brea Alepoú is working on, Subscribe to her **Newsletter.**

Brea Alepoú realized her dream was to write and tell stories after spending five years in college getting a degree. She has since been writing and letting her imagination free. With her wild imagination, expect lots of different stories; from fairies ruling, to vampires killing everyone, to the sweet loving between two men, or the love of multiple partners. She believes that everyone deserves love even if not all of her characters get it right away.

Love is passionate, hot, needy, confusing, painful, draining, fulfilling, and all-consuming.

Come join my Facebook reader group. Where I share teasers and cover reveals. Along with pictures of my cats and dog. Come have a blast and join the Heart Family.

Made in the USA
Columbia, SC
12 November 2024

46305718R00167